PATH OF
DESTINY

THE CREMELINO PROPHECY
BOOK I

MIKE SHELTON

The Path Of Destiny
Copyright © 2016 by Michael Shelton

ISBN: 0-9971900-0-0
ISBN-13: 978-0-9971900-0-7
Library of Congress Control Number: 2016901555
Greenville, North Carolina

Cover Illustration by Brooke Gillette
http://www.paintedbybrooke.com/book-covers.html

Map by Robert Altbauer
www.fantasy-map.net

For more information on Mike Shelton's books
www.MichaelSheltonBooks.com

Acknowledgements

First and foremost I thank my wife Melissa for all her patience as I have worked through multiple versions of manuscripts over many years. Her support is immeasurable. I thank my children Danielle, Emily, and Ryan, my parents and my siblings for their continued interest, support, and encouragement of my writing.

This book would not have been accomplished without the work and help of Heather, Crystal, Kelsey, and others at Precision Editing Group, as well as my beta readers. I really appreciate all the feedback and support they have given me.

Bringing my book to life visually was Brooke Gillette (cover) and Robert Altbauer (map). They took my simple thoughts and ideas and interpreted them perfectly into wonderful visual representations of my world.

The Path of Destiny is a work of fiction. Names, characters, places and incidents are the products of my imagination and are used fictitiously. Any resemblance to actual events, locales, or persons, living or dead, is entirely coincidental. I alone take full responsibility for any errors or omissions in this book.

-Mike-

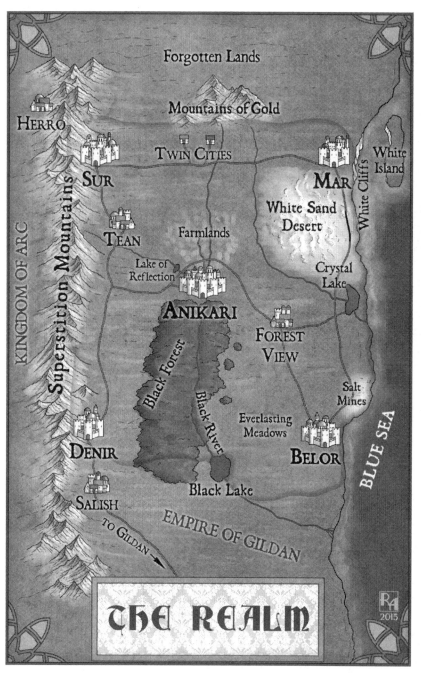

See Color map at www.MichaelSheltonBooks.com

Chapter One

Darius San Williams followed his best friend, Kelln El'Han, down the dark stairway in the back of the school library. Black boots clicked on wooden steps, stirring up dust and Darius almost sneezed. The stairs curved away from the lighted doorway and darkness met the two young men down below.

Hearing voices from above, Darius pushed himself back against the wall. Muttering, he mentally punched himself for following on another of Kelln's harebrained adventures. He had known Kelln now for five years, since entering the academy at eleven years old. Normally one to obey the rules, he hoped beyond reason that he wouldn't find himself standing in front of his father, trying to explain how the two of them had found trouble once again.

"I thought I closed this door before we left for lunch," said an older lady with a hoarse voice from the top of the stairs.

"You should've slid the shelf back over the opening," a younger snappy voice answered back. "We're going to get in big trouble."

"What? You think someone went down there?" said the first. "No one would be crazy enough to do that. It's too dark down there."

"All we were supposed to do was to get one of the history books for King Edward from the private storage and close things back up," interrupted the second lady. "No one is supposed to know the doorway is even here. You weren't even supposed to tell me, except you were too afraid to go by yourself."

Only a few yards away, down the stairway, Darius continued to hold his muscles taut. His dark bangs hung just above his grey eyes. The two young men were barely out of sight of the ladies at the top of the stairs and strained to hear their whispered voices.

Five minutes earlier Darius had been studying, or trying to study, in the old academy library of Anikari, the capital city of the Realm. Both of the young men, at sixteen years old, were in their last few months before graduating and were supposed to be getting ready for their final examinations. Kelln had wandered off, as he often did when told to do homework. When he came back, he grabbed Darius and whispered something about a secret door he'd found.

Kelln had noticed the opening next to the moved bookcase and he'd led Darius down the narrow stairway behind it.

"You and your bright ideas, Kel," whispered Darius. "Once again."

"Shhh." Kelln put his finger on his lips. "I was bored. We'll be fine."

Darius sighed. How many times had he listened to that phrase? Kelln always said his Belorian blood protected him from trouble. Darius wondered if that was about to change. His friend's bright red hair would surely give them away this time and maybe Darius wouldn't be able to smooth things over with the school authorities.

Darius tried to listen to what the ladies were saying but couldn't hear it all. The two boys crept up a few unsteady steps to hear better when Kelln stepped on an old board and a loud creak ensued. Darius dropped to his hands and knees and froze. He wondered if his pounding heart would give them away. Kelln now was lying down flat on the stairs next to him.

"What was that?" said the younger lady. "Is someone down there?" she called down the stairs in a loud whisper.

Darius almost answered. Maybe if he gave up now the punishment wouldn't be so bad. He had always been able to cover for Kelln and take a part of the blame. Being a noble did have some advantages, but he could already hear the lecture once again from his father about how the son of a noble should be acting. That he should be studying and readying himself for a minor apprenticeship in the Realm's government after graduation.

His stomach tumbled at the thought of getting into trouble and not being able to see Christine if his father pulled the reins in tighter on his social activities. Christine was from the farmlands, and in his father's opinion way below Darius's status as the son of one of the King's councilors.

Kelln put his hand over Darius's mouth. Darius almost bit him. *Kelln's Crazy! Crazy!*

"Probably just those rats," cackled the older lady. "Maybe they like to read!"

"Rats!" mouthed Darius behind Kelln's hand. All Darius could envision was the secret door closing above them with wild rats to keep them company.

"Just lock the door and let's put the shelf back before anyone notices. No one went down there," continued the older lady.

The door closed with a loud thud.

Silence! Thick, black, empty silence!

All Darius heard was the blood pumping through his veins. He'd never been in such darkness before. Kelln took his hand off Darius's mouth. However, Darius couldn't see anything around him at all. He put his own hand up against his nose and still couldn't distinguish his fingers wiggling. Panic began to creep up inside him. His breathing quickened. Why did the dark do this to him?

"Darius?" whispered Kelln.

"I'm here. What do we do now?" Darius didn't like the dark. It had always been embarrassing for him to admit. "We might die in here."

"Not for a while. We could go days without food," laughed Kelln.

"Kelln El'Han!"

"I'm sorry, Darius. We have to keep our sense of humor in times like this."

"This isn't very humorous. If we could at least see, we would be able to think of something. I am sure I could find a way out, but I can't even think in this darkness. And what if there *are* rats? Ugh."

"Wait," said Kelln. "I took some of those new sulphur sticks from the chemistry lab this morning."

"Why didn't you say so?" Darius didn't mean to sound so irritated at his friend, but he really didn't like the dark. He took a deep breath and tried to remain calm. Kelln was the son of the city's most famous sword maker, and Darius was the son of the King's first councilor, Richard San Williams. They had become fast friends immediately upon entering the academy. There always seemed to be adventure around Kelln, and Darius always stood up for him in front of others. But they had ran into their fair share of troubles.

"They're in my book pouch," Kelln offered.

"And where is your pouch?"

"I took it off my shoulder when we got down here. I must have set it down on one of the steps, but it might have fallen further down to the floor."

"All right, let's find it." Darius got up on his hands and knees and heard his friend do the same. Even with their eyes trying to adjust to the dark, they couldn't make out anything. Darius backed down the steps and started feeling along the floor, dreading what he might find instead of the pack. *Rats!* The words echoed through his mind.

"Christine's not going to like this . . ." Darius half said to himself.

"Seems you worry a lot about what Christine thinks these days," teased Kelln.

"Well . . . uh."

"Well what, cat got your tongue . . . or maybe the rats?"

"Shut up and find your sulphur sticks," laughed Darius. "Remember what happened last time you had one of your great ideas?"

"How was I to know the rain would make the city walls too slippery to climb back over?"

"If we had come back when I or Christine suggested, we would have been fine." Darius stood up and peered around the darkened room. It felt oppressive and he wished that Kelln would hurry.

A year before, Darius had made friends with Christine, a beautiful, intelligent, fair-headed girl from the farmlands. She had tripped and fallen in front of the city gates and Darius had helped her up and escorted her home. He'd tried to keep their friendship from his father, but it hadn't worked and his father found out. As a noble's son, he was expected to maintain certain decorum, and hanging out with those outside the city walls was not proper. It was one of the things about being a noble that Darius couldn't seem to understand. Why should anyone be treated differently than anyone else?

"I found the bag," yelled Kelln, interrupting Darius's scattered thoughts of Christine. "Now if I can find the sticks."

"What are we going to light?" asked Darius. "The flame won't last long."

"I have a few pages of writing paper in here," said Kelln as he continued to rummage through his pack in the dark. "As soon as I light this thing, look around for a candle or lamp to light. There has to be something down here." Kelln took a few moments to get things ready. "I've got them; are you ready?"

"Go ahead." Darius readied himself to glance around. He didn't know which direction to look first.

He heard a scrape, and then Kelln moaned, "Oh."

"Oh what?" asked Darius with anticipation.

"I broke one of the sticks." The sulphur sticks were something that the chemistry department had been working on for some time. Earlier that month they had been able to get them to work a few times. Somehow Kelln had gotten hold of a few to test. Another thing that amazed Darius about his friend was how he always ended up with the means to get out of a difficult situation.

"All right, I'm trying again. Here I go."

The small flame caused Darius to blink a few times as light created dancing shadows around the end of the long room. Kelln's face reflected a specter of orange behind the burning stick, his unruly hair glowing even redder in the strange light. Kelln lit a piece of paper and started to walk around the large room.

Darius darted through the enormous room. All he noticed were books. And dust.

"Books!" he said out loud.

"What?"

"Light a book. That will give us more light."

"What book?" asked Kelln .

"It doesn't matter. You're not going to read it. Just grab one. I'll keep searching for a candle or lamp."

Darius knew Kelln had found one when he heard the ripping sounds and watched the room grow in brightness. He headed toward a desk in the corner, where a small lamp sat.

Kelln moved toward him in a slow crouch, shielding the light with the palm of his hand. Suddenly Darius yelled and sent a chair crashing to the floor. Kelln ran to him, almost causing the flame to die out.

"What happened?" he asked.

Darius paled and his voice shook. "Rats."

"Rats?" asked Kelln.

"Huge ones," said Darius, holding his hands about six inches apart to show Kelln. " . . . Well, I only saw one."

"Ouch!" yelled Kelln as he dropped the burning pages. The flame must have gotten too close to his skin, and now the fire started to die out on the dark wood floor. The paper taken out of the book turned to ash before their eyes.

Darius reached over to help but couldn't grab the paper fast enough. Before either of them could do anything, the small light blinked out of existence, leaving them once more in thick darkness.

Darius scooted back against the old wooden desk and took a deep breath. He could hear Kelln moving around on the floor.

"What are you doing?" asked Darius, noticing for the first time how his voice echoed around the room. The darkness put him on edge once again.

"Trying to find something."

"Like what?"

"I don't know. Something. I don't see you doing anything."

Darius closed his eyes to compose himself. With the surrounding darkness there wasn't much difference, but it became easier to think. He breathed in again, then let the musky air out of his lungs with a slow puff. A picture of a flame came unbidden into his mind. He thought about the flame and how nice it would be to have light in the dark basement room. With his eyes still closed, he perceived flickers of light reflecting through his eyelids. Before he opened his eyes, Kelln gasped audibly.

"Darius. Darius?"

"What?"

Darius finished opening his eyes and found himself staring at an orange red flame dancing above his upturned right palm. The flickering light both frightened and excited him at the same time. The small, unbelievable flame started wavering and he panicked and yelled out.

The flame shrunk to barely a pinprick.

"Don't let it go out," Kelln yelled.

Darius closed his eyes, brushed his bangs to the side with one hand and concentrated again. He opened his eyes back up and watched the flame grow larger, bright enough to distinguish the entire room. He wasn't sure what was happening, but at least they would be able to see.

"Been holding out on me?" Kelln asked, his voice quivering.

"Kel, I, uh," Darius stammered, and he couldn't tell if it was from fright or exhilaration. He had no justifiable reason to believe what he was doing. "I had no idea."

He wondered what Kelln would think of him now. Was he a freak? Would he tell everyone? Magic was not looked upon favorably in the Realm, especially in Anikari.

"This is so fantastic," Kelln said, his mouth opening wide.

"Not everything is fantastic, Kelln." Darius pushed his friend's favorite word back at him.

"Well this is. Like the wizards and magicians from the stories. What else can you do?"

"What else?" Darius became frustrated and the flame soared larger. "This isn't a game! How am I going to explain this to anyone? They'll lock me up or kick me out of the city. I don't even know if I *can* do anything else."

"How did you do the flame?"

"I was just thinking about a flame in my mind and how much I wanted to see, and it happened."

"Great need and strong emotion," Kelln stated.

"What?" Darius rubbed his eyes with the fingers of his empty hand. A headache started to emerge, but through the simple pain he felt a sense of wonder and excitement.

"Don't you read anything? Wizards of old used 'great need' and emotion to perform their magic."

"I'm not a wizard." How could he be a wizard? Wizards were normally thought to be hereditary and neither his father nor mother was one. "A full wizard hasn't existed in the Realm for over a hundred years."

"But the Empire of Gildan has them. The Emperor there is one, and his entire family I hear are wizards. And the Conclave of Wizards in the Kingdom of Arc advise their king," Kelln recounted.

"All of a sudden you are an expert on magic and wizards?" Darius's voice rose louder than intended. He took a deep breath and tried to reason it out, but reason didn't make any sense in this situation. He looked inward and felt his heart stirring with new feelings.

"I have heard my father talk of a wizard in Belor," Kelln continued. "What if you are a wizard, Darius?"

"I am not a wizard." Darius repeated himself. As soon as he said the words out loud, doubts and fears rushed in. He again sensed something stir within him. An awakening. Something calling to him. He didn't like what it might mean, and he dismissed his friend's words. But there was the fire burning above his palm. He couldn't just ignore that, could he? But if he didn't ignore it, he knew he would be exiled out of Anikari, or worse, kept in a prison for the rest of his life.

"Not a wizard?" Kelln flapped his skinny arms around him in mock excitement, his green eyes sparkling. "Oh, I'm sorry. I forgot that you *always* make fire come out of your hands. Just a normal occurrence for you."

"Shut up, Kel." Rare frustration flew out of the young noble.

They both jumped back as a row of old lamps high up on the wall roared to life with flames. They lit the room from one side to the other.

"Great need and emotion. Fantastic."

Darius glared at Kelln's flippant remark. He rubbed his hands together, putting out the small flame, which they no longer needed. As he did so he felt a receding of the power throughout his entire body. He knew that his father didn't like him befriending some of the people from the farmlands, but having magical abilities would send his father into a tirade. Ever since the wizard rebellion a hundred years earlier, the people of

Anikari had been apprehensive about magic, to the point of not allowing it in the city under any circumstance.

"I wonder what all these books are for?" Kelln changed the subject. He reached up on a shelf and pulled one down, dust falling down over his simple white shirt. At least three dozen rows of books from floor to ceiling filled the length of one wall of the room. The ancient volumes of books sat on old brown-stained shelves.

With the added light, the two young men noticed their footprints in the dust behind them along with the prints of the ladies who had been downstairs before. The dark wooden floor showed years of dust. A few old portraits and maps hung on the wood paneled walls opposite of the shelves, with a few smaller study desks lined up under them.

"Those ladies made it sound as if this room is secret." Darius turned and picked a book off the shelf that he was leaning on. He blew off the years of dust on the cover and sneezed three times.

"*The Battle of Denir, volume 3*," read Darius from the front of the book. He opened the ancient book up to see handwriting that was faded and old. "Anikari III," he whispered.

"What?" asked Kelln coming closer.

"This was written by Anikari the third," said Darius.

"You mean King Anikari's grandson? The last Anikari king?"

"I'm sure of it," answered Darius as he thumbed through the pages, "The final large battle between the Realm and the Gildanian Empire over 400 years ago. Their empire tried to take over our young Realm."

Kelln glanced down at the book he held. "*The Kingdom of Arc and Its Founding*. These must be books written by the kings and emperors of the past."

Darius ran his fingers across another volume: *Genealogy of the Kings*. He opened up the last page. Written in a flowing script was a lineage of the last few kings. "Kelln, look here. This book ends with King Charles, but King Edward isn't listed after him. Instead it says Alric, but someone has scribbled it out. What do you think that means?"

"Alric? Who is Alric? Never heard of him."

"My grandfather's name was Alric, but it's a common enough name around the Realm. I barely remember him though."

Kelln wrinkled his nose. "Forget the book, Darius. Who knows with royalty."

Darius put down the book. "You're right; it doesn't have anything to do with us. King Edward does need to have another child though. I've heard rumblings from my father about needing an heir to the throne."

"I will let you nobles worry about that. Whoever is king doesn't affect me much, I suppose." Kelln shrugged his shoulders, then motioned for Darius to turn around.

Darius turned around. They stood at the far end of the room, peering down its long rectangular length.

"Fantastic sight, huh?" said Kelln.

Darius raised his eyebrows. "Yes. Quite fantastic, as you say. One of your most interesting adventures." The lamps on the walls lit the length of the room. Even covered in years of dust the site was reminiscent of rooms in the castle itself. The finest wood, gold lamps, and leather-bound books sat in eerie silence.

"Come on now. Admit it. You like my adventures." Kelln slapped his friend on the back.

"After this I think I'll want to stay right here in Anikari and live a nice peaceful life with a beautiful wife," answered Darius.

"Like Christine?" Kelln teased. "Not me." Kelln walked down the long room, looking for a way out. "I want to travel the entire Realm. See Belor, Denir, and Mar. Maybe even beyond to the Empire of Gildan or the Kingdom of Arc. It's boring around here. Come with me."

Darius smiled at his friend's enthusiasm. "You're right. I want adventure too. But I'm going to be a general in the army, win battles and keep the Realm peaceful for the rest of you."

"Lofty goals." Kelln raise his eyebrows at Darius.

Darius laughed as both boys reached the far end of the room with no sign of another door. Darius thought about knocking on the door up the stairs until someone heard them. He just didn't want to face his father again. There must be another way out.

"What about your father?" asked Kelln. "Doesn't he want you to follow in his footsteps; be a councilor for our mighty King?

Darius grunted. "You know I can't stand the politics. The councilors have forgotten what they are supposed to do. They are appointed to protect and help all people, not just the nobles. I want to help the Realm become great once again and protect all the people, not just the nobles."

"What about your magic?" Kelln asked.

Darius stopped in the middle of the room, his shoulders slumped. "I don't know Kelln, what should I do?" Looking at the lamps on the wall, he was reminded again that magic was not gone in Anikari as everyone supposed. "Maybe I should just forget this ever happened?" He moved his arms around the room, pointing to the dozens of lamps that he had lit.

Kelln, with rare seriousness, shook his red topped head from side to side. "I don't know, Darius. It is quite fantastic, but I don't know what to do this time. It really could be dangerous."

Chapter Two

Kelln and Darius continued to look around the walls of the cavernous room for a way out. It seemed like hours passed, but still no sign of any kind of outlet had been found.

No door. No window. Nothing.

"This building must be one of the oldest ones in the entire Realm," Kelln whispered. "There has to be a way out."

"The Realm is over five hundred years old, Kelln. I'm sure there are a lot of old buildings around. But I agree there should be another way out of this room. Let's start at the other end once more, back behind the shelves."

Reaching the other side of the room, the two young men stopped moving and stood in silence for a moment, each in his own thoughts. Their physical builds were opposite. Darius took after his father, Richard: large build, broad-shouldered, with dark hair and grey eyes. His skin color was lighter than his father's though, and closer to his mother, Elizabeth. Kelln stood about six inches shorter than Darius, with bright red hair that never stayed combed. His skin was fair, full of freckles, and his voice came a few pitches higher than Darius's.

"Darius." Kelln's voice finally held some sense of worry and exhaustion. "I'm out of ideas. You?"

"Kel." Darius motioned Kelln over to a cabinet that was hidden behind a smaller bookshelf.

"What's that?" Kelln asked.

"I'm not sure, but I feel something. Something important is inside."

Kelln raised his eyebrows at Darius, but reached down to try and pry open the black cabinet. They both pulled hard but couldn't move the door. No apparent lock existed. They moved their hands and fingers around the back and underneath. Kelln stepped back.

"A stupid box with no door. It's not like a secret passage is hidden inside or something. Come on, Darius, leave it alone. We need to find our way out of here."

"Tiring of adventure already?"

"That's not fair, and if you have to know, I'm hungry."

Darius laughed hard. As he did so he ran his hand over the front of the wooden case. His hand was guided by an unknown invisible force. As his laughter died, they heard a click, and the front swung open.

"But . . . how . . ." Kelln stumbled over his words.

"I felt something from inside and thought about it, and when I laughed the cabinet opened."

"The laughter," Kelln stated. "It was emotion again, Darius."

Darius didn't answer. At the moment he didn't want to think about his newfound abilities or what made them work. Besides facing his father, how could he ever face Christine? She was special to him and he didn't want something like this to ruin things.

Darius peered inside the black case. It was darker inside than it should be, but a golden, polished sword stood upright inside the case. Darius reached his fingers forward.

"Are you crazy?" Kelln batted Darius's arm back.

"It's fine, Kelln. The sword is reaching out to me." How could he explain to Kelln the feeling that was emerging in him? How could he explain the calmness he envisioned everything with at that moment? The edges of his vision were sharper. His mind opened and there seemed to be pure knowledge flowing into him. Part of him wanted to push it away, but part of him was intrigued and excited. In that moment the possibilities that were opened to him were endless.

"Great. Now you can talk to objects. Aren't you taking this wizarding a little too far?"

"I'm not a wizard, Kelln. How could you say that? The books say wizardry runs in families. You know my father. He certainly isn't one."

Kelln shrugged his shoulders, but didn't seem convinced. "Wizards of earth, mind, and heart," Kelln mumbled.

"What?" Darius asked.

"Everyone knows there were three types of wizards. I wonder which one you are?"

Darius glared back at his friend without a response. He seemed to be an unsolicited fountain of magical knowledge today. He guessed it was the stress of the situation. In times like these Darius was calm and liked to think, while Kelln seemed to want to talk.

They both turned back to the sword. Hesitating only a moment longer, Darius reached in and grabbed the hilt, pulling the shining golden sword out of the dark case. The lamps in the room started dimming and their flames started flashing in random patterns. Darius felt his mind pulled away from the room and flowing back in time to when the sword was created.

He watched an old man, red-faced and sweating, leaning over a hot forge with wizards casting spells into the molten metal. Three wizards and what looked like a Cremelino horse stood around the forge with colors of magic hanging in the air and being drawn into the sword itself. The odor of hot fire burned Darius's nostrils and throat when he tried to breathe. He saw men at arms guarding the forge as a small group of others began to attack. He gasped at what he was seeing. His mind raced back to the present and knocked him to the ground. The lights flashed off and the sword clanked against the floor.

"Darius. Darius. I told you not to touch it. Where are you? I can't see anything. What's going on?" Kelln's voice, bordering on panic, spat out questions.

Darius moaned from the ground. "I'm fine."

"If you're so fine, can you bring the lights back on?"

Nothing happened for a long ten seconds, then a blinding light lit the room around Darius, causing Kelln to turn away. Darius held the sword, now shining white, out in front of him. After a moment the sword dimmed to a low glow, and Kelln turned back around.

"What in Anikari's name was that? That was fantastic!" Kelln looked shocked to the core. "Your face looks sunburned."

"The forge." Darius felt dazed. "I saw the forge in my mind. I watched them making this sword. I stood right next to the fire. Three wizards were chanting spells over its making."

"Earth, mind, and heart. The three types of wizards. That makes sense." Kelln reiterated his earlier comment.

Darius turned the sword over in his hands. "There's an inscription here that was burned into the metal when it was created. I don't understand what the symbols mean though."

"You're worrying me. What did you get yourself into?"

"Try being in my head right now, Kelln. I can sense things I couldn't sense before. I can feel the sword, the room, the library upstairs. Everything is clearer to me. This sword was meant to protect the Realm. That is what I must do, Kelln. Protect the Realm."

"Before you run off and become General Darius San Williams and save the Realm, do you think you can use that power of yours too find us a way out?" pleaded Kelln.

"I think I can." Darius smiled as he strode back across the room. The lamps remained dark, but the low glow of the sword gave off enough light to see. He stood in the middle of the room, over a carpet, and closed his eyes. It seemed easier that way. Only seconds later he walked over to a rug on the floor and knocked on it with his sword.

"Listen."

"Hollow," said Kelln. He started pulling back the rug, almost knocking Darius off his feet.

In quick fashion they pulled up a secret door that led to a steep stairway down under the room. They both stood for a minute looking around the room. Kelln ran over to grab a book off the closest desk.

"What?" glared Darius. "You can't take that."

"It's only one. It might come in handy someday when we travel. Call it a souvenir of our greatest adventure . . . so far." Kelln smiled. "Anyway. Are you going to leave the sword here?"

Darius was silent.

"I didn't think so."

With that, they headed down the narrowing stairs to a small tunnel. The sword still glowed, lighting their way. If possible, it was even darker there in the small, dusty tunnel than back in the room. They were not sure where they were; somewhere between various walls in the old castle-turned-school. The building had been constructed over 250 years before. At first, it had been used as an ambassador's castle of sorts. Ambassadors and other important people from countries near and far had stayed here waiting to do business with the King and his councilors and wizards. King Edward's father, King Charles, had built a newer building closer to the castle for visiting dignitaries about twenty years earlier. At that time, the old castle had been made into a school.

A few old wooden doors in dark, recessed doorways dotted the sides of the tunnel. At the end of it all hung a metal door, larger than the others. Running to the potential exit, Darius reached it first and tried to pull it open by its large handle. Nothing! It seemed to be locked.

"Try the sword on the door," said Kelln.

Darius put the sword in the slit between the door and the doorframe. He brought the blade up to the top of the door and brought it down with as much force as he was able. They heard a cracking sound and sparks flew out from the door frame. Darius shielded his eyes for a moment as the sword brightened again. The latch of the door now sat cut in half.

Kelln pulled on the heavy door a few times before it came open. Water drops flew inside, dotting their faces with the heavy drizzle that hung in the spring air. Stepping out of the tunnel they turned back and closed the door. They both glanced at the sword and without saying anything Darius started to hack away at the bushes around the hidden doorway.

Ten feet later they found themselves standing in mud up to their ankles, next to a small hill in the back of the school property. The archery fields and small sports stadium were a little over the rise to the east.

"That sword is fantastic," exclaimed Kelln. "What does it feel like?"

Darius ran his forefinger up and down over the astonishing sword. There was not even a scratch on it, and it sat in perfect balance in his hand. He still experienced the power flowing over him.

He handed the sword over to Kelln. "Here."

Kelln took hold, the sword dimming to its original gold shine. Kelln waved the sword in the air a few times.

"Do you feel anything?" asked Darius.

"Nothing, though my dad would love to see this. Its workmanship is flawless and the balance is perfect. If this was used as a pattern, we would be able to arm our men better against any attacks from Arc or Gildan."

"I've heard from my father there are problems in our own Realm. Down south in Belor."

Kelln frowned. "I've heard too, but I don't like the way my father is talking about it."

"What do you mean?"

Kelln handed the sword back. "Nothing. Forget it. "

Darius could tell his friend didn't want to talk about it. It was rare that Kelln didn't want to talk, as besides getting into troublesome adventures, talking seemed to be his favorite pastime.

Darius moved bushes back in front of the door and the path they had cut so their footsteps weren't so obvious.

Kelln went back to talking about the sword. "It didn't start to glow again when you took it back. I guess there is no need now."

"You've suddenly become quite the expert on magic artifacts I see." Darius smiled at his friend.

"My father's family is from Belor. It's part of our culture and past. I grew up listening to stories of the old magic. The days of wizards and the magic of the Black Forest were regular dinner conversations."

"You believe all that?"

"Sure. Why not?"

"I just don't know what to believe. I know that the nobles say their fear of magic came from the wizards' revolt a hundred years ago, but it also just might be a story to justify their persecution of the farmers."

"Darius! Are you daft or what? I saw fire come from your palm, lamps light with no fire, and a glowing sword. If this isn't magic, then tell me what it is."

Darius paced and grew serious. "I've been brought up my whole life to not trust anything magic. It almost destroyed our kingdom once. Promise not to tell anyone?"

"But . . ."

"No one. Kelln. No one. You hear me? Not until I know what is happening to me for sure. If my father ever found out I don't know what he would do."

"Fine. Sure. You don't have to get angry."

Darius didn't want to get mad at Kelln. He was just plain afraid. During the wizard revolt, wizards had tried to take over the government in Anikari. It had been a long and bloody battle. In the end the stronger wizards were all killed, and the lesser ones exiled outside of the city. Over the years those weaker wizards had mixed their blood with the farmers, but the nobles still talked down to them and referred to anyone outside the city as outsiders.

Darius still felt the power flowing through him. Now that he had done so once, he knew without even thinking that he could pull forth a flame again. That in itself alarmed him. He had no training in these types of things. What did it all mean?

"Promise?" he asked again to make sure. He stuck his right hand out to shake Kelln's right hand, then left hand to left hand, the ultimate promise, signifying the entire body, both heart and mind, would abide by the promise.

They ran through the field to the nearest road and began to head back toward the school. It was later in the afternoon now and they hoped that classes hadn't started up again. A drizzle in the air made everything wet. They would have to find a place to clean up first.

Without paying attention, they almost ran directly into a group of other boys walking down the dirt road back toward the school.

"What are you guys doing," said one of them to Darius, "skipping out of school?"

"Huh?" Darius hesitated. He recognized these boys and had never liked them. They were younger sons of some minor nobles who always tried to act tough. Darius had run into a few of them just a week earlier when they had been bullying a younger student. Darius had helped the young man and stood up to the bullies. Remembering the sword in his hands still, he slid it behind his back.

"Don't worry," said the boy. "We won't tell."

The other boys laughed and started joking among themselves about what they had just done.

"What's going on?" asked Kelln.

"We were messing with some outsiders, that's all. Nothing too important," said the apparent leader of the group.

"Some outsider boy thought he was real tough, but we showed him," said another.

"You mean we shoved him," laughed a third. "Shoved him right in the mud. He looked like a pig. Stupid outsiders!"

Darius's breath quickened and his face reddened. He tried to walk away and ignore the other boys. "Come on, Kelln. Let's go."

The first boy continued talking to them, however. "His sister was an excitable one though. I still say she was cute enough under all that mud and water. She just has to learn her place in life. I mean there is an order to things, right? Us nobles, the merchants, then the outsiders."

"I am not a pig," mimicked one of the boys in a high girl's voice. "My name is Christine."

Darius, a few yards away with his back to the young nobles, turned around so fast that everything blurred in front of him. Some residual effects of his manifestation of power still clung to him. He felt a new anger build, which he hadn't felt before. It was the power reacting to the other boys' conversation. "What did she look like?" asked Darius with new interest.

"Before or after she was covered in mud?" the leader laughed with the others.

Darius, with hardly a step, appeared suddenly in front of the braggart. He stood at least twenty pounds heavier and three inches taller than the younger noble. "Before!"

"Well . . . she . . . " stumbled the leader of the group as he backed away, "she was tall for a girl, maybe fourteen or fifteen with blonde hair."

"And the boy?" quizzed Darius. He sensed his newfound power surging within him. The force needed a release. He tried to keep the rage under control. He was not used to these types of feelings. He tried to push it down, but anger continued to build and his head pounded.

"Uh . . . A few years younger than the girl. Jain, I think it was. He was . . ."

Before anyone knew what happened, the leader of the boys crashed to the ground with a thud. "Ouch . . . Hey . . ."

Events happened so fast that no one really noticed Darius's outstretched hand actually hadn't touched the other man, yet he sat on the ground just the same. Darius wanted to hit him again, but he maintained control over the power, just barely.

Thoughts of Christine being pushed around by these boys was hardly more than Darius could handle. Christine Anderssn was one of the nicest and sweetest girls he knew. Her parents, Stefen and Caroline, and her siblings, Jain and Emily, accepted Darius's presence with Christine quite well. Stefen was a very educated farmer who raised cattle and grain. He taught his children many things, including how to read and write. Increased tensions had risen recently between the farmers and the city people, but Christine's family seemed to always keep a positive attitude and to do their best.

Two of the other boys in the group jumped at Darius. Kelln, still trying to figure out what had happened, jumped in between them.

"Don't!" he said as he tried to stop them. They pushed him aside but the delay gave Darius time to pull the sword out from behind his back. He held the blade by the hilt with both hands over his head. It glowed again.

Everyone else seemed to freeze in time. Mouths hung open. Fear spread across the leader's face as he looked up from the ground, wiping the red blood off his nose. The other men stopped in mid-stride. None of them held any weapons at all and they recognized that the sword could slice all of them within a few moments.

Kelln was the only one to move. He took a step toward Darius and grabbed his arm. Darius tried to pull the hand away, but soon he seemed to focus on Kelln. He blinked his eyes, wiping the misty rain from them with one of his hands

The leader of the other men stood up and joined the others running back toward the school.

"Not a good way to keep a secret," mumbled Kelln.

Darius pushed Kelln away and took off running. How could he have let himself lose control like that? That wasn't like him. Darius was afraid of what the power was doing to him. At first he had felt a profound sense of his destiny to help others and secure the Realm. But the anger was new. He needed to learn to balance it with a purpose.

His thoughts turned to Christine as he ran. He hoped she wasn't hurt. His heart pounded with thoughts of her being pushed around by those boys. He ran harder, down the hill from the school into the merchant section of town. The large stone buildings with their colorful flags were blurred in his vision. Horses tied up with their carts waited to be unloaded. Ladies with silk dresses and bonnets had servants holding umbrellas for them in the drizzle. His steps slapped loudly on the wet cobblestone street. The guard at the north gate gave him a quizzical stare and a shake of his head as Darius ran out of the city with the sword swinging in his hand.

Darius panted so hard he thought he would faint. Power continued to surge through him, pushing him harder and harder. He let the power fuel his body. The exhilaration was amazing. He had never felt such raw strength. *It doesn't feel evil.*

Into the farmlands he ran. Orchards of fruit trees with spring blossoms blurred by as he pushed himself harder down the dirt road. He passed cattle grazing in the fields and spring vegetables just poking up out of the ground. Two deer ran across his path, running off behind a small whitewashed home with a thatch roof, reminding him he needed to be more careful. He loved these farmlands and the fields. To him they signified a simpler time and way of life. One that did not hold to so many prejudices that the nobles in the city had developed over the years. His father was one of them. Senior Councilor to King Edward, his father, Richard San Williams, seemed to detest the "outsiders," as he called them. Darius didn't understand. These were good, hardworking, simple people.

He knew he needed to slow down, but he couldn't until he saw Christine. Digging his feet into the mud he stopped in front of Christine's small wooden cottage and gulped in breaths of fresh air. He hooked his sword through his belt and leaned over, hands on knees, until he found his breath again. The smell of fresh rain and alfalfa filled his nostrils.

The rain stopped and Darius pushed his wet, brown hair out of his eyes. Christine stood on the small front porch. Spring flowers sat in pots lining the landing to the side of the door. The thatch roof was steep and almost as low as Christine's head. Her simple dress held spots of mud, but she seemed to have cleaned herself up.

She looked from Darius's face to the sword hanging by his side. "What's wrong, Darius?"

Darius continued to try and slow his breathing. Taking a few steps onto the porch, he reached out and grabbed Christine in a hard hug. "I'm so sorry, Christine. I know it isn't fair."

"But how did you know?" Her eyes opened wide.

Darius rubbed at his eyes, trying to get the rest of the rainwater out. He reached over and held Christine's hand. "Let's take a walk."

"In the rain?" Christine asked. Her long blond hair usually held a slight wave, but now hung down the sides of her slender face. She ran inside and grabbed a dry cloak to wrap around her.

Darius didn't say anything but pulled her gently along. The two friends walked in silence, heading farther west into the farmlands. From the dirt road they ducked under a forest of trees onto a small path. A breeze fluttered the oaks and birches, dripping drops of water onto their heads. Darius glanced at Christine out of the corner of his eyes. Her long blond hair still stuck to her head with the previous drizzle, but her green eyes sparkled with intelligence and beauty. He breathed in deeply and then tried to exhale the frustration of the day out of his lungs.

"Where did you get the sword?" Christine asked, breaking the silence.

"One of Kelln's adventures," he muttered.

She nodded and raised her eyebrows as if knowing there was more to the story than he was willing to tell at the moment.

Soon the two emerged from the trees onto the top of a gently sloping hill.

Looking down, Christine whispered in a soft voice, "Look. It's beautiful!"

Darius nodded, afraid that by speaking, the scene might disappear. As the sun broke out from the rolling dark clouds to the west Darius and Christine beheld a field of bright green, in which the recent drops of rain sparkled in the emerging sunlight like the stars on a clear night. Beyond the grass, to the west, lay a small, beautiful lake of clear blue, reflecting the disappearing rain clouds. They listened to thunder rolling through the dark, shadow-filled Superstition Mountains in the distance.

As if on cue they both began to descend the small hill. Their wet shoes flattened the raindrops into the soft carpet of grass.

"The rainwater sparkling on the grass looks like jewels or silver." Christine twirled around with her arms held out from her sides. Her dark blue cloak flew out around her wet cotton dress.

"Or like diamonds," said Darius.

"A field of diamonds," said Christine with excitement in her voice. "Let's call it our field of diamonds."

"All right," agreed Darius as he walked toward a lone oak tree in the field. Its gnarled trunk was the width of three normal trees. The newly emerged, irregular green leaves spread a canopy over a considerable area. He felt like a small child hiding the secret of a faraway place. When younger he had always dreamed of being a famous explorer or traveler.

He climbed up on a limb for a moment to view the landscape better, but it was hard to see through all the leaves, and the droplets of water from the branches above kept getting in his face. He poked his head through some of the leaves to see better.

"I would love to have this big tree at my house," said Christine.

"Why?"

"When I was younger we had a huge walnut tree almost this big. My dad built the biggest swing coming down from it. He would push me and Jain for hours." Christine paused, as if seeing it play out in her mind once again. "But one winter the snow was heavy and the tree fell. The other trees never seemed the same."

They walked down to the edge of the small lake and threw a few stones in, watching the reflection of the clouds and sky break into tiny ripples traveling to the center of the lake.

"Christine, I don't know why they treat you so badly. Someday I will change things. I love the Realm and I want all the people to be treated fairly. Someday, somehow, I will make that happen."

He knew she probably didn't believe him. What could he ever do? He would need to try and talk to his father. When his schooling was done he would train to be in the army, rather than as a councilor like his father wanted. He would protect the Realm from invaders and work to bring her people together. He didn't want to just sit around like his father, in an office, running errands at the whim of the King. He needed to do something.

"Darius." Christine lifted her hand to his face and wiped some remaining droplets of water off with a tender touch.

"Something happened today. You seem different." She looked him in the eyes and leaned in closer next to him.

Darius wrapped his arm around Christine in a tight embrace and together they watched the clouds continue their exodus toward the mountains. Darius wanted to tell her, but just couldn't find the right words to say.

Chapter Three

The city of Anikari was the center of the Realm. It was where the King resided and where the central government made their laws. The Realm had been founded over five hundred years earlier by a man named Anikari. He had brought together the smaller kingdoms of Belor, Mar, Denir, and Sur, and along with his capital city of Anikari, formed the Realm. Bordered on the south by the Empire of Gildan, the west by the Kingdom of Arc, the north by the forgotten lands, and the east by the Blue Sea, the Realm had been at peace for quite a few years under King Edward and his father, King Charles. Only recently had resistance been forming in some of the cities and minor skirmishes had been fought on the borders with the other kingdoms.

Being the center of the Realm, Anikari hosted many tournaments, contests, and celebrations every year with the partial purpose to keep her people at peace with one another. In late spring before school ended for the noble's children and before the heat of the summer set in, an archery contest was held. Today was no exception. The archery contest would be the last fun thing before the young men had to hunker down and start studying for their graduation exams. After that they would spend the summer running errands for the King and his councilors before advanced training, internships, or apprenticeship started up in the fall.

Three weeks after Darius had found the sword, he and Kelln walked across the green practice field behind the academy. This was where they prepared for the archery contest. With his hand Darius shaded his grey eyes from the early morning sun. On the other side of the large grass area on the competition field, a dais was raised where the King would sit and watch the contest. Flags from the four major cities, as well as Tean and Forest View, joined the Anikari flag on top of a tall pole. The light breeze did little to lift them up.

The two young men stopped in front of a group of younger boys practicing their archery skills. Darius leaned down to one of them who seemed to be struggling.

"Here, let me show you a better way to hold it," Darius said to the young boy.

The youngster looked up at Darius with a startled look in his eyes. He handed the bow to Darius. "You're the councilor's son, aren't you?"

"Yes I am. My name is Darius."

"I want to be a councilor someday," said the young boy.

Darius reached down and showed the young boy how to hold the bow for a more steady shot. "And why is that?"

"They get to do all the exciting things."

Darius thought of his father and sighed deeply. His father seemed to be behind closed doors with the King more and more lately. He was hardly ever home. When he was it was only to tell Darius that he shouldn't go to the farmlands and that he needed to act more like a noble. He loved his father, but as he got older he realized that his father just didn't understand him and what he wanted to do in life. All his father wanted was to look good in front of King Edward. It was hard for Darius to watch happen. "Not everything is exciting as a councilor. They spend a lot of time in meetings."

The boy shrugged and then thanked Darius for the help. He and Kelln continued walking across the practice field. Darius continued thinking about his father and hoped that he would be there today to watch him. It was his father who had taught him how to shoot. They used to go out each week and practice. Though those memories were now so far between that he couldn't remember the last time they had spent any real time together.

"Darius, pay attention!" shouted Kelln.

Darius looked up to find that he was walking in front of some other archers practicing.

"What were you doing?"

"Nothing." Darius moved out of the archers' way.

"We better get over to the sign-in area or you won't have any chance this year," said Kelln.

"Any chance?" Darius repeated. "I'm going all the way!"

"Oh, so you've set your sights on the entire tournament," mocked Kelln. "Maybe I better give up now and just watch from the sidelines."

"Maybe you should." Darius laughed as he pulled back his bowstring. Feeling the string taut in his hand, he slowly let it go. "Because when I let this baby go, you are going to see more bulls-eyes than you've ever seen at the noble's tournament."

"Aren't we the big shot today?" laughed Kelln. "But I guess you are one of the favorites to win this year."

"I just hope I can concentrate. Christine's going to be here."

"Seems like you two are inseparable these days," Kelln teased.

Darius blushed. "Enough about me. Do you think you're ready?"

"Archery is new to me, but I think I can do all right. If it was a sword tournament I would have you beat." Kelln puffed up. "Well, I used to be better than you. With that new sword of yours I don't know now."

Darius shook his head and glanced around. "Kelln, not a word. You promised."

"No one is around, Darius. I know you have been holding it and practicing with it. But you don't even talk about it at all. Come on. What about the power? What's going on with you?"

"I don't know. Sometimes it's here. Sometimes it's not. When it is, I can sense everything around me. It makes me think and see more clearly." Darius stopped talking and turned to his friend. "It's hard to explain."

"Sounds fantastic."

"And scary."

"Yeah, I guess so, but what else can you do? You know, the fire in the palm thing was great!"

Darius saw someone walking up from a distance. "No more, Kelln. Not now. I need more time to figure it out."

"Later, though. You have to talk about it." Kelln had tried to get Darius to open up for the past few weeks since they had found the sword in the library basement. He wasn't ready though. He knew that Kelln didn't understand. Kelln would have just rushed into things and shown his abilities to everyone. That was Kelln though. Brash and fearless. Darius tried to determine how he felt about it. Was it evil or not? He needed to be very very careful and make sure that no one knew about it until he understood what he could do. He would have to be prepared to defend his magical abilities or else he might be banished.

"I'm going to get a drink. See you in a few minutes," Kelln said, walking away.

Darius tried to put his focus on the tournament and push the thoughts of magic to the side. But it was hard. He couldn't even explain how afraid he felt. He hadn't told Christine about it either, which pained him more than anything. He hated keeping secrets from her, but he didn't know how to bring something like this up. *Hey Christine, nice day today, isn't it? Did you know I might be a wizard?* Or *don't bother lighting that fire in your stove; let me do that for you with my finger.*

"Hey Darius," someone yelled.

Darius turned around, saw Sean, and gave an outward moan. Sean San Ghant, nineteen years old, and the ambitious son of a minor noble, constantly drew attention to himself with his loud mouth. Unfortunately, he was also one of the finest archers in the Realm.

"Is your girlfriend going to be here?" he said with his usual mocking and whining voice.

"What?" said Darius, caught off guard by the question.

"Come on, don't pretend, Darius," he said as he put his arm around Darius. "I've seen you with your little farmer girl. But what would your father say? Oh so scandalous. So many secrets, my friend. What other mysteries do you hold inside?"

"Cut it out, Sean." Darius pushed away from him. There was no way Sean could know about his magic. "Don't start this!"

"Come on, Darius, I'm just teasing. You are so touchy lately." Sean stood a few inches taller than Darius and rubbed his short-cropped blond hair with his hands. Darius thought it an annoying habit that just angered him more.

Darius turned away and studied his bowstring to take his mind off of the older boy. Ever since they were young boys Sean had seemed to have it out for him. He had sucked up to the councilors and tried to get the King to notice him, and now he was distracting Darius from preparing for the tournament. Another ploy, he was sure, to help him win.

"I guess if you can't get a city girl . . ." said Sean behind his back.

Darius turned around with a glare, "Sean, why don't you just shut up. She's ten times the person you are, and much smarter." Once the words left Darius's mouth he realized how stupid and immature he sounded, but he couldn't think of anything else to say at the moment.

Sean just laughed.

The power surged through Darius, flaring his anger further.

Sean turned to walk away and Darius flung his hand toward the ground where Sean stood. Dirt rose up over the grass, forcing Sean to trip and fall.

Kelln, coming up behind Darius, choked on his drink, spraying drops of water all over the front of him. He was trying not to laugh. Darius turned to him with a glare that told him to shut up.

Sean stood up and turned toward Darius. He seemed confused and embarrassed.

"Watch your step, Sean." Darius smirked.

"What's the matter here?" one of the coaches asked, walking up to them.

"Oh it's just Sean being himself," Darius said.

"I just asked him about his farmer girl," Sean scowled while wiping the dirt off his knees.

"What happened to you?" the man asked Sean.

"Nothing."

"The contest starts in fifteen minutes. Both of you should be getting over to the tournament field. I don't want any more trouble."

"Yes sir," mumbled Darius as he turned away. He had to be more careful and think about the contest now; calm himself down. He let out a deep breath, then walked away. The power rose up in him too easily these days.

"I thought you said . . ." Kelln started.

"I lost my temper," Darius mumbled.

"It was funny though."

"Yes it was, wasn't it?" Darius joined Kelln in a good laugh. "But I don't like losing control."

Darius and Kelln ran over to the competition area. Darius squinted into the sun when he heard someone else call his name. He looked over and his face broke into a wide smile as he saw Christine. He walked over to them.

"Next year I'll be here," said Jain to Darius as he walked up. Christie and her sister, Emily, sat on the ground. They had found a spot in the shade overlooking the tournament field. "Then they'll see that the city people aren't always the best at everything."

Darius smiled at Christine's younger brother. He had grown six inches the previous year and at barely thirteen stood eye to eye with Christine, who was two years older. His hair was darker than his siblings, taking more after their father. Always ready to jump in to defend himself, Jain had recently begun learning from Darius how to shoot the bow and arrow.

"Yeah, if you live that long," laughed Christine.

"Look!" Christine's younger sister, Emily, said. She was a mini version of her older sister, complete with blond hair, a slender build, and almond-shaped green eyes that sparkled in the sunlight with anticipation. At eleven years old, she was four years younger than Christine, but Emily was forever trying to be like her older sister. She pointed toward the entrance to the field. The rest of the crowd stood up with anticipation. Trumpets sounded, signaling the approaching procession. Darius said goodbye and hurried back into line with the rest of the competitors.

The contestants lined up all together, shoulder to shoulder. Kelln stood next to Darius, with a big grin on his freckled face. Even though he had always been good with the sword, this was his first archery competition. He had been practicing with Darius and even though he wouldn't win, his skills were better than average. The thrill of being there was apparent on his face, and he elbowed Darius in the ribs with excitement.

Darius glanced over at him, offering up a smile. The air seemed to be filled with anticipation. This would be his last competition. He had won his grade bracket for three out of the last five years. He hoped he might win the King's Cup and a medal in his final year before graduation from the academy. It would help him in his placement in defending the Realm.

The trumpets sounded again in unison. A large archway had appeared overnight in the south end of the field, built by the King's carpenters. Fresh vines and flowers covered the arch. It was large enough for at least four riders riding side by side. First came nobles from the surrounding cities of Denir, Mar, Sur, Forest View, and Tean. They each wore their city colors; Denir in blue, Mar in yellow, accented by a multitude of other colors, Sur in gray, Forest View with green and black, and Tean with earthy brown. No one in the competition this year was from Belor. There were rumors of someone declaring himself a new leader there just a week before. A man known only as the Preacher.

Next entered the nobles and the mayor from Anikari. They wore the royal purple and red of the capital city. They were always held in higher regard than the other Realm cities. The lower councilors came in next. They, along with the King's personal councilors, made up the King's royal advisors. Each one today was being pulled by two large pure-white Cremelino horses in small single chariots. Darius's father, Richard, along with his mother, Elizabeth, entered next. He tried to grab his father's attention, but his father wasn't looking around.

After all the others were lined in place, King Edward DarSan Montere made his grand entrance. His chariot stood larger than the councilors' and was pulled by four of the famous Cremelino horses. The King wore the royal crown on his head and held the royal staff, and his purple robe swirled around his red coat. All of the colors of the Realm streamed from the back of his chariot. The King entered last as an ancient sign of humility. Darius laughed inside at the irony of it.

The crowd cheered. The Realm always loved their kings and queens. King Edward was no exception. However, some of the outlying cities were more subdued in their cheers. Tensions had been rising lately among some of the other cities in regards to taxation and fear of approach by some neighboring kingdoms. King Edward was in his early forties and still held the sturdy frame of his athletic youth. A crown sat atop his brown hair. Almost ten years earlier, the King's wife and only daughter had died during a spreading outbreak of a plague. For some reason not known to the general public the King had never remarried, and thus there was currently no heir to follow him.

Darius glanced at his father. Always right next to the King, making himself available for his every wish. As soon as he saw him, Darius's stomach knotted in anxiety. He remembered they hadn't spoken much that week. He had wanted to discuss with his father the trouble with the farmlands, but hadn't found a chance. His father just seemed too busy to care about him anymore.

The King seated himself and the crowd sat back down again. The competition was ready to begin. Darius took a deep breath. He couldn't afford to become angry today. He had to control himself.

"This is fantastic, isn't it?" smiled Kelln. "I can hardly wait for my turn."

As the younger group went, Kelln shifted from the right to left foot and back again in anticipation.

"I go first, so all you have to do is aim for the big hole in the middle of the target that will be there after when I'm finished," laughed Darius, glad his best friend was there. Without any other siblings, Darius considered Kelln almost family to him. He would do anything for his best friend.

After the younger students went, Darius and Kelln's age bracket began. Darius heard his name called and walked up to the line. Over the crowd he distinctly heard Christine's voice cheering him on. He smiled inside. He breathed in deeply, called up the calmness, and relaxed.

As he lifted the bow up, nocked his arrow, and pulled the string back, he made everything else disappear from his mind. He focused on the small black dot in the middle of the target, as he had been taught to do so long ago. His father had given him his first bow when he was five years old. He'd always had the special ability to put everything from his mind. Almost as if he were pulling the target to him. Now he wondered if all along it had something to do with the strange power he now held.

In fact, his father teaching him to shoot was one of the best memories of his childhood. Perhaps today his father would receive some satisfaction and inward reward if Darius did well. He desperately hoped so.

Darius drew upon the power within him and the target came into focus more easily than ever before.

Concentrate! Focus!

He let the string and arrow leave his fingers. The arrow jumped out as a wildcat springing on his prey. He heard the crowd cheer before he was sure of the results himself. The arrow struck dead center. The second one a little off to the side from the first. The third arrow held deep, dead center in the target, scraping against his first arrow.

He had one more turn. The best three out of four arrows would count. If he shot another bullseye, his worst one would drop out and he would have a perfect score. Not a common occurrence.

Darius pulled back on his bowstring, but as he started to let the arrow go he felt and heard a loud crack. He jumped, yelled, and grabbed his hand. The arrow shot into the ground about five feet in front of him.

He heard a few laughs, but mostly condolences rose from the crowd and other competitors. Darius had broken his bow, and the string had struck hard into his hand, making an instant welt. An official came over to assess the situation. Darius sat down on a bench and hung his head low. He wondered how his bow could have broken.

He sensed someone looking at him. From down the row of competitors he eyed Sean's toothy, over-confident smile. Darius picked up his bow with his good hand and breathed in deeply. Images flashed across his mind. The break seemed unnatural to him. He made an educated guess on what had happened; Sean had sabotaged his bow somehow. But there was no proof.

Even though Darius's last arrow would be the one not counted, he still was expected to win his age bracket. There were four more boys to go, Kelln being one of them. The problem, it seemed, was that Darius had no bow now for the finals. There was a long-standing rule that no bows could be lent to another competitor. A long time ago there had been problems with loaning good bows around to friends. Some boys complained of the ruling being unfair.

Darius sat, gazing down at nothing in particular while the officials tried to continue. He tried not to think of Sean. He tried to keep his anger in check. He didn't want to make a fool of himself here. He calmed himself. A few moments later a pair of shiny brown boots appeared in front of him. He brought his eyes up.

"Here," was all Kelln said as he shoved his own bow toward Darius. A sad smile lingered on his freckled face.

Darius realized what Kelln was trying to do. "No, Kel. I can't take your bow. Don't you know the rules?"

"I asked, and since I haven't gone yet, I can give you mine," he said with a genuine smile.

"But that means you can't go. I can't . . . I can't . . ." said Darius, pushing the bow back.

"No, Darius. You have a chance to win. I want you to have it!" He thrust the bow into Darius's hands.

The two young men were unaware that the entire tournament had stopped to watch the interchange until they heard the crowd cheer. Darius was moved. He knew how excited Kelln had been and how hard he had worked for his first archery tournament. He pushed it away from himself, back into Kelln's hands, but Kelln was adamant and wouldn't take it back.

"Thanks, Kelln. You're the best!" said Darius as he stood up and shook Kelln's hand with his good hand. A lump formed in his throat and he wiped his eyes from something the wind had blown in.

"Now you'd better win, after all of this commotion," Kelln laughed as he motioned toward the crowd. Turning, he whispered, "Don't you dare let Sean beat you."

"Oh, don't worry about him," Darius said with a twinkle in his eye.

"Darius?"

Darius laughed. "Don't worry."

Darius stood, holding a cool wet cloth on his hurt hand as the competition resumed. He wasn't worried about using Kelln's bow. In fact, he had used the bow many times practicing together. He felt terrible about Kelln not being able to be in the competition after all of his practicing and promised himself that he would win for both of them.

I won't let him down.

The announcement soon came naming Darius one of the finalists. Christine waved at him, and her brother and sister shouted with enthusiasm. He also heard the crowd applauding the finalist from the older age group. He missed the name, but watched Sean step out onto the field and take a flourishing bow.

I'm just going to have to put him in his place.

Sean had placed second in the competition the previous year. Even though Darius had won his age bracket, an older boy had won the entire competition that year. The prior year should have been Sean's last, but because he was still only eighteen he was allowed to either compete in the junior or the nobles' tournament. Darius knew Sean decided to hang back a year at this competition to feed his ego and try to win.

Sean stepped up to the line and stretched his muscled arms, puffing his chest up as he did. The pompous frills of his lace shirt moved in the slight breeze. Many of the younger girls thought Sean was an idol of perfection, and Darius heard a chorus of sighs from the crowd. Most of the adults thought the young noble a little extreme, but they tolerated him for his charm.

Sean shot his first arrow. It sailed through the air with only a slight quiver and barely missed the bullseye, but it was still an incredible shot. Darius thought he noticed disgust run across Sean's face, and he relaxed a little. Sean's next two were flawless, even touching each other in the center of the bullseye. Darius started getting nervous again.

Darius tried not to watch the fourth arrow, but couldn't help himself. He blew out a mouthful of air after Sean's arrow hit the target. He hadn't realized he was holding his breath for so long. It was a good shot, but not perfect. Darius still had a chance to beat him, if he placed three arrows in the exact center of the target.

Sean trotted down to the target to retrieve his arrows as he soaked in the crowd's applause. Darius went to the line to prepare for his shots. Sean stood on the side with a bored stance as if he had already won the tournament. He motioned for a young page to bring him some ale.

Darius' power pulsed inside him and anger strained for a release, but he cooled down and found the void in his mind to concentrate on the target. He put everything else out of his mind, drew the target to him, and shot. The crowd erupted. The shot flew perfectly. Without breaking his concentration, he strung and shot the second arrow. Again, perfect, even touching the first one.

Sean shifted from one leg to the other in nervous anticipation and Darius smiled to himself. He still had two more shots to beat Sean's arrows. All he needed was one more in the center. He proceeded in a slow and deliberate way just to keep the suspense a little while longer. He glanced at Christine in the field, his father next to the King, his mother in the front of the stands, and back at Kelln a few yards behind him. Kelln smiled and gave him a slight nod of his head. Darius found himself enjoying the moment.

My father will be proud of me if I win today!

His hand throbbed from the welt. Still he had to concentrate. It was not over yet. He pulled the string. It rubbed his hand the wrong way, and he let go before he pulled back all the way on the string. The arrow wobbled out at half speed and fell to the ground about half way to the target.

"Ow," Darius winced and held his hand in pain. The crowd held their breath then let it out in a long collaborated sigh.

Sean walked out onto the field to pick up Darius's arrow, which stuck into the medium-length green summer rye grass.

He turned to Darius. "I guess your farmer girl will be a little disappointed in you today."

Darius couldn't believe Sean was doing this here, in front of the entire tournament crowd. In addition to Sean's antics, the throbbing and pain in his hand added to his frustration. He could feel the power pushing at him again, responding to his emotions. Sean had been doing this to him since they were young. Usually he let it roll off his back, and did not let it bother him, but he gritted his teeth to hold in the growing rage.

"Sean, just get out of the way," Darius said through clenched teeth.

"Oh, the boy is hurt," Sean taunted. "Maybe his little farmer friend can rub some mud on it."

Without thinking, Darius leaped out and ran toward Sean. He tackled him to the ground, and despite his sore hand punched him hard in the ribs. The officials dragged Darius off of Sean and sent him back toward the line of competitors. By this time Christine, Jain, and Emily came down closer to the sidelines.

"Jain . . . No. It's not your fight," Darius heard Christine yell. She was doing all she could to hold Jain back from leaping out at Sean himself.

"Yes it is my fight. He insults all of us with what he says," Jain answered back, but he remained off the field with fists held tight at his side.

Darius's father and mother moved closer to him, but stopped a dozen yards away. No one knew what to do. The judges grouped together and conferred with each other and then the King. Darius saw his father march with long strides toward King Edward.

Darius continued walking back toward the shooting line, his face red and his breathing hard. He was ashamed at how his temper had controlled him. He needed to do better. What if he had let his power show?

"Darius, you are a disgrace and a coward. Maybe you belong in the farmlands with those outsiders." Sean stood up and pointed toward the sidelines. "I win the competition."

Darius, whose back was still to Sean's, tensed up and stiffened. His nostrils flared and his face grew warmer. Back at the line now, he reached down and picked up his bow. With his hand swollen and in pain, he turned to face Sean, strung his arrow, and pulled the string taut. Power filled his body and it needed a release. It was glorious to feel so much power and clarity at one time.

Sean, who still stood in the middle of the field between Darius and the target, just opened his mouth in surprise. Despite the throbbing in his hand, Darius held the bow steady, the string pulled as far as it would go, and aimed right at Sean's head.

The strange power he now possessed coursed through his veins. It heightened his senses. All at once he could hear and see everything going on around him. He heard undertones of his father apologizing to the King. He heard Jain mutter to Christine that he hoped Darius would shoot Sean. He heard Kelln, in a small and barely audible whisper that was for his ears only, plead with Darius to stay calm and remember that

Sean was nothing to them. The mutter of his friend reached him and he took a deep breath and settled into an icy calm.

Whispers ran through the crowd. Everyone waited to see what Darius would do. His face filled with anger, then turned to determination as a slight white glow appeared around his bow. Sensibility prevailed and overcame his anger and a slight smile curved his lips. The bow returned to normal and he hoped that no one had noticed the glow and would put it off to a trick of afternoon sunlight.

Darius turned his head slightly and saw the King stand up. His father, to the side of the King, clenched his teeth in anger. A few nobles whispered to each other. Christine tried to yell out but only a whisper emerged from her dry lips. All this Darius saw and heard in the blink of an eye.

Sean gaped wide-eyed still out on the field, not moving a muscle.

"Nothing to say now, Sean?" he taunted Sean in return. "No jokes on your quick tongue?"

Darius pulled the string back just a bit more – almost to the breaking point - and the crowd gasped.

Concentrate! Focus! He controlled the power and it exploded through him to do his bidding. He perceived each hair on Sean's head. He distinguished each feather in the arrows already stuck in the target. All at once his body hit ultimate calmness and balance. He breathed, smiled broadly, and knew his aim would be true.

In one fluid motion he stepped to his right two steps and let the arrow go.

The crowd sucked in a collective breath.

Sean stood frozen.

All eyes were on the target.

Darius's fourth arrow flew an arrow's width away from Sean's head and hit in the exact center of the target, fitting tightly against Darius's previous ones. The hushed silence turned into wild cheers of amazement.

Sean fell to the ground in exasperation.

Kelln whooped with joy. "Fantastic!"

Christine let out a deep sigh.

Darius looked down the field to Sean and said, "you aren't worth it," and walked away.

Before sitting down on a bench next to the other competitors he added a shout: "And I don't think you won, Sean."

The crowd laughed and cheered. They were definitely entertained that day. Sean turned a deep shade of red as anger and embarrassment filled his face. He walked off the field, turning around once to mouth a general threat at Darius that no one heard.

The last finalist took his shots, but the crowd hardly cared. They had never seen such a competition before.

Kelln brought Darius some ointment and a cloth to put on his hand.

"I almost blew it, didn't I?" Darius looked around to make sure no one else was near. "The power rages in me and has to get out, Kelln. I barely overcame it this time. What if I don't next time? That's not how I want to live my life. I need to protect the Realm, not jeopardize it. What am I going to do?" He hung his head down, visibly shaken.

Kelln smiled at his friend. "But you won, Darius. Maybe you need that temper to get things done. Maybe that's how it works. You gave us quite a show today. People will be talking about this for a long time!"

"No, Kel," smiled back Darius. "*We* won." He handed back the bow to Kelln. "Thanks for trying to cheer me up."

"You looked so calm at the end. You were taking a big chance," added Kelln.

"I was not taking any chances, Kel. If you could have seen like I did. There was no chance to lose. Everything stood out in so much detail. That's what calmed me down."

"I think I'm jealous."

"Don't be. Most of the time it gets me in more trouble than it's worth."

"That's true. Now that I think of it, it has been you getting us into trouble lately instead of me. I think I like that."

They both laughed and Darius began to outwardly relaxed, but inside he still wondered what he was going to do. He may have to leave Anikari if he couldn't control himself.

The awards ceremony was held to give out the individual awards and the overall tournament award, the King's Cup, a large golden chalice. When the speaker announced Darius's name, the crowd went wild cheering, yelling, and clapping. Darius felt a slight embarrassment over the incident. It wasn't that Sean didn't deserve it, but it was not how Darius wanted to act. He needed to be better than that. Darius stared down at the medal that hung on the end of a sculptured piece of brass with a picture of a bowman shooting a bullseye.

Afterwards, with the award around his neck and the cup in his hand, Darius started out toward the competitors' gate to see Christine and his friends; his parents would be a little longer as they wound their way out from the rest of the nobles.

"Way to go, Darius." said Jain. "Congratulations. You sure showed that fool."

Darius just smiled.

"Yes, congratulations, Darius," echoed Emily.

Christine didn't say a whole lot. He knew she did not agree with his fighting behavior. She just gave him a hug, but it was enough to make him feel better.

After talking to a few more friends who seemed to ignore Christine and her siblings, the four of them turned back toward the stands. It felt good to win. He felt proud that all the work and practice had paid off.

Christine stopped and gave another surprise hug to Darius. "Thank you," she smiled. "Thank you for standing up for us. You said you would change things and I think today might be a start."

"I just hope it is a good change, and that I didn't ruin anything. It was dumb of me to tackle him," Darius admitted.

Darius knew that even though she did not like the fighting, she was proud of Darius defending her. He wondered at times how such a strong feeling had developed between him and Christine the past year. They came from such different places in life.

Darius's father and mother approached. Their clothes were exquisite. His mother in a deep burgundy gown with gold jewelry, and his father with his royal purple cape over a red shirt. He was sure his father would be so proud of him. It was he who had taught Darius to shoot and had made him practice for so many years.

His mother gave him a hug and took the cup into her hands to study her son's award. "You did well, Darius," she smiled, "but next time . . . a little less excitement?"

Darius knew that was her way of being proud that he won, but not of the way he reacted to the situation. He didn't blame her.

He gave her a hug and smiled. She was always there for him, even when his father hadn't been. She did not express concern about the time he spent with Christine like his father did. His mother did not crave the limelight like his father, and although she attended state functions with him, she didn't linger around with the other nobles' wives very often.

Elizabeth stepped back as Darius's father approached. Darius was excited about how well he had performed and eager to hear from his father. He bounced on the balls of his feet and for the first time realized he now stood taller than his father and almost as broad. Richard stepped up to Darius. His father's trimmed beard gave his face a grave look.

Darius held out the medal for him. "Isn't it grand? Aren't you proud . . ."

"I don't know what you were thinking out on the field, Darius." Richard's blue-gray eyes flashed with anger. "You almost lost the competition for that kind of behavior. As you shot that last arrow the judges were deciding whether or not to disqualify you. You were lucky you . . ."

"Didn't you hear what Sean San Ghant said?" interrupted Darius, not ready for such treatment. "He insulted my friends. No, he did more than that; he smears the good name of the Realm with how he treats others."

"I don't care what he said. You are a noble's son, Darius San Williams. The son of a councilor. You are lucky I was here for you. I had to do a lot of talking to the King to keep you from being disqualified. He thought it might be good for you to lose. Teach you a lesson."

"If that's all you care about, looking good to your King, you take the medal. You obviously won it for me." Darius resented his father's one-sidedness. The nobility had lost touch with the people and only looked out for themselves. That is not what he wanted. He wanted to feel proud as a citizen of the Realm. He wanted to fight to defend something that meant more than all of them. The power surged at his anger again. This time he didn't hold it back.

He ripped the medal from his neck and threw it toward him. "You don't care about how I feel or why I do what I do. You don't see the injustices going on right in front of your own face. None of you do. Take the medal yourself. Go show it to your nobles and congratulate yourselves for being so mighty and just. Congratulations, you won the worst father award!"

It was one of those statements that as soon as Darius voiced the words he wished he could take it back. It wasn't that he didn't think it was true at the time, but he knew he shouldn't have said something so hurtful. He was having a hard time controlling himself once again. The words did stop his father though, and Darius walked away without any more interaction.

Before turning outside of the field arena area, Darius turned his head halfway around and saw his father still staring after the back of his son. His mother stood in her silent role by his side. The earlier look of disgust changed to hurt on his father's face and Darius almost felt glad. Almost. But deep inside he was more hurt than glad. It was his father. The man who had taught him so much. The man he wanted to please. The man he didn't like much right now, but the father he loved and wanted to make proud someday. *Someday!*

He turned his head forward and resumed walking away with his friends.

Chapter Four

Richard San Williams, councilor to the King, second most powerful man in the entire Realm, walked away from the archery contest in the bright hot sunlight with his mind filled with dark thoughts of sadness, disappointment, and hurt. He guessed he deserved most of it. Richard didn't even observe his wife, Elizabeth, turning toward some other friends.

He walked in a random manner, with his head looking at his dark boots pressing down on the summer grass. He wasn't sure where he was going until he got there. Now he sat on a dusty old log covered in multiple shades of green moss and fungus. The log had been in this empty field almost as long as Richard could remember. Parts of it now crumbled and decayed, turning back once again into the dirt it had once grown so proudly from. Yet, somehow, the majority of the log always was there for him to sit on when he needed to think things out.

The previous winter brought an abnormal amount of rain, and with the usual summer storms, the brown and green grass in the field surrounding the log had grown almost knee high. Even with the log hidden in the tall grass, Richard found the spot easily enough. He took off his purple cape and laid it across the log in front of him.

Sitting down, memories flooded back into his mind of when he turned eighteen. Now almost twenty four years ago. He wondered where the time had gone. He thought back over the years, through scattered thoughts until he reached that long-ago day.

"But they tease us, Father. It's not fair," Richard yelled at his father. *"Why don't you do something with your life?"*

Richard's father, Alric Williams, winced. "Richard, I am happy and have all I need. I have a fine profession. Being a bricklayer should be good enough for you too."

Richard laughed and laughed as his father's face reddened. "Good enough for me? Being like you is not good enough for me. You possess no ambition to be better. You almost seem to be hiding from everyone. Your family suffers for it and others treat us like the outsiders . . . like we are worse than the farmers."

"That's enough," his father roared.

"You're right. This is enough. I can't take this anymore. I'm proud to be from Anikari and I am going to make something of myself, starting today."

"And what are you going to do?" his father asked.

"Anything, but stay in this house. I would have left long ago if it hadn't been for mother being so sick." His mother had died a few months before from a two-year sickness that had taken many in the city.

"We own a good house here."

"We live slightly better than the poorest peasant at the edge of the city. I want more, Father. I want to live up there." He pointed up the hill

toward the nobles' district of Anikari. "Not at the edge of the farmlands. It's embarrassing."

"Embarrassing?" His father's face reddened. "Then leave."

He turned from his father and ran out the door.

He remembered running as hard as ever, finally stopping and sitting down on a tree that had fallen in a violent summer storm the previous month. Its wood was hard and held a deep, rich brown color back then.

This was where he found himself every time he had an important decision. It was why he was here today. Sitting on this same tree in the same field which somehow always remained for him to go to when he had problems. All around him the city grew with settlers from Gildan and Arc as well as the other cities inside the Realm. There were even a few families from the eastern empires, most of whom had engaged in the trade of wood, skins, and other products that were plentiful in the Realm. But through it all, the field and the tree remained untouched.

Almost twenty-four years ago Richard had left this field in search of his young destiny. While traveling the Realm searching for his place in life he had inadvertently saved some of King Charles' fields in Tean from thieves, and had been rewarded a small sector of land in the far corner of the city. He'd built homes out of stone, not brick, and raised more money. Fifteen years ago he had been given a position over trade in the Anikari city government, and had earned his *San* title of nobility. Eight years ago he had been named as one of King Edwards's councilors, and now he was the senior councilor. He ranked as the second most important man in the kingdom in the directing of the affairs of the Realm. His life was a far cry from the shabby way he had been raised.

Of course, he would never be king. One had to be of the royal line for that. He would never realize the high noble title of *Dar* added to his name. That was only reserved for the royal family. However, Richard had made something of himself on his own, and he was proud of what he had done. It was enough to be a councilor in the great Realm, and more so to be a senior councilor.

He knew Darius looked at things differently than he did. His son did not hold a desire for nobility or riches or the finer things his life could offer. That's because he had grown up around the good life. Richard gave his son everything that he hadn't had growing up. Darius wasn't familiar with what being poor and disgraced was—how it made you feel inside. If he had grown up the son of a poor bricklayer he may see things in a different view. Richard found it so hard not to get angry with his son.

Richard kept hearing Darius's sizzling comment as he had left the archery contest. The words seemed to repeat themselves over and over in his mind, like they held a life of their own, boring deep into his tired muscles and bones. He breathed in the summer air to steady his heart. The councilor recognized they had been moving away from each other the last few years. They used to have good times together. What had happened?

"I have given him everything." He stood up and began to talk out loud to himself. "I give him a good home, food, schooling, money . . . everything he could want to live in comfort. Nobody in the kingdom—even the entire Realm—has the kind of training and education he has. He doesn't understand how hard I work so he can enjoy what I didn't. He just doesn't understand. And with all this he stills finds a way to embarrass himself and me, by letting his anger get the best of him over some stupid outsider girl!"

Richard stomped a foot on the log. A decaying piece broke off under his boot. He thought of all the things he had given Darius again and wondered what else he had to offer. He didn't have time to give more. King Edward kept him so busy, and it was his duty to serve the Realm.

What else does he want?

He slammed his foot down again in anger on the log, breaking off a larger piece of the crumbling, rotting wood.

Then a voice came to him, almost bringing him to his knees. *"Give him love and understanding!"*

Richard turned around, almost as if he expected someone to be behind him. Of course there wasn't. The field was as empty and hollow as his heart felt. Yet the voice continued speaking again. *"Give him real love."* He realized that somehow through the years he had forgotten how to give love.

The sun had become warm during the competition and now beat down onto his uncovered head. He pushed some of his brown hair out of his eyes and wiped the sweat off his forehead. He had never been religious to any large degree, though he knew his wife was. She had taught Darius God's words and the right way to act. Through the years he himself had drifted away from religion. "Tell me what the answer is!" he bellowed.

Richard had never in fact taken the time before to think much about love. He remembered meeting his wife, Elizabeth, at a city function. She was the daughter of a rich city merchant. He had been infatuated with her beauty and sense of loyalty. Richard had felt more alive around her and pursued her from the first moment.

But his role now required so much from him. Maybe it was time to turn his attention back to his family. Maybe it wasn't too late. He left the field and headed toward the castle with new determination.

He couldn't stay away too long. He never could. The King would be waiting. The King was always waiting for something. He was a good king and Richard had served him long. He would understand what Richard needed. *He must understand!*

* * * *

"Richard, where have you been?" asked King Edward as Richard entered the large private study of the King. "There is important business to wrap up with the trouble in Belor. Seems as if some fanatic is preaching that the Belorians are the chosen people and we are their enemy. It's rumored he has used wizard powers."

Richard nodded his head, only partially listening to the King.

"Can you believe that?" King Edward continued. He absently rubbed his light brown beard with his hand. "A wizard in the Realm again, like in the days of the old kings. Like those who caused us so much trouble before. They want, or he wants, independence. Don't they understand they would be lost without us to protect them?"

The King stood up and stepped away from his red-velvet and gold-inlaid chair, which sat behind his mahogany desk. He began to walk the twenty or so steps toward Richard across the hard marbled floor. This was his private working chamber. His favorite paintings and tapestries adorned the walls on the east side and a large polished-stone fireplace sat on the west. The white marble flooring had been brought across the blue sea from one of the eastern empires by his great grandfather. The adjoining room was where the people in the Realm brought petitions or other business for him; the throne room. This room was where the actual work and decisions of the Realm occurred.

The King had not changed his royal clothes since the competition, except to take off his purple cloak. His footsteps echoed throughout the room as he walked toward Richard.

"There were some things on my mind, Your Highness."

The King, showing little compassion, but curious over his senior councilor's depressed spirits, asked, "What is bothering you, Richard?"

"It's my son. I'm afraid I have lost him."

"What do you mean?" The King jumped with sudden interest. "He didn't go somewhere, did he?"

"No. No. We just don't understand each other. He doesn't even care to be around me anymore. It wasn't always this way."

"That's what boys do, Richard. He'll come around." The King appeared relieved. "He will learn. He must!"

"Oh yes. I will make sure of that, much to his dismay I am sure." Richard paused a moment as if he was thinking carefully about what to say next. "But I need to spend more time with him and my wife."

"Richard, you are invaluable to me. I need you here."

"Edward, I have served you for many years. I do everything you ask of me. My wife and son, I am sure, think horrible things of me because I can't tell them most of what I do for you. I haven't told them I was staying such late hours to help you on negotiations for peace or trade, or meeting informants to stop rebellions and plottings. I have given you more than a normal man would."

"Richard, you are not a normal man."

A look of confusion spread across Richards face. This was not a normal reaction for his king. "What . . ."

The King cut him off with a flip of his hand and raised his voice. "You are one of the few I trust to work with me. There has been quite a bit of dissension in some of the other cities. I've tried to make these uprisings seem not so serious. I don't trust some of the lower councilors. They would use these things against me to their advantage. They see me as weakening, without having an heir to the throne." King Edward's voice rose in agitation and he stopped in front of Richard. "I always know that you won't ever betray me. That is why I need to keep you here days at a time and through the nights to work on important negotiations and assignments I trust to no one else. I fear trouble on the border with Gildan is coming again soon, and now this the growing unrest in Belor. Do you betray me now?"

"Betray you? NO!" exclaimed Richard. "Never would I do that. I just need to spend time with my family. I don't want to lose them. Is that so wrong?"

"In another time, or with another person maybe, it might be fine. You have no idea how important your family is to me, Richard. But I need you. I am sure you don't want to lose everything I have given you or could give to you, do you?"

Richard was becoming extremely confused about what the King was implying. It didn't seem to make any sense. "I am not asking to leave, my King, but only that others handle some of my duties. There must be others you can trust? Jonathon or Aaron perhaps?" His felt his face reddened in frustration as he named the other upper councilors to the King.

"Enough of this foolish talk. I don't know what you have been thinking. My father took you as a poor runaway boy and gave you land to make something of yourself. I have never stopped promoting you, until you stand almost equal to me in the kingdom. I pave your way with gold, money, art, prestige, learning, and power. I give your family everything any man in the entire world would hope to have. You have more power and riches at your disposal than many kings or emperors do. If you want less than that, then you will get nothing. I need you at my disposal always. That is what is expected of you as my senior councilor!"

"Edward!" exclaimed a bewildered Richard, wondering what had gotten into his good friend. He realized his hands were shaking. "I have never seen you like this. You have gone mad. I am not asking to leave you, but my family . . ."

King Edward paced the floor a few times, his face turning red, opened his mouth, then shut it again as if continuing to think. He slowed and motioned for Richard to sit down on one of the Belorian-made chairs, which sat in front of his desk. He moved the chairs closer together. Richard sat in silence and rubbed his hands back and forth on the carved wooden handles. Years of wear made them almost as smooth as glass.

The King took the other chair facing the desk and turned it toward Richard. He sat motionless for minutes, looking up at a large painting of the Everlasting Meadows.

Edward took a few deep breaths, leaned forward, and spoke as if in pain. "Richard, I am sorry about your family. You are not aware how important they are to me. I . . . am." The King stumbled for his words before continuing. "I wasn't going to tell you until you needed to know." He paused, and Richard wondered what bothered the King so much. Usually so direct and confident in his speech, this was unusual for Edward. There was nothing pertaining to the Realm that Richard didn't already know.

What was going on? What is the King hiding from me?

"My family? What of them?" Richard leaned forward.

"You know I don't have a son or daughter to follow me as heir to the throne." His speech slowed.

Richard nodded. This was public knowledge and had been a worry to the King, the councilors, and as well to the Realm in whole. Everyone had always wondered why he hadn't re-married. Many said he couldn't find space in his heart to love again. Many councilors were already planning and positioning themselves for the day when a new king would need to be chosen.

"Richard." He looked him straight in the eye. "There is one who is alive today who is of the direct royal line. Even more direct than me."

The royal line. Who? I know everyone! "But you have no brothers, sisters, or children."

The King paused as he tapped his fingers on the arm of the other chair. He gazed with intent into Richard's eyes and said one word that shattered Richard's world. "You!"

Richard jumped back as if something had hit his chest. "But how? What are you talking about, Edward? This is nonsense! Are you just trying to keep me here by any means? Because this won't work." Richard stood up, red-faced.

"Sit down, Richard. Now!" he commanded, then softened his features. Blue-grey eyes, almost the color of Richard's, pierced his gaze. "Your father, Alric, and I were brothers," the King spoke in a whispered tone. "In fact, your father was my older brother by almost twenty-one years."

"But he was so poor." Richard could not believe what he was hearing. His heart pounded and he felt dizzy and light-headed. His father was only a poor bricklayer in the outskirts of the city.

"Let me explain." The King paused. "My father, King Charles, banished your father for something he had once done. It was before I was born. He even made him change his name from Montere to Williams. Your father left the city for a while and cut off all ties with everyone he knew. When he came back with his wife and son no one knew him for who he really was.

He took the last name of Williams, a common enough name in these parts. No one would ever know him to be of the royal line if everything went according to my father's plan."

"What plan?" Richard wiped the sweat from his forehead.

"If my daughter wouldn't have died she would have been Queen after me. You must wonder why I didn't remarry and have more children. My father told me on his deathbed in case something like this happened."

"Well . . . I . . ." Richard couldn't find the right words to say. The implications of what the King said were more than he could get his mind around. Was he to be the next king? The thought seemed blasphemous.

"The banishment of your father and his current family was permanent, signed with the royal seal, in blood, and is kept in my personal safe in the upper room of the castle. You were one year old at the time, so of course you don't remember."

Richard's thoughts of being king crumbled with King Edward's word of his entire family being banished. He shook his head in confusion.

"My father was quick to restore the line. A little less than a year later, I was born," the King said, pointing a finger at himself. "What my father, your grandfather, did was wrong, but I am not able to overturn his oath and decree."

"I cannot believe this. How can this be right? Wouldn't others know?" Richard thought about his poor father. No wonder he could do nothing else but hide. "The pain he must have had to see us raised up in poverty when we should have been in the palace." *And I treated him so horribly for it!*

The King looked at Richard with compassion and continued. "Stories were told at the time that King Charles's eldest son had died in a war out in a ship on the Blue Sea. My father mastered the tale himself. He told the people he had sent your father off to fight in the war. No one else knew. Your family moved to the Crystal Lake area for a few years. Alric DarSan Montere became Alric Williams. He changed the way he dressed and talked, and picked up new work."

King Edward paused for a moment to let it all sink in. "After a few years your family returned to Anikari, living at the edge of the city, and nobody knew who you were. Even though my father had banished him, when my father died I found your father. I kept in secret contact with him until your mother and then he died, and I promised I would take care of his family. He was a good man, Richard. So you understand now why you must stay here with me, and why you must say nothing to anyone, including your family. No one must find this out until the right time, until I am ready to die."

Richard looked confused. Everything was coming too fast! His head spun and his body went numb. "Why is it so important for me to stay so close to you? As you said yourself, his family was included in the banishment. I cannot be king."

"But your child can," King Edward said.

A spark of understanding flashed in Richard's eyes and astonishment swept his face. "So . . . my son . . . Darius, he could be . . ." Richard tried to breathe, tried to believe the wild tale.

"He *will* be the next king," finished Edward. "He was not yet born when the banishment was made. The crown will be restored again to the direct line and no faction can vie for authority over it. But he must not know yet."

"What do we do, Edward?" Richard through his hands up in the air. "Have you really thought about this?

King Edward leaned forward and punched one fist into his other hand for emphasis. "I have thought about this every waking hour for years, Richard. There is still training he must go through. He must become one of the strongest kings we have had, in order to keep the people safe. He must be trained in the ways of the military, nobility, and trade. He must become a leader and understand the politics of this Realm like no one else. He would be in too much danger if he found out now. There are many who would like to see no rightful heirs to the throne. If Darius found out now, his life could be in danger. If he died, there would be civil war for sure. Do you understand, Richard? Do you understand now?"

Richard couldn't find any words to speak, but only nodded his head as the King continued. "You must learn all you can now so that when I pass the crown to him at the right time, you can be by his side. You will be your son's councilor, if I can leave that instruction for him. A unique ruling team that has never happened. It will give you and him the extra strength that will be required." The King's eyes gleamed in excitement.

Richard was stunned beyond belief and sat still for a few moments, then with a pale face excused himself to go to his own office. Before exiting the room, he whispered barely loud enough for the King to overhear, "He will now have another excuse to hate me."

He wondered if his family would ever forgive him for the terrible secret he must keep. They hated him for what he wasn't . . . or maybe was. Now he had to be even more deceitful. Yet he grasped the situation now and recognized he had no choice in the matter. He wouldn't risk the life of his son or civil war. Despite what others may think, he loved his family and the Realm.

Richard walked out on the western balcony, outside of his office. The landing overlooked the city. One day his son would be the king of this city. Not just this city, but as far as the eye could see. From the Superstition Mountains to the Blue Sea. He would rule from the forgotten lands to the border of the Gildanian Empire. He put his hands on his face and cried. He cried for the pain he had caused and still would need to cause his son. He cried for his father, whom he now understood, and he cried for what his son would have to go through to keep peace in the land.

Chapter Five

"**F**ather, come quick," called Jakob, Haman's only son.

"What is it, Jakob?" Haman walked around the side of the large barn to find out what distressed his boy. His long legs carried his wiry frame up next to the fence where Jakob stood.

Jakob pointed out across the grassy field toward a group of Cremelinos that seemed to be running, all together, around in a large circle. The large pure-white horses continued to speed up until the sight to behold became a dizzying blur.

Haman Widing, his wife, and his son, were the current master caretakers of the herd of Cremelinos on White Island—an honor passed down from father to son for more generations than any could remember. Although White Island sat off the eastern coast of the Realm, opposite Mar, it was the responsibility of one family. This family was paid and supported by each king. A small village had grown up over time in a western bay of the island to support all of the activity.

Everyone in the village shared the responsibility to care for the white horses, from farmers growing fields of hay, to groomers, doctors, and caretakers. In current times four distinct herds covered the island. Haman, as master caretaker, cared personally for the largest herd. From this herd the king chose those that would pull his own carriage.

As the man and boy watched the strange behavior, one by one each horse left the circle and raced toward them. Haman put out his hand and the lead horse approached, touching Haman's hand with his mane. No man other than a caretaker touched a Cremelino without their permission. In fact, once they allowed a rider, that rider bonded to them for life.

A soft voice filled Haman's head as the horse stayed in contact with his hand. It took a few minutes of concentration for him to recognize what was being said.

Master caretaker, a wizard has found his power again. A true wizard of royal birth walks the Realm again.

Haman could feel the excitement in the horse's voice.

"Father, what did she say?" asked Jakob.

"They are excited about a wizard in the Realm again."

"A wizard? Really? I want to see a wizard, papa. Is he old like in the stories? Does he do magic? What's his name?"

Haman tousled his son's hair and laughed. "So many questions."

Tell him he is five years older than your son. His name is Darius and he will impact the entire Realm and beyond for either good or evil.

Haman relayed the message to his twelve-year-old son.

"I would like to meet Darius," commented Jakob.

The other horses joined the man and boy next to the fence. One of the younger ones reached his long white mane over to Jakob, touching his skin slightly, and spoke.

Soon you will meet him, but he doesn't understand who he is yet. You will escort me to him to be given into the care of another. I will watch over the young wizard. It is the beginning of the prophecy.

Jakob jumped. This was the first time one of the horses had had direct communication with him. "Papa. It's wonderful. I heard her voice. She spoke to me."

Haman smiled a large, toothy grin and rubbed his hands down his thin face. Looking down at his son, he felt the pride he was sure his father had felt when Haman had heard his first Cremelino voice. He felt the connection with himself, his son, and the Cremelino.

His son looked up at him and brushed away some of his blond bangs. "She said there is a prophecy about Darius the wizard, and I will meet him. What do you think that means, Papa?"

"I am sure I wouldn't know, Jakob. Things of wizards are not known much to man. I hear the Jordanian empire have their share, and I have heard of a few from the Kingdom of Arc, and of course there are rumors of great wizards across the Blue Sea to the east, but none have walked the Realm for a long time."

Haman reached out again to the Cremelino nearest him, while his son still touched the smaller female. They both heard the words at the same time.

Forgotten lines of ancient magic and the power of the throne
One will make them both his own if his heart sees the true power. . .

Jakob took his hand away. It became clear the Cremelino was not going to share any more of the prophecy. "I'm going to go tell Mom!" Jakob yelled as he ran off toward their small home.

Haman cleaned up a few things in the barn before heading back. The sun hung low above the harbor. Shading his eyes with a tanned hand, he could just make out the strait of water between the island and Mar. He spotted a speck on the horizon. Watching for a few moments, he saw the shadow continue to grow; a ship coming to port. A large one.

"Hmmm," he said out loud to himself. "I wonder whose ship that is."

All of a sudden, the herd started neighing and rearing up in the air. They seemed frantic about something. Haman tried to make soothing noises, afraid they would overrun him. He'd never seen them this way before. The lead horse came back to him and bumped into his hand.

Another one comes on the ship. A wizard. A wizard of evil power. One that is not natural, but learned. One that could destroy the prophecy. Keep him away from us.

The words were more frantic and louder than he had ever heard. He tried to soothe the worried horse by running his hand over the horse's mane and nose. "I will always protect you. I will open the back gate and you can run inland. No one will hurt you."

Thank you, caretaker. Make sure that man doesn't leave the harbor on his own. He is dangerous.

"Who is he? How will I know which one is him on such a large ship?"

You will know. A pure heart like yours will sense the evil in his.

Haman ran to the wooden gate and threw it open; thankful the other herds were on the far side of the island this month. It was early summer and new grass was growing in abundance all over the island. It was normal for him to rotate the herds to graze in different fields.

The Cremelinos ran through the gate in a hurried blur of white. The lead horse turned toward him and sent a final message.

Don't let him see your son and don't tell him about the other wizard.

This was the first time they had spoken to him without direct contact. His surprise must have shown through.

We can do much more than you think, kind caretaker. In a short time, the true testing of the young wizard will come. If all goes well, we will be with our masters once again.

And with that they were off so fast that by the time Haman closed the gates, they were specks of fading light running into the coming night.

The middle-aged man walked with concern toward his home. The small but sturdy stone home sat up on the hill next to the fields where the white horses roamed. The village sat about two miles west inside the bay. As he looked out, the ship continued to grow in size, coming closer to the island port. Even though the air was still warm, he shivered at the thoughts the herd leader had shared with him earlier.

Opening the door, he was met with the aroma of baked bread and stewed meat, and he took a moment to breathe it in. The tasty scent wasn't enough to take the stain of worry from his heart, but it helped. Haman looked around the room and smiled at his wife and son. He would protect them at all costs.

Later than night, Haman took a lantern and headed into town. The large ship stood in the dock, and he watched sailors, with their sea gait, moving supplies from the town's small warehouses. He entered the nicest tavern closest to the docks. Immediately he recognized who the Cremelinos were talking about. His heart lurched and terror filled him as he looked on the man.

He stood with confidence, tall and broad with short-cropped auburn hair. An aura of power and command circled him. Men were falling over themselves to please him, and gathering around him to hear him talk.

Haman stayed in the background by the wall, but moved closer to where he could hear what the man said. The warmth of the large fire in the hearth spread throughout the room, casting strange shadows on the listening group of men.

"You must protect yourselves from the Realm," the man said. "You should be free."

Free from what, Haman thought. They had a good life here, and were free from most of the Realm's doing, except for the raising of the Cremelinos.

As Haman thought about the horses, the man stopped talking and turned toward the caretaker. Haman tried to hold the stare back, but he felt as if the man dirtied his soul with his gaze. He then took two steps forward, toward Haman.

"You must be the caretaker?" asked the man.

Haman didn't know how the man knew, but he just nodded in the affirmative.

"I would like to meet and observe these Cremelinos I have heard so much about. Such beautiful horses that our king keeps must be a sight to behold. Could I by chance be taken to one?"

Haman was glad he had let the horses move inland, and also happy he didn't have to lie about it. This man surely would discern if he did.

"I am sorry, sir," said Haman in an even manner. "Just today I have let them out to roam the middle of the island. The grass grows tall there and will help make them strong. It's too far and dangerous to go out during the night, and hard enough to even find them in that vast area during the day."

"I see. How do they know when to return?"

Haman wanted to tell the man they would return when they sensed his evil gone, but didn't. "They are fickle animals, with a mind of their own. They will probably be a few days at least. Who knows?"

"Who knows?" the man repeated. "I am sure that you as caretaker must know."

Haman only shook his head. It was all that he could do not to run from the man. His stomach felt sick and his head pounded.

"Hmmm. A caretaker that doesn't know where his animals are. Not much of a caretaker I would guess."

The flippant remark stilled the other men in the room. They all held the highest regard for Haman and his ways with the Cremelinos. Haman kept his tongue still.

The man seemed to think for a moment, then smiled a smile that didn't reach his eyes. "Well, I must be off in the morning. So maybe another time. I must get back to Belor to check how my city has been doing in my absence. I am sure to have work to do there."

"Yes. Maybe another time would be better," echoed Haman, relieved the man would not be pushing the idea to visit them sooner.

The man turned back to the group, ordered some food, and resumed his tales of the eastern kingdoms and their higher level of thinking.

Haman soon turned and left the building, taking a deep breath only after exiting into the night air. He hoped he never met that man again. He felt sorry for the Belorians if they didn't see past his evil.

In the morning Haman returned to the harbor to make sure the visitor had indeed left. The ship was pulling out of the harbor as another one came in. This one flew the King's personal flag. As the first ship passed to the starboard side of the incoming one, the man seemed to stop and stare at the two men standing on the new ship's bow.

Haman saw a frown form on the man's face and he waved to his captain to stop. Haman watched as the other boat came up beside a dock. After securing the ropes two men came down the walkway, apparently leaving a captain to stay onboard.

The two men approached him and Haman saw they were younger than he had first thought. Not much older than sixteen. One stood tall with dark brown hair, carrying himself like a noble, while the other was shorter, with bright red hair, not unlike the color of the man going to Belor.

"Hello, sir." The first one spoke to Haman. "Can you tell me where I can find the caretaker?"

Haman frowned only slightly. These two were young to be here on their own. "Who can I say is asking?"

The second boy spoke up. "I am Kelln El'Han, and this is Darius San Williams, son of councilor Williams. We recently graduated from the academy and we have been given a task from the King to pick up a few more of his Cremelinos."

Haman opened his mouth wide and his face paled. He looked up at the ships in the harbor and noticed the man from Belor still looking in their direction. *Darius.* That was the name spoken by the Cremelino.

Trying to distract the man on the ship and protect the young men, he pointed toward an inn. "If you will go and wait in that inn, I will fetch him for you."

The boys smiled their thanks and Haman walked in the other direction. Hiding around a corner of one of the warehouses he watched the man on the ship shake his head and then proceed to direct his captain to finish pulling out of the harbor. Only when he was clear of the harbor mouth did the caretaker return to the inn to find the two young men.

Opening the door, he spotted them at a table. The redheaded one was flirting with a young barmaid. Haman tried to compose himself. The Cremelinos had said this man, Darius, was a wizard. He approached slowly and sat down opposite them.

"You are the caretaker?" asked Darius. "Then why the misdirection?"

Haman did not feel evil coming from this young man as he did the other one. He took a deep breath and let it out in a big puff. "You said your name was Darius? Why were you chosen to come here?"

"My father is councilor to King Edward. This is one of our first assignments after graduation from the Academy. He thought it relatively safe to send us here to choose a few of the Kings horses to bring back." Darius paused as if listening to something. "Is it safe here?"

"Forgive the trouble," Haman said. "My name is Haman, master caretaker. There was a man here last night who was leaving as you came in. He looked to cause trouble; I needed to make sure you were kept safe."

"But you didn't know who we were," Kelln jumped in.

"Darius," Haman whispered. Noticing that he had said it out loud, he recovered and continued speaking. "The man was on his way to Belor. He was evil, and I am told a wizard."

The two young men looked at each other with wide eyes.

"The Preacher," stated Darius.

"Yes, that is what some of the men referred to him as," added Haman. "Anyway, he is now gone and you are now here to pick up some Cremelinos for the King. Unfortunately, they are deep inland, grazing, and may not be back for a day or two. Why don't you come to my house and we will see about some breakfast?"

"Fantastic." Kelln hopped up. "I'm starving."

"He's always hungry." Darius said to Haman as he stood up with his friend.

Thirty minutes later they entered into Haman's simple cottage. Everything was arranged neatly and the smell of bacon and bread hung in the air. After introductions, Haman's wife,

Nhila, shooed them out of the kitchen until everything was ready.

Jakob bounded in the front door and stopped short in front of the two visitors.

"This is my son, Jakob. He helps me care for the Cremelinos."

"And how do you like caring for King Edward's horses?" asked Darius.

"Oh, just fine." Jakob puffed out his chest. "One day I will be head caretaker like my father."

"They are beautiful horses," continued Darius.

Haman saw Kelln glance at the kitchen more than once. He remembered being a young man once. A full stomach seemed to always be the object of his desires. Now he looked at his young son, Jakob. Growing quickly, he was almost thirteen. He would make a fine caretaker.

"Are you here to take some away?" asked Jakob.

"Where are my manners?" Haman scolded himself. "Jakob, these young men are on the King's errand and are here to pick up four new Cremelinos. This is Kelln and Darius."

Jakob went pale and his eyes widened. He looked at his father. Haman shook his head slightly from side to side. He hoped his son would keep the secret they had heard about Darius. It was not theirs to tell.

The two young men looked at the boy and wondered what silent exchange was happening. Suddenly the boy closed his mouth and squinted at Darius. He seemed to be thinking about something before he spoke.

"You will be taking five with you when you leave," stated Jakob with a barely audible voice.

"Five? But we only need four." Kelln looked confused. He looked once again at the kitchen.

Haman's wife called them in and Kelln bounced to his feet. His stomach grumbled and they all laughed.

Darius put his hand on the young boy's arm to ask a question. "What do you mean we need five?"

"Four for the King and one for you, Darius."

Darius shook his head in confusion.

"Jakob, what are you talking about? Darius didn't come for one." His father stepped up close to his son.

"Darius needs to give the Cremelino to someone. Someone special who will need it. He will know who."

Just then a horse neighed from outside the window. Everyone jumped and looked around in surprise. Jakob was the first one to the door. The others gathered behind him. There in front of the house stood one of the pure-white Cremelino horses.

"There she is," pointed Jakob. "She came back before the other ones."

Haman gave a loud sigh and turned to Darius. "Sir, I am sorry if this causes you any problems. But sometimes these Cremelinos do have a mind of their own."

Darius stood gaping at the horse as if listening to something. His face grew pale and he took a step forward and then stopped.

Kelln reached out to his friend. "Darius. What's wrong? You all right?"

Darius turned back to the group as if he hadn't heard their comments. "What did you say?"

"Are you all right?" Kelln asked again.

Darius turned to Haman and Jakob. "You're right. We will be taking five back, and I know just who I'm going to give it to."

Kelln gave him a questioning look, but Darius didn't offer any additional information.

Haman's wife ushered them back inside to eat their fill of bread, bacon, fresh fruit, and milk. After filling their stomachs they retired to the porch. A slight breeze blew in off the Blue Sea, giving a salty tang to the warming summer air.

"So what are you boys going to be doing after your summer service to the crown?" asked Haman.

"I'm trying to find a way to travel if I can get out of doing an apprenticeship. I've already worked with my father for years," said Kelln, stuffing into his mouth a sweet roll that he had taken from the kitchen on his way out of the house.

"Travel where?" Darius asked his friend. "You know your father's going to have you sweating over that forge of his."

Kelln frowned. "I'll find some way to see the land."

Haman smiled at the boys' banter. "And you, Darius?"

Now it was Darius's turn to frown. He sighed deeply. "My father wants me to stay in Anikari and apprentice to be a councilor."

"Doesn't sound like a bad life to most people," Haman mused.

Darius stood up. "But I want to do more than that. I want to fight and defend our great land. I want to help others and bring our people closer together."

"And you can't do that as a councilor?" Haman smiled at the boy's enthusiasm.

"All the councilors do is sit around and have meetings. They don't know what is going on around them. They all think they are better than the farmers and everyone else."

"What's wrong with farmers?" asked Jakob, sitting down next to his dad.

"Oh, Darius likes the farmers," added Kelln with a mischievous smile.

Darius blushed bright red and headed out toward the well. "I think I need a drink of water."

The group all laughed as Darius's step quickened and his ears turned a darker shade of red.

Chapter Six

A week after delivering the Cremelinos safely back to the castle stables Kelln walked back home from eating dinner at a nearby inn. His mother and sister had gone to visit a relative and his father had left to Belor a few weeks earlier. It was not like his father to leave so abruptly, and Kelln was thinking about traveling to Belor to find out if he had met any trouble, if he could get out of his current duties to one of the councilors.

The night was darkening and a few lamps lit the street. Kelln heard a sound in the street behind him and turned around.

"Stop!" The guard yelled and rushed down the street toward Kelln.

Kelln's heart jumped. He wondered why the city guard would be after him. Something about the way they were running after him vaulted him to action. He took off running down the street toward his home.

The guard followed him into his home, banging the door almost off its frame. Kelln ran quickly through the small home to outdistance the guard. He didn't know why he was being chased, but he knew he didn't want to get caught. He had done enough sneaking around in the city to warrant some notice, but some of King Edward's guards chasing him didn't make sense. It must be something to do with his father going to Belor. His father had been talking about the trouble in Belor for some time but Kelln didn't think he would actually leave his forge and go there.

He grabbed a small cap from a peg on the wall and pulled it down over his red hair. With his short thin frame he jumped out of a back window and ran around the forge. The apprentices had let everything cool since his father had left. His feet kicked a few small, stray pieces of steel out of the way as he ran onto the cobblestone streets of a darker part of the city.

Guards shouted from behind, ordering him to stop and return. He turned around once to see if they followed. Their bright swords flashed in the lamplight of the late evening air.

A dark, moonless night threatened a summer thunderstorm. He ran down a few less-populated streets and found himself in the merchants' quarter. Large warehouses with their small storefronts were dark at this time of night. Kelln turned down a nearby alley and waited a moment to catch his breath and to think about where he would go. On such a dark and eerie night he didn't relish the thought of staying in the narrow, dirty alley longer than was required. It could be more dangerous than the guards. The small dark streets seemed to breed thoughts of danger and despair.

He heard slowing footsteps approach. He tried to crouch into the shadows. The men passed and he let out a sigh. Something brushed against his leg and he went to hit it away. As he did so he bumped into an old crate and knocked something down. The sound would alert the guards. He looked for a way out. The backside of an abandoned inn with rooms upstairs sat a short distance down the alley. He couldn't see well enough in the dark to distinguish if the building held any promise for escape or not, but it held his only hope.

The guards' voices floated through the air and their footsteps came closer. Jumping up, he skirted toward the building. Kelln tried one door after another. In sudden desperation he noticed an opened window on the second floor. He jumped up on the ledge of a first-story window and pulled himself up onto an overhang and into the top window, barely making it in before the guards came back into the alley.

They stood talking right below him.

"He must be in cahoots with his father," one of the guards said.

"Traitors to the King," the other one said, his voice deeper than the first.

Traitors? No. What were they talking about? Kelln stayed in the shadows but tried to lean farther out the window to hear them better.

"Nothings here," said the first one. "And it's getting cold."

A noise in the alleyway caused Kelln to duck back inside.

"Just cats," said the second man. "Let's go get something warm to drink. He can't hide forever. Someone will find him."

Kelln heard them leave, but stayed in the dark room for a few more moments, letting his eyes adjust to the old building. He got up to move and a hand covered his mouth from behind him.

Terror grabbed him for a few moments and he pushed his head back into his attacker and tried to turn around. A girl not much older than himself smiled at him. A dark black cape swirled around her when she stopped. With her raven-black hair and black leather pants she was almost a shadow. His heart beat in rapid succession. She was beautiful.

"It's all right," she whispered with a smile, and her dark green eyes picked up a few stray flecks of light from somewhere.

He lowered his fists.

"Kelln, I'm here to help. Your father sent me."

"My father! Is he all right?"

"Yes he is, but he wants you to join him."

"Wait. I don't even know who you are, yet you seem to know more about my family than I do at this point." Kelln glanced around him for any other trouble.

"My name is Alessandra El'Lan. I, too, am Belorian, though I may not appear that way at the moment. I had to disguise my red hair. Your father, Grisham, went to Belor two weeks ago to oversee the delivery of weapons to the King's men there. At least that's what everyone thought. In reality, he was bringing them to us."

"Us? Who are you?" asked Kelln. A dreadful feeling started to develop in his gut. His father had been talking strangely the past few months. The talk about a man in Belor who spoke about freedom and independence had seemed to excite his father.

"I am part of the Belorian resistance. Belor has approached the King for our independence, yet he has denied us, so we have taken up arms to convince him ourselves. It's not right that we should be under his rule. He treats us as foreigners and his taxes are heavy. We contacted your father a few months ago, and he agreed to help us reestablish the Belorian rule back to its purity!"

Information came at Kelln too fast. He knew his father had left for Belor to help deliver swords, just as the girl had said. During this time his mother and two sisters had gone to visit an uncle in a small village by Crystal Lake.

"What about the rest of my family? They are not in Belor, are they?"

"We will arrange for them to meet you and your father again in Belor after the present situation has died down." Alessandra smiled a big smile. "For now I will be your guide to safety."

Kelln wasn't sure he needed a guide, but on the other hand he sure didn't mind Alessandra's company. No woman had smiled at him this way before.

"I have to think about this first. I have been born and raised in Anikari. Now you want me to fight against the kingdom. I need to think about this."

"Don't think of it as fighting against anything, but for something. For the freedom of your people."

My people? Who are my people?

She did sound convincing. Maybe it was those alluring, dark, almond-shaped eyes. "I need to talk to a friend first." He thought of Darius and tried to pull his mind from the girl.

"All right. Talk to him, but be careful. They may be watching your house for someone to return. Your father made some of the best weapons. I am sure they would love to have his son. Meet me tomorrow morning behind the Mid-Summers Inn on the south end of town. Make sure you have clothes and a weapon to travel with."

She touched his arm with a few fingers, smiled again, then disappeared. He sat alone for a few minutes in the dark. The night became quiet once again except for the loud beating of his heart.

He absently rubbed his arm where Alessandra's fingers had touched him. He stood up and headed out toward Darius's house.

The Williams' home stood tall up on the hill in the nobles' quarter. Kelln crept past a few bored guards. The lamps in the large stone house were off, so he worked his way around until he was under Darius's second floor window. There were ornamental bushes to block the view from the street. A night guard would be walking by soon, so he hurried.

Kelln threw a few pebbles at the window and waited. He knew Darius slept lightly. This was not the first time he had woken up his friend for a late-night adventure. After a few seconds, a sleepy Darius came to the window. "Kelln. What are you doing?"

"I need to talk to you."

"Oh no. What sort of trouble are you in now? Can't this wait until morning?" Darius pulled the window open a little further.

"No, I need to talk now." He tried to sound as serious as he could.

Darius snuck downstairs and outside and together they hurried to the back corner of the courtyard. Darius brought up a flame in his hand for light and lit a lamp on the wall. Kelln raised his eyebrows.

"This strange power has got to be good for something."

"Getting more comfortable with being a wizard, I see," Kelln commented.

"Kel, I am not a wizard." Darius looked around the dark yard. "And don't say that out loud. No one knows about my powers."

"Not even Christine?"

"Not even Christine," Darius answered. "I still haven't found the right time. Soon, though. Soon. I promise you. I just have to figure it out for myself first."

Kelln smiled and proceeded to tell him what had happened over the past hour. Darius had a little knowledge about the current situation in Belor.

"My father said it's getting dangerous there. He's been telling me a lot more about the Realm of late. I'm not sure why," Darius added.

Kelln furrowed his eyebrows. "Don't you know? He is grooming you to be a councilor, now that we have graduated. Your full training will start in the fall."

"He knows I'm not interested. I am still hoping to train for the army in the fall. He hasn't said anything more about my relationship with Christine since he was embarrassed at the archery contest either. But since that day he has been more patient and at least not as angry at me. Well, when you get me in trouble, his still gets mad at me then."

Kelln laughed. "Trouble? Me? It's that power of yours that has gotten us in more trouble lately. You seem to be growing more powerful."

"So what are you going to do about Belor?" asked Darius, pushing the subject of his powers away from Kelln.

"I realize I am Belorian by heritage, but I am also a member of the Realm. My parents may have ties to Belor, but I don't. Why should I go?"

"Have you been there to notice if things are as bad as it sounds?" asked Darius.

"The last time I was in Belor was about two years ago. It seemed like a nice city to me. It was clean and had new construction going on. It looked different from here, but in an exotic sort of way. I don't understand what the problem is."

"Maybe you should go and check out this Preacher on your own."

"You mean a religious man is causing this trouble?"

"No, I don't think so. They call him the Preacher because he preaches that they are better than us and that the Belorians should take control of their own land. Not exactly religion, more like some political maneuvering, it seems. He's also rumored to be a wizard."

"You mean there are two of you now?"

"Kel, I am not a wizard." Darius was adamant.

"Then what do you call it?

The two had been over this a thousand times and Darius still didn't have an appropriate answer for Kelln.

"This isn't about me, Kelln. This is about you. If you go and fight, that's civil war. You would be fighting against the armies of Anikari!" exclaimed Darius. "Maybe an army that I will be in someday. Our army could kill you or arrest you for treason."

"I know. I know!" Kelln paced the garden area. "But my dad wants me. You know my dad, Darius. He wouldn't go if there wasn't a good reason." His father had been making swords for King Edward and his father before him. He had always been level-headed, a good businessperson, and a great father.

They continued to reason back and forth well into the night. Finally Kelln stood up.

"I'll go and see what's going on, but I'm not going to fight," Kelln said. "I'll send a message or come back and let you know. Maybe your father can help."

Darius nodded his head, the two said their goodbyes, and Kelln went a back way to his house. He looked around the outside of the home and waited for a few minutes in the dark to make certain he was not being watched. Two guards sitting on the ground down the street seemed to be sleeping against a lamppost. He went in through the back and arranged some clothes together. He grabbed his sword and bow and laid down to rest a little.

He tossed and turned between dreams of fighting and dreams of Alessandra. He dreamed she had deceived him and that his father was held as a prisoner. He dreamed she loved him. He dreamed Belor was destroyed under rubble. Some of the dreams seemed so real. Others seemed like dreams. Still others seemed to be warnings or premonitions of future events.

Kelln woke in a sweat as the early summer sun streamed into his room. It was an hour before he was to meet Alessandra. He looked outside. The previous night's threatening storm had passed on. It was the kind of clear summer day that made him remember lying in the field with his dad and finding shapes in the clouds as a young boy. He pulled a cap over his head and walked out to find the mysterious girl from the night before.

Noises made him jump and glance around. He thought someone watched him. That everyone was calling him a traitor for leaving. Doubts crept back into his mind as to what he should do. If he fought, he could possibly be fighting against friends he knew.

He was so deep in his thoughts he almost bumped into Alessandra. She wore men's dark leather pants again, a dark shirt, and a dark cape. Her hair was tucked up under a hood, but in the light of day and up close he could see the soft features of her face. She looked even more beautiful than the night before.

"How are we getting out of the city? I am sure they will have guards on the lookout for me," Kelln asked Alessandra, to see if she did have a plan. "They found me easily last night by watching my home."

"We are going out through the tunnel where the Black River runs out of the city, then through part of the forest until we reach the Everlasting Meadows."

"The Black River? The Black Forest? Are you crazy? Haven't you heard all of the stories?" Kelln looked at her in astonishment.

"Yes, I know them all. I'm sure most aren't true."

Kelln gulped. "Most?" He had to think hard to stop his legs from shaking.

"For us it's the safest way." She smiled, picked up her bundle with one hand and stretched her other hand out toward Kelln. "Let's go."

Kelln stood for a moment, wondering what he was doing. Something drew him to her, but he was smart enough to not be led away by just a pretty face. He reasoned that going to Belor and checking it out would not be treason. He needed to talk to his family and make up his mind for himself.

He grabbed her hand and walked with her to the river.

Chapter Seven

Sitting in the field of diamonds later that morning, Darius told Christine about Kelln. She didn't seem to be listening and he repeated himself.

"Do you believe in God?" she asked all of a sudden. Her blond hair bounced around as she turned her head with the enthusiastic question.

Darius sat silent for a moment, stunned by the apparent change of subject. "I . . . uh . . . Well, I know my mother does. I go with her to the worship service most weeks. I guess I feel something in here too." He pointed to his chest.

"That's kind of what my parents say. My dad says if you are doing what's right you will feel good inside. That's what God is. Dad says that God will help us and tell us what we are supposed to do. That God created everything, including you and me," Christine said, as if deep in thought.

"Why are you worrying about this? I would trust your parents. They seem happy."

"How are you and your father getting along, by the way?" said Christine with a concerned voice, another jump in the conversation topic.

"Better, but it's kind of strange. On a personal level we don't talk much about anything, though I do see him looking at me when he thinks I'm not watching. He knows you and I see each other, but he ignores it for now. He's been telling me a lot more about the happenings of the Realm lately. He sent Kelln and me to White Island, as you know, and he has taken me to a few meetings with the councilors. I guess he's trying to push me into doing what he does . . . politics. That's what Kelln thinks."

"Why does he not like me or the other farmers?" asked Christine. "Why can't he and the King and the other councilors do something about all the trouble? "

"I don't know, Christine. Like I said, I don't understand him at all anymore. It goes back to the time of the wizards' rebellion. Many of the nobles just can't forget what their ancestors went through."

"But it wasn't us."

"No, but they put everyone outside the city in the same group now. It's easier that way for them. It gives them someone to blame for things."

"Does he believe in God?" asked Christine.

"I don't know what my father thinks!" Darius stood up and threw his hands wide. "He does what he wants for reasons I'll never understand. All of them do. All the councilors sit in meetings and decide what is right and wrong and good and bad for us. Yet very few of them actually get out and see what's going on."

Christine stood up next to him and put her hand on his arm. "It's just not fair. They're not any better than us." Tears came to Christine's eyes and Darius put his arm around her. It felt like the best thing in the world. The problem was he wasn't sure what was going to happen now that school was done and they were getting older. She molded her slim body into his arms and he felt the beat of her heart against him.

"What's wrong, Christine?" asked Darius with concern. "Why all these questions?"

"Today Emily came back from the city with a bruise on her face," cried Christine. "Some girls beat her up. She's so young, eleven years old, just a little girl, and it's starting already for her. It gets worse every year. I don't know where they get it from, but someone is spreading lies and rumors and whatever about us, and everyone in the city believes it."

Darius was not sure what to say. He was in an awkward position, being from the city himself. He tried to hold her and tell her that things would be all right, but he couldn't convince himself totally that they actually would be.

"It's so beautiful here," Christine whispered, looking across the field and lake. The summer grass grew thick and green, and wildflowers scattered themselves throughout the field. "If God created this, why can't he create beauty and love between people? Unless he thinks we aren't worth it."

"Christine, don't talk like that. I am sure God thinks you are just as good as them . . . uh . . . us," started Darius, not knowing what he was going to say from one word to the next, but knowing that he had to comfort her somehow. "You said your family believes God speaks to your hearts. What if he speaks to everyone, but some don't listen? What if someone besides God speaks to us also, and others listen to him?"

Christine stopped crying to listen to what Darius was saying. "Who else do you mean?"

"I'm not sure. But don't you think that if a good God exists that there is someone bad also? Keeping things in balance? Wanting to bring hate and anger to people?"

Darius sensed the power building inside him, giving him the words to say. Everything became clearer in his mind. He felt a power of intelligence flow through him as he felt the plight of Christine and her people. Once again he felt the need to go out and protect the Realm from these evil influences.

"You mean like someone evil? Like from the old days, when the Black Forest was evil?" ventured Christine.

"Sure. Maybe. I'm not so sure," stumbled Darius. The power faded back from him. He hadn't learned to control it enough yet and times like these were frustrating. "But it could be, couldn't it?"

Christine laughed. "For a minute you sounded like a philosopher from our fables, Darius San Williams. Your words seemed so right and clear. I think you're right! God does speak to us all, but some just don't listen! But how do we get them to listen?"

That's a good question, Darius thought. He looked around the field then back at Christine. She had become so beautiful. He had seen changes in her since they had met. Saving her in front of the messenger's horse had been the best day of his life. She was intelligent, and she sparked something deep inside him. She was confident and stood up for things she believed in. He wanted to say something to her to show his feelings. He wanted to share with her his newfound powers. But he still couldn't figure out what to say. He was just plain scared.

"Darius . . ." repeated Christine. "Have you fallen asleep standing up, or what? What are you thinking about?"

The question caught him by surprise and his answer flew out without a thought. "About you." He felt his face grow warm at the words.

"What about me?" Christine probed with a smile. Her intelligent green eyes met his light gray ones.

Darius felt his face flush a few shades darker. "Without you, my life would be dark and lonely."

Christine stood on her tip-toes, leaned over, and kissed him on the cheek. Fire seemed to burn from her lips, spreading throughout his body.

He reached his arms around her and with his broad shoulders pulled her into him. This time he was able to open himself to his power and he let it engulf them. As thoughts of joy and love spread through him, he transferred them to her. He could feel her feelings for him. They matched his. She relaxed in his arms. The sensation was euphoric and magical.

Long moments later she pulled back from him and looked deep into his eyes. "Darius? How did you do that? You made me feel so much joy. You've made me forget my pain and anger. It came from you. I felt a power of love that I've never felt before."

Darius was embarrassed with the attention. He had to be more careful with his power. All he wanted to do was to show her love and kindness. "You deserve to be happy, Christine."

He wanted so desperately to tell her everything – it was the perfect opening, but he retreated once again. How could he explain something to her that he couldn't explain yet himself? He needed more time – he would tell her soon.

Little by little he was gaining more control over the power, but without anyone to teach him it was difficult to know what he could or couldn't do. As Kelln had said, it seemed to come to him with great need and emotion. The power came to him when he thought about something happening. Sometimes he needed his hands to move in a specific gesture; other times just a feeling from inside would provoke a magical outcome. It was exciting, yet made him more afraid than anything else he faced.

Christine leaned into his strong arms and Darius kissed her deeply on the lips. The fire moved through him again as he felt his power stir and his heart burn.

He would tell her when the time was right.

Chapter Eight

The journey to Belor by Kelln and Alessandra began by wading through a waist-high portion of the Black River at the south end of Anikari. They walked under a bridge, leaving behind the sights and sounds of the largest city of the Realm. Kelln tried to stop shivering but couldn't. The water numbed him from the waist down as they trudged through it for a hundred yards, holding their packs up above their heads. It was the only sure way out of the city without someone seeing them leave through a proper gate. It was cold and uncomfortable, but it worked.

After that, they kept beside the river and journeyed south through the Black Forest. The first night Kelln couldn't sleep. He was sure some forest animals or wandering thieves would attack them. Alessandra calmed him and assured him everything would be all right. She talked of a power and force that would protect them. He didn't ask any questions but thought about her words as he tried to go to sleep.

Kelln enjoyed Alessandra's company, but, being used to the crowds of the city, he began to miss the constant sounds that were present there. To pass the time he started asking questions.

"How long will the trip take? Are we safe? Why did I have to leave in secret? I haven't done anything wrong. Where is my family?" And the list went on and on.

Alessandra answered him in short statements, not giving any more information than she absolutely had to.

After a few days they emerged from the Black Forest and met the Everlasting Meadows. For some reason the openness made him uneasy. As far into the distance as he could see, there was only grass and small plants; nothing over a few feet high. The lack of trees made him seem tall but vulnerable. The meadows seemed to stretch on forever until grass blended into the sky. It was breathtaking and astonishing to observe so much land at one time, without any trees or hills to block the view. Later that night Alessandra first told him of the Preacher.

"He is a great man. One who has seen our plight and our future. He is gathering us as an army to fight for our freedoms," Alessandra said with conviction.

"Where did he come from?" asked Kelln.

"He is one of us. Born and raised in Belor. Seeking direction and purpose, he sailed across the ocean and studied in the eastern kingdoms. He said it was there that he found God and his purpose."

"I believe in God, but I didn't have to sail around the world to find him." Kelln's sarcasm appeared a little too harsh.

Alessandra stood up as if to emphasize her point. Her face reddened, brighter in the glow of the fire. "What do you know about God, being from Anikari? They have no God there. If they did, they wouldn't treat us as they do. God is in Belor."

He told himself he would remain calm about the matter until he learned about everything for himself. He wanted to know more about Alessandra, but she became so defensive about what the Preacher did. Kelln didn't have anything against religion really. He had always believed in God. What bothered him was that the words from Alessandra were not her words.

Kelln found himself holding back a laugh when she said that God was in Belor. "God is in Belor? Can I see him when we get there?"

"Kelln El'Han!" Alessandra stood with hands on her hips. "You know full well what I mean. He doesn't live in Belor. It's just that his presence is felt there."

Kelln only lay back on his blanket roll and gazed up at the stars. He had rarely seen so many. They stretched from horizon to horizon and even beyond that, he imagined. He wondered how many other worlds were out there. He felt incredibly small. Like one blade of grass on the entire plain. All this talk about God made him a little embarrassed he didn't understand more about religious things.

He wanted to know more, but never knew where to look. Maybe Alessandra was right. Maybe he would find him in Belor. He smiled to himself as he fell asleep.

Two days later the two entered Belor. Even though anciently Belor had been its own small kingdom, ever since the days of King Anikari it was part of the Realm. Ruled overall by whoever was the King in the capital city of Anikari, Belor like Denir, Mar, and Sur, all had its own governor and local leadership.

There were signs of a few skirmishes, but besides that, the city looked as Kelln remembered it from a few years earlier when his family had visited there. He soon found his father working in a metal shop and forging weapons. They hugged and spent a few moments in talk about Kelln's trip through the forest, and then his father excused himself to get back to work.

The zeal in his father's eyes was different than Kelln had seen before. His father was a happy man, giving time to his family even when he was busy making swords. Now it seemed he was obsessed with making swords and didn't have much time for his family.

Kelln didn't like the change.

He was told the rest of his family would join him soon. Two weeks later they did.

After a few weeks, Kelln itched to leave and do something. He was getting tired and bored of Belor. He asked if he might take a couple of days and go to the sea, but they did not allow him to leave the city. He felt like a prisoner, yet his father assured him it was for his protection. He did not make many friends. Most were still wary of him since he came from Anikari.

There was Alessandra. Once she was all cleaned up, her beauty captivated him even more. Her hair, though died dark, was thick and luxurious. He tried to spend time with her, but she was usually too busy for him also. He stumbled on his words around her when they talked. He wished they were more like Darius and Christine; those two could talk for hours.

Alessandra was gone most of the time, even disappearing for days. He figured out, though she would never confirm it, that she went off and helped others escape from other cities around the Realm and returned them to Belor. He thought it strange for a woman so young to have the responsibility she did, but she performed the task well.

Kelln passed most of his time practicing with his sword and his bow. He was also given the charge to teach others. In the Belorian palace library, Kelln had found various books that proved interesting reading about the history of Belor and the Realm. He thought of Anikari often and of his friends, especially Darius. He wondered what they were all doing.

Kelln decided to find out for himself what was going on in Belor. Things just didn't seem that bad, and he was concerned that the man they referred to as only the Preacher was stirring up trouble. The key to finding out about Belor was to find out about him.

The Preacher was a man in his late thirties who stood tall among the Belorians, who were a short race by heritage. He stood well over six feet with a broad-shouldered build. His short hair was auburn and he wore two gold wristbands, one above each wrist. His deep red cloak seemed to always sway in slight movements from his body as he walked or preached. His voice was commanding yet at the same time compassionate. As large and powerful as he was, his charisma made people follow him.

The Preacher seemed to have a way of becoming one with the people and leading them into whatever direction he desired. That is what Kelln didn't like about the whole situation. This one man seemed to string them all along like puppets on a huge stage. The first time he saw the Preacher a strong feeling of danger loomed up inside him. It was obvious to Kelln that the man craved power, but held it under a cool mask of compassion.

"We cannot be held prisoners in our own land." The Preacher spread his arms wide to the gathered group. They stood transfixed in the town square in front of Kelln. "God has declared that all men are free. Those in Anikari are no better than we are. We have a right to be free and to direct our own way. God has declared it so."

The people cheered and Kelln sunk back farther in the crowd and continued watching. The Preacher, stood on majestic steps that curved upwards in a vast structure that held a massive dome on top. Kelln had been intrigued with the architecture of the city since he arrived. Where Anikari was built with straight lines and brick and rock, Belor was all curves, domes, and circles. To decorate most of their buildings they used a type of colored rock-and-mud mixture that hardened when it dried. He liked the effect.

The Preacher rambled on for more than half an hour. *God said this and God said that.* Kelln could almost recite the speech word for word. It was the same every time. The Preacher would go on and tell them how the Belorians should not be slaves to the rule of King Edward. They had God on their side and God was their king. That is why he was known only as "the Preacher."

Kelln didn't disagree with the religious aspect of a supreme being and that all men should be equal. Darius and he had discussed that very thing after he had met Christine. But Kelln did not perceive God in the Preacher.

He tried to look at the conflict from their point of view. The people were taxed just the same as others in the Realm outside of Anikari. Perhaps they had been treated unfairly at times, but not any more so than the other outlying cities, he would guess. He just did not understand the level of alarm that this leader made things out to be. They now were taking up weapons and training to go to war.

Situated between the Everlasting Meadows and the Blue Sea, Belor had a great advantage in hunting, fishing, and farming. Yet they needed to trade these for wood, brick, and metals from the rest of the Realm. Kelln reasoned that by fighting against the Realm they cut themselves off from the necessities they actually needed.

One day, after one of the Preacher's famous talks to excite the people, Kelln was walking behind the large palace that the Preacher used as his headquarters. He heard voices arguing up ahead and he stopped behind a doorway. He recognized one as the Preacher's booming voice.

"I have them in my hands. They will follow me now."

"All I was saying was that we are getting short on food and need to make sure that we don't cut off all trade from the Realm," another man with a higher voice debated. "Our population has swollen in recent weeks and we were not prepared."

"The people can cut back. Sacrifice will make them stronger," the Preacher spoke again.

"But sir, you can't mean that. The people will starve."

"Sometimes there are sacrifices to be made," the Preacher said.

"The governor should be here. Where is he?" asked the man.

"He is of no concern to you, councilor. You will obey my orders or you will join the other councilors in the dungeon. The Realm will recognize me as the legitimate ruler of Belor and leave us alone or the people will die fighting them."

Kelln heard the councilor squeak out an affirmation that he would obey the Preacher's words, then heard him walk away.

Hoping to not be seen, Kelln turned back the way he had come and he ducked into an alley that would bring him out into the merchant's district. He couldn't believe the Preacher would starve his own people. The thought appalled him and made him even more fearful of the Preacher. He was a man who wanted power, not peace.

Of course, it seemed to him that he was one of only a handful who seemed to grasp the situation this way. The Preacher seemed to get them all extremely excited in fighting for their independence. They fought for good things—freedom, equality, and religion—but Kelln wondered if the Preacher went about it all wrong. He drove the people into a frenzy, in which they had no choice but to follow him. They lost sight of the real meaning of freedom and peace. They took away the peace they did have by starting a battle with the Realm. And among it all, the Preacher declared himself their undisputed leader. He lived in lavishness in the old domed palace he used as his own headquarters.

Kelln had to find out more of the Preacher's plans and then, if required, he would send word to the capital and warn them about what was happening. Darius would listen to him and then tell his father. He loved his family and didn't want to see them hurt any longer by the Preacher's evil influence.

Chapter Nine

Again the voice came. It wasn't louder, yet it seemed closer. Darius thought he heard someone, or something, breathing. All he could do was stare into the black nothing and wait. He reached for a wall. Anything solid to hold on to. Before he reached anything, something reached him instead, and grabbed hold of his hand.

"Darius," a female voice whispered. He tried to jump back.

"Darius," it said again as the unseen hand shook him harder. He yelled out and tried to push the hands away. Darius opened his eyes. The bright light forced him to closed them again.

Darius heard his name once again, but this time the voice sounded more familiar and closer. His eyes were slow to open the second time. When they did they began to focus on a woman . . . his mother, Elizabeth. How could she have gotten here? As if to answer him, she spoke.

"Darius I have been trying to get you awake for minutes. Couldn't you hear me or feel me shaking you?"

Darius looked around, eyes darting to take in his surroundings. Feelings of familiarity flooded back into him as he realized he had been sleeping and dreaming. His mother,

Elizabeth, stood next to him. He looked up at her again, seeing love spread across her face after a brief hint of concern—or was it frustration?

"I guess I was dreaming," yawned Darius, still trying to shake the all-too-real dream from his head. His bed felt good. Since Kelln had left about a month earlier he had spent later hours with Christine and her family in the farmlands. Not having any other duties this morning he was looking forward to a morning of relaxation before heading back to Christine's.

"Your father left a note for you this morning."

"What? What kind of note?" The anxiousness drove the remaining sluggishness from his mind, and he grunted. "I had the morning off," he mumbled. It was probably another meeting his father wanted him to attend. He hoped it wasn't going to take too long. He planned to go and take the Cremelino to Christine today. A gift for her upcoming fifteenth birthday. He also planned to let her know about his powers. Finally. He was prepared to face whatever consequences would come. He dreaded telling her, but he hated more keeping secrets from her.

His mother handed him the note and he opened it with curiosity.

"It's a summons from King Edward." Darius was surprised. "I don't have much time."

Elizabeth nodded as if she knew, then walked out of the room. "I have breakfast ready. Don't run off too quickly."

Darius glanced out of the window from his second-floor bedroom. From high up on the hill he could see much of the city from his vantage point. He supposed that was why they lived in this section of the city. So his father felt even more superior to everyone. When Darius was a younger boy they had lived down in the lower parts of the city. That was when his father had spent more time with him and his mother.

His mother pretended to be busy around the kitchen as Darius ate, but he watched the worried glances toward him when she thought he wasn't looking. His mother, Elizabeth, liked to cook, so she shooed the servants out that morning.

She was still a striking woman into her early forties. With long brown hair and blue eyes, she kept up with the latest court fashions, though Darius thought this was more out of duty than real interest. She stood behind her husband, but was much softer in her approach to Darius and his interests, especially with Christine.

His mother seemed more somber this morning. He looked at her. "Mom?"

She just shook her head and kissed him on his forehead as she encouraged him to hurry to the castle. He sensed concern.

The castle wasn't too far from his house. With a brisk step he walked along the cobblestone streets that marked his neighborhood and wondered what the King wanted. A summoning by him must be something important. Due to his father's position, Darius had met the King many times.

Lost in his thoughts, he tripped over a broken stone and winced as his knee hit the ground. He hated these stones. They always came out. His father would tell him they marked the upper-class neighborhood of Anikari. He liked brick himself. His father, having grown up laying bricks with his father, was adamant about surrounding himself with stone. Darius also liked the simple thatched houses of the countryside rather than the tile roofs now popular in the upper part of the city. Thoughts of the countryside brought thoughts of Christine back to his mind and he smiled, excited to bring her the Cremelino today.

The early summer air was warm already that morning. Darius now wished he had worn something less formal. The wool coat over a silk shirt, along with the woolen pants tucked into his high black boots seemed to hold in the heat. A summons by the King, however, did warrant the nicer attire. He ran his hand over his hair once again making sure it wasn't sticking up anywhere.

He arrived at the castle. Other young men a few years older than him were walking in through the same gate. He recognized many of them from the academy from when he was a few years younger. They weren't all sons of nobles, but most seemed to be from the city.

An old, wrinkle-faced guard stood at the south gate to the castle and nodded to him as he entered. "Darius, looks like something exciting going on today."

"Nothing exciting ever happens around here, Robert, not like when you were out traveling the Realm." He had grown up listening to all the stories of the guards. They had recounted their adventures to him of when they traveled away from Anikari in guarding the Realm.

The guard seemed to get a dreamy look in his old, tired eyes. "That is true, young sir. It's not like it was in the days of King Charles or his mother. Those were the glory days of the Realm. Seems like we are kept closer to home now, lad."

"Not me. I am going to go out and fight for those glory days again, Robert." Darius smiled and hurried through the broad stone archway, and climbed the smooth carved granite steps.

He followed the others, even though he was familiar with a short cut to the palace court. The King's court sat outside for the most part. Up front stood a raised dais where the King and his councilors were covered by a large canopy. The rest of the court had benches of varying lengths spread throughout. The castle surrounded the open court on all four sides, except for the small walkways where the young men had just entered.

This was where King Edward held large meetings, gave out sentences, made official announcements, and did everything that was outwardly important to the Realm and city of Anikari. This differed from the inner throne room, where the Throne of Power resided. It was in there that petitioners would gather once a month and where matters that were more private were discussed.

Darius looked up at one side of the castle wall, and even though he had seen it many times, he still marveled at its size. Legend said the castle had only taken ten years to build, a feat that was amazing for this size of structure. Of course, it was also rumored that a few wizards had contributed their help. He wondered again at the potential of his power. Would he be able to build something some day? Would he be shunned for it or, worse yet, kicked outside the city, like the wizards of old? Maybe living in the countryside with Christine wouldn't be so bad after all. He blushed at the thought and turned his attention back to the gathering.

Looking around the large area, others were already sitting down. Within minutes, more than 200 other men arrived. With a quick glance Darius noticed he was most likely the youngest of the group, by at least two years. The others all most likely had completed their one or two year apprenticeship program.

Royal guards stood at attention around the perimeter of the courtyard. Darius sat in nervous anticipation, wondering again what was going to happen. He wished that Kelln was there. It had been a month since his best friend had left for Belor. He was anxious to hear what he had found out in the southern Realm city. If he didn't hear from Kelln soon he would plan a trip there himself. His father had said that things were getting worse there and may turn to fighting soon.

The power within him began to gather, even without any prompting, rising up in him as preparation for any trouble. It seemed nervous too, if that were possible. At one point, his feelings almost made him get up and run away, though he didn't know where. Only his strict upbringing and teaching kept him in rooted to his hard seat.

The men seemed to quiet down as they looked up toward the podium. Darius's father, Richard, stood up in the front. He looked Darius in the eyes, but gave no outward indication he saw him. Darius sensed a strange air of sadness and exhaustion on his face.

Richard motioned for all to stand.

In came the King in his entire royal splendor, from his brilliant golden crown atop his head to his purple cloak swirling around his tall frame. The King's eyes seemed to settle on Darius for a fraction of a second - it was the first time that

Darius really noticed that King Edward's eyes were similar in color to his own.

King Edward proceeded to sit on a throne that was a smaller and less ornate version of the Throne of Power. Richard motioned for all of the men to sit.

"Our loyal King Edward, friend of the people, protector of the people, and one of the people, has summoned us here today," began Richard.

Darius had heard these lines before. A rhetoric that was repeated each time a king spoke. The King stood and walked to the podium. His fierce, greyish eyes looked at each young man. An excitement ran through the room and Darius' own heart began to pound louder.

"My young men of Anikari and of the Realm," the King's voice boomed. "You have been gathered together this day for an exceptional purpose. You have grown up in a world of relative peace and safety. That was not always so. Many people among your ancestors and mine fought for this long reign of peace that began with my father and that has carried into my reign. It is not I who established the peace. It is you. You the people. You the young and the brave and the loyal."

Darius still wasn't sure what was happening, but he joined many of the other men as they moved to the edges of their seats. Anticipation filled the air.

"The peace I have spoken of is becoming fragile. There are those in, and out of, the Realm who would like to watch us fall and fail. In order to protect our peace and our people I have selected you, a chosen group, to become what will be known throughout the lands as the King's Elite Army."

The King paused, letting his words sink in. Darius's heart leapt with joy. He was finally going to be trained in the army. That is what he had wanted all along. He wondered why his father had said nothing to him, or why he had experienced a change of heart from Darius being trained as a councilor. He looked at his father, but got no response back.

"You will work and train hard to become one together. A group so cunning, strong, and brave that no one would dare take our freedom and peace away. You will be trained, as warriors of old were, to become one with your weapon, one with yourself, and one with the Realm."

"Woohoo!" yelled out one man.

"Off to battle!" shouted another.

Darius heard cheers and handclaps emerge from the others, rising to their feet. He found himself bewildered and full of questions, but joining the others in praise of their King. He felt a sudden sense of pride. Who wouldn't? He would be trained as in the legends of old. He looked around the room and realized again that he was the youngest by at least two to five years. What did that mean? Was he being given special treatment because of his father? He hoped not. He wanted to prove himself on his own. He couldn't wait to tell Christine the news.

Darius thought once more of Kelln. Maybe he could get his father to allow Kelln to join him also. He could ride to Belor and back in a week's time and bring Kelln back to Anikari before they started training.

The King sat down and Richard returned to the podium. The crowd resumed their seats. Darius's father looked tense and stern as he began to layout the finer details of the plan. Darius half listened as he daydreamed about what the King had said. Every young boy dreamed of being a great warrior, like in the ancient tales. His power flared inside him with those thoughts.

" . . . We will leave late tonight," was all he heard to shake him from his dreams. *What?* He almost said out loud. *Leave where?* The King hadn't said they were going anywhere. Didn't they have to get ready and train first?

To answer Darius's silent question, Richard continued. "We will be going up into a special camp that has been set up in the Superstition Mountains. There you will not be distracted. You will leave here when I dismiss you, to go home, pack any clothing and weapons you have, and return in three hours' time. Everything else will be provided for you. An escort will accompany you to make sure everything goes according to plan. This news . . . this idea of a new Elite Army will be kept confidential for now. The location of your training will be guarded and kept secret."

Darius felt his world slam shut. Why this sudden move to the mountains? How could his father do this to him? It must be a plan to keep him away from Christine. Thoughts of her made him swoon in his seat. He had to tell her. He had to hold her one more time before he went. He had known that he might have to leave for short periods of time to defend the Realm, but not like this. Not so suddenly and secretly. He thought about escape, but he realized it would never work. Not now. Maybe later, after he had time to think about the situation. His heart ached, and he choked back the lump forming in his throat. What would he do without her? He wasn't prepared to deal with this now.

The new soldiers were dismissed one by one with their escorts, guards from the perimeter of the yard. The escorts were coming down to the end and an escort hadn't been assigned to him yet. Time was running out, he thought.

He would have to figure out a way to get rid of his escort for enough time to get to Christine's house. He felt a sudden pushing in his mind to get the Cremelino to Christine before he left, almost like a voice pleading with him. It shouldn't be too hard. He was fast. If he needed to, he would even use his powers, but only as a last resort.

All of the boys were gone except for him. His father walked up to him and said, "I will be your escort, Darius."

Darius's heart sank. How could he get rid of his father?

* * * *

The sounds of the busy city floated through the air, but empty silence sat between Richard and his son. Horse hooves on the cobblestone were heard coming around a corner, children playing outside, the distant sound of a voice singing. Yet the quiet surrounding Richard and Darius was palpable.

Their steps matched each other as Richard realized his son was now an adult, full-grown. Each one walked, deep in his own thoughts. Each one wanting to say something to the other. King Edward had been talking to Richard for months about this idea, yet he had kept hidden from even Richard the ages of the men he had in mind. Richard had supposed they would be seasoned warriors, men who had been trained already. Instead the King wanted young men in their early twenties, and then Darius, his son, was younger than them all.

His own son, leaving to become someone that Richard didn't have any control over. Edward had assured him that it would be the best thing for Darius. A chance to become strong both physically and mentally. A chance to become a leader without Richard or the King around. His age would force him to either succeed brilliantly or fail miserably. Richard didn't like the odds.

He looked over at his son, walking beside him. He had become large and strong in the last few years. He knew Darius must hold tremendous grudges against him for this. He just wanted what was best for Darius . . . to be raised right and to be prepared for his future role.

The one thing he didn't understand about his son was his attraction to the young woman Christine and the other outsiders. He wished he were able to make him understand his heritage and his obligation. He was a noble and a city man, and was better than the uneducated farmers living in wrecked houses on dirt roads outside of the city. He tried not to think about what else his son was. *A future king?!*

Richard could imagine what his son was thinking about him. He knew that Darius didn't agree with the way Richard saw things. He knew his son wanted to stay out of politics. But Darius didn't know the truth. The one thing that Richard couldn't tell him. Now this sudden quest would upset him even more. He could see his son's clenched jaw, the anger building in him.

"You will learn a lot, Darius." His father interrupted his son's solitude. "This can be a great opportunity!"

"But why so soon?" Darius turned to face him. He stood only inches away from Richard and looked him in the eyes. "I know I wanted to go train and protect the Realm, but not this way. And I am sure you noticed that I am younger than everyone else there. Are you setting me up to fail? Is that what this is all about? You want me to fail so you can have your way of me following you in politics?" Darius let all his frustration rush out at once.

"It is what the King wants. I . . . ." Richard's voice trailed off. What could he tell his son? He wished he could spare him the pain.

"You what?" asked Darius.

Richard looked at Darius with a tender glance. "I wish it weren't so. At least not this way, but the King has his reasons."

Richard almost saw the walls break down. Could his son finally understand his feelings? But as quickly as he thought he saw a softening, firmness replaced it moments later and Richard realized an opportunity had passed.

"Right!" Darius said. "Reasons I bet you can't tell me right? This is what you want anyways. To keep me away from Christine."

Richard stopped. They stood in front of the house now. It had been a mistake to show his feelings. The councilor had thought he saw a spark of understanding within his son, but once again Darius wouldn't even try to understand. How could his son be so blind and rebellious?

Anger came to Richard and he grabbed Darius by the shirt, looking him straight in the eyes, up close. "I don't care what you think of me anymore," Richard snapped, not holding back. "I've given you the best I could. It may not be the best to you. Maybe nothing is. You treat me like you are better than me because you see the way things should be. You want everything peaceful and everyone getting along. You can't have it all. The world doesn't work that way, Darius. There are nobles, merchants, outsiders, and thieves. This is an opportunity for you to make something of yourself. Don't mess it up!"

Rage filled Darius's face. He reached his hand toward Richard and pushed him on the chest with the palm of his hand. Richard flew back ten feet, stumbling to keep from falling into the short bushes next to his home.

Darius shook with anger. His temper seemed out of control. "I want to see Mother," he said as he barged through the large front door and stood in the two-story entryway, "by myself."

Richard felt real fear for the first time in his life. Darius should not have been able to push him that far. He didn't understand what had happened, but he sensed a power from his son that confused him and brought a thousand questions to his mind. Questions he didn't want to think about – and didn't have time to figure out.

He sat down on the front steps, honoring his son's wishes for some time with his mother, not out of concern for Darius, but out of fear of what else could happen.

He hoped Edward lived for a long, long time, because he was truly afraid of what might happen to the Realm in the hands of his son. He hated feeling this way. He hated the fact that he thought his son would never be ready to rule. He choked back the tears and looked off at the summer thunderstorm coming in the distance.

Chapter Ten

Darius walked toward the kitchen, where smells of food reached his senses. He stopped once in the hallway and breathed in a deep breath of air. He had lost control again. Anger, more often than not, seemed to be the driving force behind his powers. He knew he shouldn't have pushed his father, but it had felt good to release the frustration. He couldn't believe his father was acting like this was good for him.

It finally felt good to be angry. His whole life he had tried to be understanding of his father and others. He always tried to do what was right. He wanted to feel pride in the Realm, but at the moment he didn't care anymore. He wanted to feel the anger. His power boiled inside him.

He went into the kitchen, closing the door behind him with a loud bang. The cook was not in the kitchen, but a meal sat on the table. The large oak table was set for a small, informal meal. Three places were set. His mother looked up from one of the seats. He watched tears come to her eyes and some of his anger abated, leaving him feeling empty and hollow. She was aware of what was happening, or at least sensed it.

Darius went over to her and hugged her. Sitting down, her head reached only to his middle. He wondered when her hair had begun to grey.

She looked at the other two place settings. "I was hoping that maybe. . ." she trailed off.

Darius shook his head and she took the meaning. There would not be a last meal with the three of them. He gulped in huge breaths of air, trying to regain control over his emotions. He couldn't bring himself to speak yet.

Elizabeth spoke again. "It will be lonely here, Darius. I will miss you."

Her words broke his heart and he finally spoke. "I'll miss you too, Mom. But I will think about you all of the time," answered Darius. The tears of his mother softened his anger. He felt like a small kid again. All the memories of his childhood seemed to flood into his mind. He remembered her teaching him to read and write, encouraging him with his many interests, helping him with his problems. She was always there for him. She was his rock he relied upon when things got bad with his dad, or at school, or with the many other problems facing a young man. She didn't live the life of many other nobles' wives, always involved in parties and court functions. She liked being in her home. She would always be there. Never judging. Just loving.

He took a few bites of food, but was not really hungry. He was not ashamed of the tears in his own eyes. His emotions swirled inside. He wondered how so much anger and love existed in him at the same time.

"How long do you have?" she asked.

"Only a short time. Father is my escort to watch over what I do. We must return in a few hours. I need to pack."

"Then you must leave right away." Elizabeth smiled through her tears, thin lines of wrinkles showing at the corners of her eyes.

Darius wasn't sure what she meant. *Leave?*

"What do you mean? Leave where?"

"You will want to see Christine, won't you?"

It was then that Darius realized again why he loved his mom so much. She always knew what he was thinking and what he needed.

"You can go through the back door. Your father will not realize for a while. I will talk to him. I will have him bring your things to the castle."

"Mom, I love you," smiled Darius as he gave her a kiss on the cheek.

They stood for a moment longer; then she shoved some food into his hands. He would have to rush to the back of the castle grounds to get the Cremelino first. He would have to run hard. So he started running, calculating in his mind the quickest route.

He ran through the back alley and down the cobblestone streets of the nobles' neighborhood. Tall houses flanked him on either side. He made it to the school and through the fields behind the school. He wound down the hill and to some forgotten stables.

He grabbed the Cremelino by the reins, knowing that he couldn't ride the animal. The Cremelinos only took one rider in their lifetime, and that would be Christine for this horse. There were stories of people trying to ride one without the Cremelino's permission. They talked about feeling a deep burning pain inside and being thrown from the horse. He hoped Christine enjoyed the horse. Not many people owned one, and none who did lived in the farmlands. He was so excited to see Christine's face when he gave her his gift.

He took roads that skirted the city center, as far away from the castle as he could go. The homes and storefronts in this area were smaller and less attractive. A few street vendors yelled to him to buy their wares.

No need to pull me so hard, wizard. I will follow you.

Darius stopped so suddenly that the Cremelino bumped into him, almost knocking him over. Who had just spoken to him?

I did.

Looking into the horse's light blue eyes, he got a funny feeling inside his mind.

Yes, wizard, I can speak to you.

Darius looked around. Some street kids stopped and looked at Darius. He still wore his finery and stood out in this seedier part of town. He didn't want someone to report back to his father that they had seen Darius leaving this way.

"I am not a wizard," Darius growled out loud, but softly.

Call yourself what you wish, but the prophecy says otherwise.

"Prophecy?" This time Darius tried to speak in his mind, as well as out loud. He was shocked to find it actually worked. He was really communicating with one of the Cremelinos. He didn't know that it was possible. Could others do it too? Or was it due to his emerging powers?

The horse recited in his mind:

Forgotten lines of ancient magic
and the power of the throne
One will make them both his own
if his heart sees the true power. . .

More people began staring at the young noble facing his Cremelino horse. Darius looked around and decided he needed to keep moving.

I will follow you. Run, wizard, run!

Darius didn't feel like arguing again. Besides, arguing with a horse seemed silly. Talking with a horse seemed foolish also, but that was what he was doing.

The Cremelino followed behind Darius as he picked up his pace. He rounded a curve in the road and began running harder. He stopped to pass through a small back gate out of the city that wasn't used much. He was now in the farmlands. He ran faster over the pastures and farmlands, jumping fences as he needed. His legs burned and his lungs drew in deep breaths.

He brought the power up and found he could direct some to release some of his pains as his long legs carried him faster. His hair stood just above his neck and blew in the breeze. He reached the main road into the farmlands and appreciated the firmer ground. The ancient oak and maple trees became a blur of green and burgundy. He had to see Christine.

Christine's father had been quite sick lately and Christine spent more and more time helping to work the farm with the others. Darius wanted to help, but his father had insisted on Darius accompanying him to more and more meetings. He wondered now if the whole plan had always been to get him

away from Christine. His time away from her had made him
grow even more fond of her. Darius couldn't believe how
intelligent, compassionate, and fun she was. He smiled,
thinking of her soft voice and laugh. Only seeing her for a few
moments would sustain him for now.

He saw her house ahead and stopped a little ways before
to catch his breath. The Cremelino stood next to him, hardly
breathing at all. He was amazed at the horse's endurance, as he
knew that he was already running faster than was normal. His
power washed over him again to take the tiredness away. His
heart beat with excitement as it always did when he anticipated
seeing her. This time, however, he also carried a heaviness, and
he realized he would have to say goodbye for a while.

"Hello, Darius," greeted Caroline, Christine's mother. She
met him on the porch and ushered him into the house. "Will
the horse be all right out here by itself?"

"Oh, yes." Darius guessed she would be.

"She is beautiful."

Darius felt a glimmer of pride come through his mind. He
looked at the Cremelino and smiled.

Darius tried to catch his breath from the long run, but was
sweating from the summer afternoon heat. The clouds had
become thicker, but as yet no rain fell. "Is Christine out in the
field?"

"No, Darius. She isn't here."

"What do you mean she isn't here?" Panic began to set in.
"Where is she?"

"She went to Forest View to deliver food from the
farmlands. It was a sudden thing. She wouldn't let Stefen go

alone. He was feeling sick again. They won't be back until early tomorrow morning, I'm afraid. Why?"

Darius moaned and found himself speechless. He felt like someone had taken his stomach and torn it out of him. His face winced in pain and he put his hand up to his chest to stop the growing ache. Sweat started dripping off his face and he turned pale. How could his father do this to him? How could the King send him off so quickly? What right did they have to push him like this?

Oh, Darius. The Cremelino sighed in his mind.

"Sit down, Darius." Caroline sounded worried. "Here on the chair," she motioned.

After a few minutes of silence, Caroline's concern got the better of her. "What's going on, Darius? Are you sick?"

He trusted Christine's family. They had accepted him and taught him much about the simple things in life. But he knew he couldn't share too much with them. The King had ordered silence on the matter, and as much as he disliked King Edward at the moment, he was an honorable citizen and knew that to disobey the King could bring more trouble.

"I can't tell you much, but I have been called away to the mountains for some military training and I don't know when I will be back...or," his voice caught, "if I will be back."

"And you just found out?" Caroline's lips shook, holding back her own tears.

"Yes, and we leave in a few hours. I'm not even supposed to be here."

"Oh, Darius, I don't know what to say. Christine will be so . . . so . . ." She couldn't say anymore after that. Darius knew how close she and her daughter were.

Darius sat, leaning upon the edge of the chair with his face in his hands. Tears fell through his fingers. Caroline came over and put her arm around him, trying to comfort him.

Darius looked up and wiped his eyes. They were red and running with tears. "I have to go now," he whispered shakily. "I have to get back, but I brought her a gift."

"The Cremelino?" asked Caroline.

Tell her, her daughter was chosen. We are meant to bond together.

Darius paused, listening to the Cremelino in his mind.

"Yes," Darius continued. "Just tell her they chose her. Only one rider may ride a Cremelino and this one is hers. I am not sure why, but I know she is meant to have her. "

Caroline nodded, trying not to cry again. "It's a great gift Darius."

Darius stood and dragged his feet to the door. "Also tell her . . . tell her that I . . ." He began to choke up again. He tried to summon the power to help him, but it wouldn't come. His despair ran too deep.

Caroline found a piece of paper, an inkwell, and a quill. "Why don't you write a note?" she offered.

Darius took the paper and sat down at a small table by the front door. He just gazed at it for a few moments as he felt tears drip like rain over his reddened cheeks and onto the blank paper. He finally dipped the quill in the ink and scrawled a few words, folded it, and gave it back to Caroline. He smiled at her through the tears, hugged her, and went out the door.

We will be waiting for your return, the Cremelino spoke to Darius's mind as he passed by.

He walked with his head hung low, in a daze, not really thinking of anything in particular. He was lost. He was numb. He felt cold and afraid. He looked up at the dirt road before him.

Darius started to run.

I need Christine! He needed to hear her voice of reassurance. Now he was alone. So alone. He ran faster. His lungs ached; his legs ached. He let the anger build. It felt good to feel something. He vowed to remember this anger. It made him feel more alive and powerful.

He hadn't realized his feelings for Christine had grown so strong. He ran even harder. It seemed to help to have something else to focus on. He felt his insides rip apart. Alternating feelings of love and hate tore through him.

Darius. A voice in the back of his mind called, almost pleading. *Don't let this anger control you.*

Go away! He slammed his mind shut.

He raged in anger at his father for doing this. He cursed the King for his plan. He hated life right now. This whole thing was unfair and wrong. His best friend had even left him. Kelln should be here with him. Darius should be going up into the dark Superstition Mountains with his friend. He tried to run harder but he couldn't keep up the pace.

He passed through the city gate as he slowed down. He crossed through the field behind the school and stopped and fell to his knees into the dark dirt. He cried out in anguish again, in between breaths of survival. He kept the ancient sword concealed next to the hidden doorway they had found behind the school. He had removed it a few times over the past few months to practice, but had never wanted to leave it in his home. He was aware that the sword somehow magnified his power. If he ever needed power, it was now!

Darius knew he didn't have much time. He dragged himself to where the hidden door sat in the back of the hill. He pulled at some bushes next to it. He began to dig slowly at first, then in frantic scratching at the dirt. His emotions raged within him, jumbled between anger, rage, loneliness, sadness, and excitement. He could feel the sword calling to him and thought of the times he had held it before. He felt the package before he saw it. The power raged through him as it recognized the ancient weapon. He swayed at the force of it. It washed away all his weariness and replaced it with purpose.

Darius pulled the sword out of the ground and out of the burlap he had wrapped it in. He held the shinning sword up and watched it turn a golden white. Small veins of lightning traveled up the blade from his hand. In reluctance he lowered it and hooked it onto his belt, then sadly smiled at the memory of his and Kelln's adventure that rainy afternoon a few months before. Kelln had always made sure that some kind of adventure was in progress. He missed his friend.

With the sword at his side he ran again. He neared the walls of the castle grounds and noticed no other men walking in. He was late and received nervous looks from the guards. Dirt spotted his coat and pants and his face was smeared with dirty tears. He stopped at a well, cleaned his face, tried to wipe off some of the dirt, and strode into the courtyard where the other soon-to-be soldiers stood waiting at their benches.

Heads turned to follow him when he walked into the meeting area. A quick glance around showed him he was the last to arrive. His father stood up front on the podium. Anger and rage filled his face.

"Darius San Williams. Come up front!" the senior councilor commanded with a voice that left no question. Darius walked up front, his hand on his sword. Mumblings went through the crowd and a few pointed at the ornate hilt of the golden blade.

"You left your escort and disobeyed the King's instructions." His father said it as a statement, not a question. Darius didn't say a word. He just looked emotionlessly at the councilor.

Richard brought his hand up and slapped Darius so hard it knocked him off balance and almost onto the ground. With his right hand never leaving the sword, Darius reached out his left hand and balanced himself against a chair. His father seemed to pay little attention to the sword at all.

"No one—not even the son of a councilor—disobeys the King of the Realm. His words are law!" He looked Darius straight in the eye, piercing his entire soul. "No one," he added to the entire group.

With a flick of his hand, Richard motioned for Darius to return to the group. Darius walked down the aisle with a slow anger brewing deep inside him. Each slow step emphasized his feelings. His cheek stung and the slap would surely leave a bruise. He hated his father now.

The crowd gasped and Darius looked around. They were all following him with their eyes. He looked down at his hand, which tightened around the sword. Both glowed a brilliant white.

Darius turned back toward his father with rage filling his eyes. His father's arrogance, abuse of political power, and blindness to the plight of the people brought a bad taste to his mouth. He spat trying to rid himself of it. He continued to hold onto his sword, almost bringing it out at any moment. It felt good to be consumed by the anger. He hated his father more than he could ever remember, and he hated the King for being the king. No one should have that much power, he thought. *No one!*

He sat down and with a deep breath let go of the sword. The light winked out. Whispers and questions flew like the wind through the courtyard. Richard moved to the podium and demanded silence. He gave more instructions, and by the time he was done, Darius hoped the others had already begun to question whether they had actually seen the brilliant light or not.

Late that night all the young men were loaded into large covered carts. They sat packed in side by side on simple benches, their belongings packed in the other wagons. Darius glared at the guard that tried to take his sword. The man backed off and moved down the line, inspecting the other men. Just after midnight they departed. The wooden wheels creaked in slow unison as they left the dark city behind them.

Darius could feel the glare of others around him. Being the son of a councilor and defying the King had marked him as surely as anything else. He didn't know how to gain their friendship. He looked back at the city. His city. It was all he had ever known. Anikari. The center of the Realm. One of the crossroads of the western world. He who held Anikari held the power of the Realm and had great influence across the neighboring kingdoms of Arc and Gildan. A power he vowed to take down if it was the last thing he would do.

They passed through the west gate on to the road leading to the Superstition Mountains. He thought of home, of Kelln, and mostly of Christine and his anger abated. Regret and shame seeped in. He didn't know what had gotten in to him. Exhausted, sleep soon overcame him.

His sleep seemed to be devoid of dreams that night and he woke early feeling relaxed and almost new. The warmth and direction of the sun signaled morning, sending shadows across the road ahead of them. Ahead to the west, the Superstition Mountains loomed closer. He sighed a deep breath when he thought again of Christine. He thought of their favorite place, the field of diamonds, the small meadow at the edge of the Lake of Reflection. He told her when they first found it that he wanted adventure and to fight for the peace of the Realm, he just didn't know it would happen this way. He told her silently he would return for her.

"I promise," he said whispering to himself.

Chapter Eleven

Christine arrived home with her father early the next day. Her mother told her what had happened. She tried to be strong and keep the pain inside. Her mother handed her the note, but before she could read it, she saw the beautiful white Cremelino horse that Darius had left for her.

Walking up to the animal, she put out her hand and touched the horse. In that instance a new presence entered her mind. She jumped back, thinking she had imagined the voice.

Christine!

Christine looked around. Her mother had gone back inside to take care of her father, who was feeling sick again. Tentatively she reached over and ran her hand over the silky white mane of the horse. The Cremelino was large, with its back standing almost as tall as Christine. Its light-blue eyes looked out at her with intelligence.

Stroking the side of the horse seemed to soothe her mind. Christine brought out the note and unfolded the paper. There were dirty water stains on its edges. She opened it, read it, and leaned against her horse. She read it over and over again. She tried to hold herself together. She reasoned it would only be for a short time. Silent tears rolled down her tanned face. Caroline came back out and put her arm around her eldest daughter.

"What if he never comes back? What will I do?" Christine looked at her mother. She bit her lip to keep from bursting out into sobs.

Her mother had no answer for her.

Christine, let's ride. The Cremelino encouraged her silently, bringing itself down on its two front knees.

Without thinking, and without a saddle, she jumped on the back of the horse. She hiked her dress up to be able to sit forward. She had ridden bareback before and was comfortable on a normal-sized horse.

"Christine!" Her mother was embarrassed. "That's not a way for a lady to sit on a horse."

"I'm fine, Mom." She ran her hand over the horse's pure-white mane. The horse moved around, prancing for a few moments, and then as if she now understood who Christine was, settled down and stood still.

"I'll be back later," Christine informed her mother. "I just need to be alone."

With loneliness and sadness filling her heart, Christine turned toward a pasture and touched her heels to the horse's side. The horse took off with a grace and speed that astonished her. The Cremelino jumped over a fence while Christine held onto her mane.

"Woohoo!" Christine yelled out in delight.

Most everyone in the farmlands grew up riding horses, but a new feeling of exhilaration she had never recognized before came over her. She felt as if she was one with the horse.

Christine only had to touch her new horse with a soft pat and it seemed the horse recognized how fast to go and which direction. Even without the saddle, the ride was as smooth as sitting on a cushion of air. She looked down and saw the ground as a blur of green and brown.

In the back of her mind she sensed something. A connection that wasn't present before. Almost as if someone else listened to her thoughts. As she neared a fence she thought to herself that she should stop and turn back. In the blink of an eye the horse obeyed her thoughts. Christine gasped in delight. In her mind, she asked the horse to turn to the right and then left, testing her over and over.

The ride was exhilarating and amazing, taking her mind off her sorrow. She thought of what to name the horse as they ran faster and faster.

They followed a trail into the forest, emerging in a flash only minutes later into the field of diamonds. She stopped and looked toward the mountains and heard a distant rumble of thunder.

"Lightning," Christine voiced out loud. "I will call you Lightning."

A feeling of joy overcame her and she laughed. Then she dismounted, allowing Lightning to wander the field and eat.

Christine sat under the large tree and remembered when she and Darius had named the field. The sun had broken through the clouds then, reflecting droplets of rain on the ground. The memories brought tears to her eyes.

"Oh, Darius," she said out loud.

She stood up and walked to the water's edge. She looked at her reflection, shattered by ripples in the blue water. She herself felt shattered. Christine reached into her pocket, pulled out the note once again, and read it. Tears filled her eyes as she read the scribbled words repeatedly. She could hardly see the three simple words, "*I love you.*"

Christine looked toward the mountains and said, "I love you, too, Darius. Please come back soon."

Lightning nuzzled up against her, and she accepted the comfort.

Don't worry. He'll be back. The horse sent the thoughts to Christine's mind.

How do you know? said Christine back, still astonished at hearing an animal speak to her in her mind.

I don't know for sure, but I have great hope that he will. It is his path, his destiny . . . and yours.

What is our destiny? Christine asked. She still found it strange to be talking with a horse, but the Cremelino seemed much more than that. Her wisdom, insight, and knowledge were vast, but Christine felt that much was still held in secret.

The prophecies are alive now.

What prophecies? She prompted her new horse.

Forgotten lines of ancient magic and the power of the throne

One will make them both his own if his heart sees the true power. . .

Christine heard Lightning's voice in her head, but had no time to decipher its meaning at the moment. It had been an exhausting day.

I can't tell you more now, my child. I have to be careful I don't alter what is supposed to be.

Christine climbed back on top of her Cremelino. A warmth comforted her, not unlike that which she felt in Darius' arms. She closed her eyes and fixed a picture of him in her mind. She would never forget him!

Never!

Chapter Twelve

When Darius and the other men first arrived in the camp, there was no camp. It was nothing but an empty field. But it was a breathtaking sight. A small valley of grass nestled up next to a pristine mountain lake. The cool water sat between two jagged peaks in the western Superstition Mountains. The late summer season and high altitude brought a chilly temperature to the air.

Darius's anger had subsided somewhat on the journey there – now it was only a smoldering burn in the pit of his stomach. He tried not to think about Christine too much. Whenever he did he felt hollow and lost. He faced the fact he was stuck in the mountains with two hundred other young men. Biding his time, he would go along and do what they told him to in order to get back home quicker. But when he did, he surely wasn't going to follow into his father's footsteps – not after what he and the King had done to him.

Their first task was to build their own cabins. In fact, for the first month they did nothing but build in preparation for the winter. Muscles ached that he did not even know existed, but his strength and endurance increased each day. It was hard work, but Darius soon felt his muscles growing stronger and he wasn't as sore as the weeks went on.

It was a hard and lonely beginning. Thoughts of home and Christine occupied his mind and he had a hard time concentrating on the task at hand. He felt bitter and betrayed, and didn't care to do well.

"Isn't this great?" said Eliam a few weeks later. He had been friendly to Darius since the beginning and now stood in front of him with a waterskin and motioning to the cabins. "I've never worked so hard in my life, but it looks good."

Darius nodded. It did look good. The camp was almost completely built now. "Now what?"

"Now you start training." A stocky man with short grey hair and darker skin walked up next to the two young men.

Darius hadn't seen the man before and gave him a questioning look.

"My name is Cray," said the man with barely a smile. "You haven't seen hard work yet."

Eliam groaned and slapped his hand to his forehead, then pushed aside a swatch of blonde hair.

"Rest up men," Cray said loud enough for all the men around Darius to hear. "Tomorrow we start bright and early.

Darius walked away with a shrug. He really didn't care what they did next. He just wanted to go home. He tried to experiment with his growing powers when he could, but there was not much alone time. The men had been divided up into teams of 50. He was on the red team.

Over the next few weeks they practiced swordsmanship, archery, knives, and body fighting along with wilderness survival techniques. Soon cooler weather arrived, but that did not hinder their training. Early autumn would still be warm in Anikari, but it had already began to snow up on the peaks of the tall mountains around the camp, and soon would be falling all around them.

One day about six weeks after they first arrived, a new group of teachers and trainers came and among them was Sean San Ghant.

Seeing Sean again brought back bitter memories of the archery competition and thoughts of the argument with his father. Sean was a year older than Darius and closer to the age of the other soldiers and to Darius's dismay had seem to have grown taller since the archery competition. He now sported a light goatee and mustache that appeared to be the fashion of the day, and within days of his arrival many of the other men copied his style.

Darius tried to ignore and stay away from Sean, but one day, coming around the side of a cabin, he ran right into him. A look of annoyance came and went on his face, but he quickly resumed his usual smirk.

Sean crooked his finger, motioning Darius to follow him just outside the ring of cabins.

"Let's take a walk. We need to talk." Sean said.

Darius, suspicious of his motives, looked around him for support, but no one else was close enough. He decided he shouldn't be so angry for something that had happened in the past. Maybe they had both grown up a little since then. So he followed him.

"I know we have had our differences in the past." Sean began as if thinking carefully what he would say. "I have watched you and the other men here practicing the last few days and I can see that you aren't trying very hard, Darius."

Darius tried to protest but Seam put his hand up. "Let me finish, Darius. I know you don't like me. Just listen. I know you are younger than these other men, but even I have to admit you have a lot of potential. Remember, I saw the way you handle a bow." He smiled a little, and Darius relaxed somewhat. "You are the best archer here. You also have great potential with your sword, especially the one you have. Where did you get it anyway?"

Darius shrugged, signaling that he didn't want to tell Sean anything.

Sean continued. "You are quick and strong. But even with all of these characteristics perfected, many would not be the leader that you could be. You have been given everything that comes with privilege as a noble."

"I just don't like it here," said Darius.

"That's fair to say. I don't really like it here either, and I have only been here a few days. I would rather be back home in my warm house or in the Fair Weather Inn drinking ale and watching the girls, but we don't always have a choice in these matters. Sometimes there is something that guides our life that is bigger than we are. Sometimes we are being led to a destiny. We must make the best of it. This is where we have been sent, although for different reasons."

"What is your reason?" Darius said, still suspicious of anything that Sean said or did.

"I came to help teach various duties for a few months. I have not been called into the Elite." Sean paused, a quick glimpse of frustration and envy crossing his face. "I am in another type of training unit. Part of our duty is to rotate here and then to report back to . . ." He stopped as if he had gone too far.

"Report to who?" prodded Darius.

"To . . . your father," he said, looking Darius in the eye.

"My father? He's checking up on me?" Darius raised his voice.

"He is . . . concerned . . . about you, Darius." Sean said his words in a slow, rehearsed cadence.

"Are those your words or his?"

"That is what he implied. He wants to know how you are doing."

"Tell him I am doing fine!" snapped Darius.

"Are you?"

Darius grabbed Sean's arm and he felt Sean tense. Power flared up inside him and he glared at Sean in the eye. "I am doing fine, I said." He turned and started to walk away.

"Darius, what do you want?"

Darius turned around.

Sean continued. "You stated that you don't like it here, you don't want your father checking up on you, you obviously don't want to follow in his footsteps as a councilor, but you are a man now, Darius. You can't define everything by what you *don't* want."

"And what would you know about what I want?" Darius still stood a few feet away. His face reddened and his right hand gripped the handle of his sword. He controlled the power as to not let it glow. It was difficult to hold back. So difficult. He clenched his jaw.

"What do you want, Sean?"

Sean walked closer to Darius. "That's easy. I know exactly what I want. I always have. It's kind of funny, really. I want everything that you don't want. I want to be a noble. I want to be in charge. I want attention. I want to have power to rule over others."

Darius scowled, trying to fathom why anyone could be obsessed with such power.

"I really don't care what you want, Darius. But don't get in the way of what I want. But for your own good you might want to figure it out. You can't go through life whining about what you don't like. Grow up and be your own man!"

Anger welled up inside Darius and power coursed through his veins. With a well-placed shove, he used his powers to push Sean a dozen feet away to the ground, then with one jump he stood over him. Sean looked up and wiped dirt off his face. "Good. Good." He smirked up at Darius. "Now I see you want something."

"Yes. I want something. I want you to leave me alone, Sean San Ghant. Stay away from me."

Sean slowly stood up, still smiling. "Well, that's a start." Sarcasm dripped from his smug smile.

Once again Darius turned to walk away.

"Darius," Sean added without turning around. "You might want to get your anger under control. I must say I don't like this side of you."

Darius clenched the pommel of his sword but continued walking away. His power filled him with anger toward Sean, his father, and the King. They had no right to choose his destiny and what he would do. Sean talked of a greater destiny, of something guiding their lives. The only thing he noticed guiding and trying to influence his life was his father, King Edward, and some hidden agenda that they didn't want to talk to him about.

Sean was right in one thing—though Darius hated to admit it to himself. Darius needed to decide what he wanted. He needed a purpose back in his life. He thought back to conversations with Christine and Kelln. What had he told them he wanted? He wanted to make things better, to protect the Realm, to unite the people together—all people—in peace. He had always just thought that meant fighting and protecting from outside influences and from other kingdoms. Now he knew what his purpose was.

I must protect the people from influences inside the Realm—from those who have too much power.

He would not let others control his destiny any longer. He would step up and be his own man, and he was not going to get that by hanging around in the background and going through the motions. He would have to be the best. No one would push him around any longer. He would take control over his life. Starting today!

That next morning Darius woke up earlier than anyone else and started exercising on his own. Cray, the training camp commander, came by and watched Darius go through his morning drills. Out of the corner of his eye, Darius watched Cray watching him. His gray hair was cut short across his head.

He stood shorter than Darius but much more solid. Without saying a word, he nodded his head and walked away.

From that day on Darius trained and fought with one thing in mind. To protect the Realm. He did not hang out with the others, laughing, drinking, and talking in the evenings about the server girls. He closed himself off to anyone and anything but his duties and practices. He woke up before dawn and practiced until after sunset. His strength, abilities, and physical powers grew—and with that, a greater understanding and control over his magical abilities. His mind became sharper and his ability to focus grew stronger.

Chapter Thirteen

Christine kissed her mother on her cheek and ran out of the house with a few items to bring to a friend's house. Christine spent a lot more time with her friends in the farmlands since Darius had left almost two months before. Anya, Stephanie, Karel, Thomas, and she had become a common sight together around the farmlands. Karel was her cousin, and the other three lived on nearby farms.

She jumped on Lightning and rode down the road as the sun began to set. She shivered in the autumn air and noticed how eerie the shadows seemed as the sun slid behind the thinning trees. The weather was colder than usual. She thought about Darius again and hoped that he was doing well in the cooler weather up in the mountains.

Christine picked up the pace on her horse, still amazed at what her Cremelino could do. At first her friends had been nervous around the expensive horse, but its genuine beauty and gentle demeanor had helped them to accept her.

The Cremelino was her connection to Darius. Her heart still ached each time she thought about him. She knew that Darius wouldn't forget her and that he would be back when he was able. She just hoped it wouldn't be too long. The work on the farm for fall harvest and filling in for her dad helped to distract her somewhat.

Soon she arrived at Stephanie's farm, and she and Anya were there waiting for Christine.

"What are we going to do tonight?" Stephanie wore a bored expression. "Last time we just sat here and did nothing."

The last time they had stayed over at Anya's house had been only a week after Darius left and Christine still had not gotten over him leaving. Every mention of boys, or the city, or her horse, had brought tears to her eyes. Heartbroken, she hadn't wanted to feel better, because if she did she thought it meant her feelings for Darius had gone away. She had cried herself to sleep for weeks thinking about him. Even still, she kept his note in a secret jar in her room and would sometimes look at it. The days between reading, however, started to draw out longer. It had been a while since she had pulled the note out. She still longed to hear his voice again and feel his fingertips on her face, but the pain begun to dull as other mundane activities took its place.

"Let's go find the boys," said Anya, with a sparkle in her green eyes that spoke of love or at least infatuation. Anya was the shortest of the three, but of slender build. Her flirty smile seemed to tease all the boys in the farmlands.

"Always wanting to be with the boys," Christine said.

"What's wrong with that? I'm sixteen now. I have to be looking around," answered back Anya. "We all should be married in the next year unless we want to become old maids."

"Anya!" Stephanie seemed to warn her friend to stop talking about boys.

"What?" Anya paused, then realized what she had said. She turned to Christine. "Sorry, Christine. I know you are waiting for Darius. I'm sure he'll be back soon, but . . ." She stopped as if to figure out what to say next.

"What?" Christine asked.

"Don't you think you should find someone in the farmlands to marry?" continued Anya. "Darius would never be allowed to marry one of us."

Christine tightened her jaw. "Darius can decide for himself what he can do."

Stephanie tried to change the subject. "The men are having a secret meeting and Karel said that he and Thomas were going too."

"Why did he tell *you* if it's supposed to be so secret?" asked Anya.

"Well . . . Uh . . . He just did. That's all."

"What else have you and Karel been talking about?" inquired Christine. "He *is* my cousin, you know."

"And such a cute one, too," giggled Stephanie. "You should have introduced me earlier. I love his brown eyes and dark hair. He seems very mysterious. I think we should go and find out what their meeting is all about."

"You mean spy on them," smiled Anya, as if they had already agreed on it.

"I don't know." Christine sounded hesitant. "We don't know where the meeting is."

"I know. Well, kind of," announced Stephanie, as the other two looked at her. "Karel kind of mentioned it." They noticed her pink cheeks before she turned around and giggled again.

They all laughed and after a little more discussion decided to go. The gathering was taking place at a barn a few fields away, across one of the small rivers in the area.

The moonless, yet cloudless night allowed the stars to shine brightly enough to lead their way. Christine walked next to Lightning, who seemed to have eyesight that was better than her human companions. A few times she led them away from falling into the small irrigation ditches that in recent years had begun to spring up around the farmlands more and more. Many farmers were not content anymore with relying on just the rain to water their crops.

They made their way around an old corn field. Old stalks of corn sat drying out from a farmer trying to grow a late batch at the end of autumn.

Christine felt jittery, as if waiting for something to jump out and grab them, but they made it without any incident to the edge of the river.

They walked upriver a short ways until they found the double log that most children knew about from the time they were five or six. At this point the river cut into a deeper gorge. Some years ago, before corn grew in the field, a large tree had grown by the river until it was struck by lightning. It had fallen in a perfectly straight line over the river and had become a natural crossing place for many years. Then a few years ago some of the men had widened the crossing by adding another large tree.

The river below rumbled away in the darkness, rolling south, toward the northern edge of the city, carrying water from the recent storms. The girls crossed the make-shift bridge without looking back. Lightning seemed as light as a feather as she moved across with perfect balance.

"I think that's it." Stephanie pointed toward a barn with a faint light coming through a few windows as if men were moving in front of lanterns.

"Let's go around the back. If they notice us out here they might get mad," said Anya.

"Who's here anyway? I'm not sure if I like this or not," whispered Christine. She wrapped her arms around herself and shivered in the dark. Her Cremelino nuzzled up next to her as if reading her thoughts.

"You agreed to this, remember?" reminded Anya. "Now let's go. Maybe you'll meet someone new."

"Is that all you ever think about, Anya? Boys?"

"What's wrong with that? They are so cute."

Christine tried to stifle a laugh behind her hand. Anya, as fun as she was, obviously was not serious about life. She wouldn't be surprised if she were the first of them to be married.

They crept their way around a half a dozen walnut trees, toward the back of the old brown barn, being careful not to step on any of the old walnut shells on the ground. The noise might give them away. There was a pile of old wood leaning up against the back. The three of them moved toward it in silence. So far, no one had seen them, but they hadn't seen anyone themselves either.

Leaning up against the old barn, they searched to find a crack in the old bent and faded boards that they could peer through. After quite a bit of maneuvering they found a place where, if they sat down, they could see between two warped boards.

"We are wasting our time here," said an angry voice from inside the barn. "They don't care about us. And I don't care about them."

Christine peered through the hole, trying to see who was doing the talking. She thought she recognized the voice, but she couldn't place it. A barrel with a small fire tried to provide some warmth in the barn.

"I am tired of their children picking on my children. The next time I catch one of them outside of the city he won't forget where he is."

"Now wait a minute," said another voice. "I don't want you doing anything foolish that will cause more trouble. We need to unite together. All of the farmers. Then they will have to deal with us. They can't kill all of us."

The three girls continued listening as the talk went on. It became apparent it was a serious meeting of farmers trying to agree on a way to confront the persecutions by the city people.

"Let's move around to the side a little," motioned Anya. "I want to see if Thomas and Karel are here or not."

With careful steps they moved toward a closed side door, until they once again found a way to look inside the barn. Christine peered in, looking for Thomas and Karel. As she scanned the room, she recognized others in attendance.

"I say we fight them. They need our food. Maybe if we show force they will listen," continued yet another man.

Christine soon spotted Thomas and Karel. They sat toward the back in a small corner, with eyes wide open, and Jain her brother sat with them. She realized her friends were men now, and would be married in the next few years and would start taking over their family farms. That was the cycle out in the farmlands. But why was Jain there?

"Maybe others in one of the other cities will help," said a man from the back. "They don't look at us like the nobles here in Anikari do. They understand. I heard Belor is rebelling and a wizard leads them. I think . . ."

Christine had stepped on a loose piece of wood and she had put her hands out on the barn to keep from falling over. The man stopped talking and the group inside turned in the direction of where the women stood.

Anya and Stephanie gave irritated looks at Christine and put their finger up to their mouths, but it was too late. The men had heard something and a few of them moved toward the door. They turned to run, but Stephanie stumbled and fell down.

"Go ahead," she pleaded. "Run away, I'll say it was only me looking for my boyfriend."

"It doesn't matter if they see us. They won't hurt us," encouraged Christine. "It's not like we are forbidden to be here."

"But they will be plenty angry," added Anya as the door swung open to show three against the lantern light—two held swords and one a long pole.

"Too late now," mumbled Anya.

"What are you three doing?" asked one of the men in an angry tone. By this time more of the men had gathered around the door.

Thomas sighed, "Oh no."

The man who had spoken first turned toward Thomas and asked, "Do you know these girls?"

"Well . . . Yes." He stumbled with embarrassment. He furrowed his eyebrows in the direction of the girls, and his face heated up.

One of the other men came over to help Stephanie up. "Didn't you move here a short while ago?"

"Yes, a few years ago," answered Stephanie, trying to stand up on the foot she had twisted when she fell.

"Maybe she is a spy."

Mumbles in the crowd echoed agreement.

"She is not a spy," retorted Karel.

"How do you know?" came another voice as others joined in. Stephanie began to look nervous, and Anya moved over closer to Thomas. Christine glanced back and forth at the crowd of farmers both young and old. They looked like a poor lot. There was no direction or unity, but only a place to vent their frustration. She hoped they would not vent it in a fight.

Karel started to head back toward the part of the crowd that heckled Stephanie. There were other young men Christine had seen a few times from farther north of the farmlands.

"Karel, be careful," she found herself saying, until she noticed that her brother stood in the back of the crowd. He looked annoyed when he saw her.

"And Jain, what are you doing here?"

"What do you think? Someone has to do something, or don't you remember how many times you and Emily have been teased or beaten up?"

Christine realized how large Jain had grown. Muscles bulged in the side of his neck in anger. At almost three years younger than her, he was already her height.

Some of the older men just scowled as their heads moved back and forth between Christine and Jain, trying to figure out what was going on.

"You can't fight them," reasoned Christine. "They have an army."

Some of the men started murmuring about girls and children not being where they were not wanted or needed.

"You need to try a peaceful way," continued Christine as Jain got closer.

"Like what? Lay ourselves down in front of their feet so they can kick us? I don't think so. I'm tired of being pushed around."

Some of the other boys agreed. Thomas and Karel stood off to one side with Anya and Stephanie as if not really sure how they should react.

"This is enough childish talk," said one of the men that Christine knew. "If your father knew you were here he wouldn't be too happy."

"And if he knew you had gathered here without him, he wouldn't be happy either," snapped back Christine without thinking.

"He is . . . uh . . . too sick to come this far," the man tried to say without stumbling on his words.

"You know if he were here he would want a peaceful outcome, not fighting," Christine continued as she watched a few heads drop in acknowledgment. Her father was no small man of influence in the area. He had spoken up many times for continued peace, and was one of the most successful farmers. He wouldn't ask the city people for help with any matter, but he also didn't want to fight them on anything either. He said they should just leave the city people alone, sell their food, and let it pass.

"Go home, little girl," a voice yelled from the crowd. "You don't know what you are talking about. Go home to the kitchen, where you belong."

Christine became defensive and angry. "Who is saying that? That's just what the city people say to me. You don't seem much better than them right now."

The last remark caused quite a stir. "Hey, aren't you the girl that was always with the senior councilor's son? Maybe you like them better than us."

Lightning came trotting into view from around the side of the barn, where she had been nibbling on a tuft of tall grass sticking out between an old fence.

"And that horse is not meant for the farmlands," said another man.

Christine glared at the offender.

Don't let them bully you, Christine, said Lightning.

But I'm just a girl.

You can be so much more. Stop hiding behind your skirt.

Christine swayed slightly. The rebuke from her horse came with such force into her whole being.

Thoughts of Darius ran through Christine's head like a sandstorm blowing in random gusts across the hot desert. Flashes of everything she had learned from him, done with him, and seen with him flew around inside of her. She wasn't sure what to say. Everyone watched her, waiting for an answer. *What am I doing here?*

Lightning softened. *Just speak your mind. They will listen.*

Christine took a deep breath. "I am a farmer. My family is one of you, and I will always be one of you. But that doesn't mean I have to make myself suffer." She was amazed that they seemed to be listening to her.

Go on.

"There are good people in the city, and there are troublemakers. Just like there are good people in the farmlands, as well as troublemakers." She paused and looked around a little. A few eyes turned away from meeting hers. *Why aren't they stopping me? Are they that confused?*

"I learned more through my friend Darius than I have learned from any of you. He treated me as a person. Not as a farmer or city person. Not as an unintelligent girl, but as an individual. He taught me of faraway lands, of things in the forest, of languages. The most important thing he taught me is that I am as good as anyone else is. I am not any less because I am a farmer's daughter. Now many of you want to stand up with your few to the greatest army in the western world to show how brave you are. Many of them would then have a good reason to say that we aren't very smart."

Christine could tell she had some of the men thinking. A few even nodded their heads. *Why doesn't someone stop me before I say something stupid?*

Lighting whispered in her mind, *Because you're not being stupid, Christine. Yours is the first voice of reason they have heard. Do not underestimate the power you have.*

"I hate the way most of them treat me as much as you do. Most of you have no idea how they treat us women and what they say to us. It's a lot worse than what they say and do to you. We must show them we are as smart as they are. That we are organized, and can identify what we want."

"I want to fight," mumbled Jain again to one of his friends.

"And what are you going to fight with? Your shovel and hoe against their armor and swords?"

"I have a bow. And others have knives." Jain stood ready to fight.

"And they have a whole battalion of bowmen, and on top of that a whole unit of riders with swords."

"Then what do we do?" someone asked, as others echoed his question.

Christine thought for a few moments. Christine had not been prepared for the question. Even in the cool evening air, sweat rolled down her back and dripped off her face. She, only barely fifteen years old, faced a couple dozen men and boys. Now she was being asked how to stop years of persecutions.

"A petition," she said after a long silence. "We think out what we want, have our best writers put it on paper, and take it to the King. We must have demands ready, but we must also show we are willing to talk, or they will shut us off."

"They aren't going to listen to words," someone yelled from the back. "I thought the men were meeting tonight."

"She might have an idea," said the man who knew her father. "I think it's worth a try at least."

"We might as well put forth some effort," said another. "It's better than getting killed."

"Maybe we are as stupid as they say," said Jain, as he and a few of his friends walked away in disgust. "Talk and more talk. That's all we ever do."

Others joined in the conversation and began discussing their demands. Christine sat back on a large rock and took a deep breath. Lightning nuzzled up to her. *You did well.*

Christine smiled and ran her hand over her horse's nose. She didn't know what she would do without her. Anya, Stephanie, Karel, and Thomas crowded around her.

"Wow! How did you do that?" asked Anya. "I've never seen you like that before."

"You did good, cousin," smiled Karel, patting her on the back.

"I don't know." Christine tried to pull away her sweaty, sticky dress from her body. She was now feeling chilled in the cool air.

"We've been needing someone like you," complimented Thomas as he hugged her. Anya looked at the two of them and frowned.

"I think I need to go home," Christine said. She hopped up on her horse. Karel and Thomas were going to help

Stephanie and Anya home. The sleepover would not happen that night.

"Oh, to be a kid again," sighed Karel with a statement that echoed all of their feelings.

While riding on Lightning once again, she began to doubt the things she had said.

Be strong, Christine.

But my strength came from you. What if you are not around?

Your strength comes from inside, and don't worry, I won't leave you. I was sent to be with you.

Christine wondered what her Cremelino meant about being sent to her, but when she asked, she did not get an answer. The Cremelino, she was finding out, could be very evasive and cryptic in sharing what she knew with Christine.

Christine's message and idea spread throughout the farmlands. On the other hand her brother Jain became more distant from the rest of the family and more argumentative toward his position on the whole matter.

Groups of people began to stop by to talk to Christine's father, Stefen, about the idea. Though his physical abilities had begun wearing thin in his older years, his mental prowess and knowledge were recognized throughout the area. The group discussed late into each evening how to word the petition to King Edward and who would take it to him.

Two days later Christine's father informed her the men wanted her to accompany the petitioning party to the castle. She was shocked as well as overwhelmed. She had not really realized the impact she was having on the people.

"Aren't I young for this?" she questioned her father.

"You have won the hearts of the farmers, Christine."

"How? All I did was get a little angry and offer a few suggestions. I am no politician. I'm just a simple farmer, Dad."

"You are nothing simple, Christine. The men see this. You were friends with the councilor's son, you ride an expensive Cremelino, usually used only by the King or his chosen nobles, and you stated your position brilliantly from what I heard. Plus many of the wives and women support your idea," smiled Stefen. "And we all know who controls the men."

Christine laughed. "Oh, dad . . . But what if this doesn't work?"

"Then we will try another way," he answered in a matter-of-fact voice.

"What other way? Do you think it will turn to fighting?"

"I hope not . . . but . . ." He sounded so tired to her. "But we must not think of that now. In three days you will go to the city. That is petition day. The King hears open petitions from any of his subjects. They cannot turn you away."

"Will you go too?" Hope filled her voice.

"No. I don't have the strength for that anymore. I . . . I . . . I find it hard going into the city."

"If you don't like the city, why don't you fight, Dad?" A voice from the other room boomed as Jain came in. "Are you afraid to lose?"

Their father sat silent for a moment. He stared at his feet, and then with a heavy head looked up. "The only thing I am afraid of losing is you two and the rest of my family," he said with teary eyes. "I would fight the entire army myself for my family, if it would do any good. Please be careful. Both of you."

"But why?" asked Jain. "I just don't understand you."

Stefen got up to walk out of the room, "Someday. Someday you will understand. "

"You upset him." Christine turned on Jain.

"I just asked him a question. I don't understand any of you. I want to fight." Jain's arms flew into the air. His face reddened under his scraggly brown mop of hair. "I want them to know they can't kick us around."

"Maybe the petition will work . . ." began Christine. She didn't understand why her brother was so angry all the time now. "Settle down and let us try."

"The petition . . . the petition . . . It's not going to work, but all this nonsense is making you famous in the meantime, isn't it? Is that what you want?" Jain paced around the room, his voice booming. "You don't have your city boy around now, so you need to be a big shot on your own."

"Jain. That's not fair," Christine yelled. "I just made a suggestion . . . You know I would never . . ."

"When your plan ends in failure, then we will put *my* plan in motion," interrupted Jain.

"And what is your plan? To get yourself killed?" Christine slammed her hand on the kitchen table. It hurt but she didn't care. Her brother was being foolish and stupid.

"Not to get killed. But to kill."

"Do you even understand what you are saying? You're still a boy. What has gotten into your head? You have never killed anyone before," argued Christine.

"No, but I want to. I want to kill anyone from the city I can get my hands on. None of them are good. None of them."

He turned to walk out of the room, when he noticed Emily standing around the corner, crying.

"What about Darius?" she asked Jain, with tears dripping down her face. "You don't want to kill him, do you?"

He stopped as if he was going to say something, then just continued toward the door, slamming it on his way out.

Emily ran to Christine and embraced her. "It will be all right," Christine whispered to her younger sister, wondering if it ever really would be.

Chapter Fourteen

The next three days dragged by. Christine tried to help her mom around the house to take her mind off things, but it didn't work much. She found herself thinking about Darius more often as she tried to wonder how the petition would work. She knew Darius's father would be at the King's side, and she knew that he didn't like her much.

Christine wished Darius were here right now to give her suggestions and comfort. She wondered if he still remembered her. She wondered if he even cared anymore.

He still cares, whispered Lightning to her.

How do you know? He could be anywhere. I may never see him again. Tears of frustration came to her eyes and she wiped them off with a quick brush of her hand. She knew he cared. She had to trust in that. Without that she would completely fall apart.

He will find his way back to you. Somehow, he must! Or all will be lost. All will be lost.

Lightning's words confused Christine. They faded out of her mind. She was beginning to not only hear, but to sense somehow, her Cremelino's feelings. Feelings of worry, urgency, and power. She didn't know what it meant. It frightened her somewhat that she felt so close of a bond to her horse. She needed to talk to others and determine if her ability was normal with these Cremelinos. She knew how magic was looked upon in the Realm. She couldn't risk others finding out until she knew more about it. And where could she find someone to talk to about magic? For now she would have to deal with it on her own.

The day to deliver the petition came and Christine, along with two men—one in his twenties, Alvyn Alstryn, and one her father's age, Martin Halverssn—headed toward the castle.

The sky shone bright and sunny, but the coolness in the air made her wrap her hooded green cloak around her more tightly. She dressed in her nicest clothes; a simple dress with lace on the edges, which her mother had made for her. Lightning walked with them. They passed through the market area, and people gawked at them out of their tents and small shops. A few offered their goods for sale, but most just turned their heads away and ignored them. The smell of freshly baked rolls made Christine's stomach growl. She had been too nervous to eat that morning.

A few wayward children playing in the street ran in front of Christine, almost tripping her, until their mothers called them back to their homes. The small group with Christine passed through the outer city and into the city center. Here, stone and brick houses rose three and four stories tall. The streets were kept clean by a night crew. Carriages and horses passed them by, carrying nobles to seemingly important places. Their distrust of the outsiders was obvious as they turned away their faces when they passed.

The castle loomed up in front of them as they headed up the steeper cobblestone street. More guards were around to keep a watch on anyone who approached. As they got closer, they joined a group of other petitioners coming from other directions in the city.

All the petitioners were ushered through the palace gates, into the castle, and down long hallways with far-reaching ceilings. They were guided into a waiting room. It was too late in the year to hold the petitions outside.

Once a month King Edward held a time in his throne room for any commoner in the Realm to make a request of him. It was the only time the small group from the farmlands would be allowed without an appointment. They would never get in any other way. They would have been given excuses and delays, hoping that the farmers would just give up. But today they were admitted inside, and by Realm law and long-standing tradition the King could not send them away.

A servant took them to a waiting room with the others. Christine's head swam as she looked around the room. She supposed since it was a waiting room it was considered simple by the castle's occupants. However, she had never been in an actual room so large in her life. The ceilings were taller than their barn. The heavy red curtains hung open and were tied with gold tassels. Light streamed into the room, reflecting the sunshine onto the polished tops of four tables placed throughout the room. About thirty chairs were scattered around the room, each with sturdy, high backs and golden cushions. Christine filled her lungs with a deep breath. She now understood some of Darius's bewilderment and perplexity with the farmlands, if this was the type of place he was used to seeing.

The others in the room tended to keep to their own groups. Some were from other cities, marked by their colors either in a sash, on a hat, or by some other strategically placed design. Christine's group was obvious for being the only ones from the countryside, their clothes being less colorful and fancy than the others in the room—but Christine's dress was only a small notch below the others. She smiled at that. At least they wouldn't stick out too much.

A few groups at a time were taken out and led into the King's throne room. Christine realized they would be in the last group. After seeing the waiting room, she could not imagine the throne room. Her head spun, seeing wonders that she couldn't imagine around her. Glass and gold cases holding rare and special objects decorated the room. The light from the window and the additional lamps sprayed sparkles of light all around the room.

Christine reached out to touch a case, but a guard shook his head at her with a frown of obvious disgust. Her eyes moved to the tapestries. The scenes of long-ago battles, of kings, and of other kingdoms were woven with exquisite detail. Each tapestry hung larger than any room in her house.

Christine suppressed anger at seeing all of the opulence and wealth that was contained in this one room. It was more than existed in all the farmlands north of the city and perhaps all the way to Sur as well. Many farmers scraped by a living, some even starving at times. They were being treated in an unfair manner by a city that threw wealth around like a toy. It was unfair. Her anger felt good. It distracted her from feeling insignificant around so many others of wealthy upbringing.

The group in front of them moved away from the King. She could see, for the first time in her life, the Throne of Power. A thing of stories and legends and myth. The pure size of the opulent throne amazed her. Seated on it was the King of the Realm, the supreme leader, King Edward DarSan Montere himself.

In the back of her mind, almost as a whisper, she heard Lightning's thoughts: *Such power in that throne.*

Lightning was tied up at a small stable outside of the castle. Christine wanted her close by for support. *You can feel its power?* she asked her Cremelino.

Yes, can't you? Close your eyes and feel it through me.

Christine did and gasped. It pulled to her and emboldened her. This power was not something to fear but something to use. She wondered if this King even knew what he had. It was wonderful. She was amazed others didn't seem to know it was there. But in her amazement she also wondered why her Cremelino could feel it and how she could make Christine feel that power also.

Use the power and speak with passion. Good luck, child.

Darius's father, Richard, stood next to the King. She saw Darius's resemblance in him. Richard looked older and more tired than the last time she had seen him, but that had been earlier in the summer.

"State where you are from and what your request is," Richard stated formally with a bored voice, hardly even looking at the group.

"We are from Anikari, from just outside of the city, great King," said Christine's older companion. "We have here some demands . . ."

The King raised his brows at the word "demands."

"I mean requests," Martin continued. "We feel we have been treated in an unfair manner, both as a group of people personally and in trade. We are requesting that you read over our petition and join with us to find a mutually satisfactory and happy solution." He stopped and took a deep breath. He had practiced the lines, trying to sound educated and flexible.

"We will consider them when we have time," Richard answered. He took the petition from Martin and handed it to the King. "As you can appreciate, we are very busy today. It may take a while."

"I think you should consider them soon," stated Alvyn. They all looked at him in surprise. The young farmer's lips snarled in anger. The group of three hadn't planned on him saying anything. "We think it is a fair arrangement. But . . ."

"That is enough." King Edward stood up and his voice echoed around the room. "I hope you are not telling me how to run my kingdom."

"The kingdom is not just inside the walls of the city." The young man from the farmlands stepped forward half a step. Guards around the King stiffened and moved to intercept him.

"He is just concerned, Your Majesty." Christine spoke for the first time. It was as if Richard and the King had not noticed her before. She spoke softly but with power.

"And who are you?" asked the King, turning toward Christine with a mocking smile. He told the guards to hold their peace with a motion of his hands.

Christine sensed Lightning in the back of her mind, urging her to go on. Through Lightning, she pulled from the power of the throne.

"I am Christine Anderssn, my King," she said with a perfect curtsy. "I understand that a matter as important as this may take time to discuss with your advisors. Please read over our petition and we will return next month for your answer."

Christine could tell the effect that the small amount of power Lightning shared with her had on King Edward. He stirred uncomfortably in the presence of her confidence.

Edward opened his mouth, scratched the side of his head below the jeweled crown he wore, then closed his mouth again.

Before he could speak, Christine turned toward Richard. "How is Darius doing, councilor?" she asked in her most polite manner.

Richard covered up a small cough of surprise and stuttered. "He . . . is . . . fine. Do you know my son?"

Before she could even answer, Richard must have put her name together with the girl that Darius had been friends with. He had only seen her on a few occasions before, and even then it was from a distance.

"I think you know who I am." Christine gave him a sweet smile. "If you see Darius, tell him I hope he returns soon." She found herself struggling to hold back the tears.

The King remained silent through the short exchange.

Christine turned back to the King once again. "We will return on next month's petitioning day for your answer. That should be enough time." She motioned to the other men. "We'll be going now. We don't want to take up any more of the King's time."

She turned and the other two followed her. They left through the large doors, which a steward closed behind them, leaving King Edward and senior councilor Richard Williams alone inside the throne room.

* * * *

The King sat in thoughtful silence with Richard at his side. In time he turned toward his councilor.

"Did you feel that, Richard?"

"Feel what?"

"The power."

"No, My Lord. I didn't feel anything."

"It was that girl. She did it. She stirred the power of the throne somehow. I have never felt that much of it before. You have heard the stories like I have. My father felt it a few times, but I never have. I always wondered if it was because . . ." He stopped and looked around. They were alone, but he knew that a few guards and stewards stood just on the other side of the doorway. He lowered his voice. "Well, you know why."

Richard shrugged. He too was concerned about Christine.

"Can she know where Darius went and why? I told them not to tell anyone," the King said with flashing eyes.

"She only knows he left, but no one knows why. No one but us."

"Ah, that is true, my friend. Not even Darius comprehends why he is off training. But keep an eye on her; she could be dangerous. We can't have her and her people causing trouble now. With the Belorians and Gildanians generating trouble, I can't deal with the farmers now. Watch all of them, but keep a special eye on her. The power she stirred in the throne is not something to trifle with."

Richard's eyes widened but no words came from his opened mouth.

"You have read the histories as much as I have, Richard. The throne has its own power. Each king feels it, more or less, and that power helps him to judge rightly and give him the confidence to be king. I don't feel it as much as my father said he did, and I think I know why that is. But this girl, she drew some of that power to herself. I felt it."

"Is she a . . . a . . . ?" Richard rubbed his forehead with his hand.

"A wizard? I doubt it. But when the lesser wizards were banished outside the city they ended up mixing with the farmers. Who knows what remnants have trickled down the bloodlines through the years?"

Richard paced back and forth a few times. "We play a dangerous game here, Your Highness. If the outsiders got hold of the power of the throne, God help us all."

"Richard, the farmers are the least of our worries. I need some information on the man in Belor right now. What do you have there?" The King switched the subject back to more important matters.

Richard motioned to the far end of the room, and the steward walked out the doors and back again with a man in tow.

The man wanted to trade secrets about the Belorians for gold. The King needed all the information he could get on the fighting in Belor, so he bargained for half the money the man wanted if the information was new to him. The amount was nothing compared to the full king's treasury.

"They are training with swords and other weapons. Talk is, they will attack soon," the man spoke in seriousness.

"How do you know this information?" questioned Richard.

"I hunt in the meadows and saw a group of Belorians practicing. They looked well-trained. They were disciplined and excited. A very tall man led them. He had dark auburn hair and seemed to pulse with some type of power. They did everything he asked them to." The man paused and then added, "They wouldn't really attack us, would they?"

"That will be enough for now," said the King, as he motioned for Richard to give him the gold. "You can go now. Your service is appreciated, but keep this information to yourself."

After the man left, King Edward spoke to Richard. "Have someone follow him. If what he says is true, shut off all food and trade into Belor and organize our soldiers to march to the city immediately. I want to find out who this man is who thinks he can defy me!"

"Yes, Edward," agreed Richard.

"And, Richard, have someone glance at that petition for me," ended the King. "I am sure they will be back next month."

Richard raised his eyebrows at the King, but said nothing.

Chapter Fifteen

"Push yourself, Darius. Come on now. Don't take your eyes away. Concentrate. That's good. Don't look down."

Darius gazed across at his present opponent, the man who had become his sword master since coming to the training camp. Cray Dreydon was about three inches shorter than Darius, but fifty pounds of well-toned muscle heavier. His short gray hair and dark-skinned face made him seem a bit younger than rumor said he was. Someone had told Darius that Cray was sixty years old. By looking at his stocky build, one would never have believed him to be one of the best swordsmen in the Realm. Neither his size nor age hindered his movements. He was as quick as a jackrabbit fleeing into his hole from a fox.

Sweat poured down Darius's face, slightly blurring his vision. This high in the mountains the autumn air was cool in his lungs. To become a team commander, this was the last test to endure. He had become a master of the sword since coming to the Elite camp in the Superstition Mountains. He felt the power rise up in him again. It seemed to happen more often now, and it felt more familiar each time. Each night he practiced trying to recognize it and control it. It was hard not having anyone to show him what to do.

Darius pushed the power back down at the moment. He wanted to win this test on his own abilities. He didn't trust his newfound powers yet, but he trusted himself. Anyway, the sword on its own still maintained a type of link to Darius even when his power wasn't active. He needed to keep it from shining too brightly though. The few times he hadn't controlled the brightness had brought too much talk and rumors around the camp.

The two stood up on the wall, as it was called, consisting of a wooden bridge built between two trees. It spanned forty feet in length and hung suspended twenty feet in the air. It was only two feet wide, which didn't leave much room to maneuver around an opponent. You had to attack him straight on.

Just a few more minutes. I have to hold on for a few more strokes.

Darius knew he needed to concentrate. Most of the group that had come up into the mountains with him stood twenty feet below, watching and cheering, though he wondered briefly whom they cheered for. His dedication and focus to practicing his fighting skills had brought grudging respect, but he had not taken much time to develop friendships.

The adrenaline pushed through his veins as he sliced forward with his gold sword, reflecting orange in the setting sun. He felt proud for being the first to make it this far. He had to last only a few more minutes without falling in order to complete this final test.

His arms and legs ached, almost cramping from the tenseness. He should be more relaxed, but it was hard while facing Cray. He lunged forward as he glimpsed an open spot. To his surprise, it caught Cray off balance. Of course, the end of his sword was dulled with a wrapping of burlap, so no one would be hurt. Darius became one with his training as he lunged forward again into Cray's right side.

Cray's foot slipped and he began to fall off the high-strung bridge. Darius gasped and slowed for a moment as Cray hung on with one hand. Men on the ground stood below, ready to catch him if needed. Darius looked at him hanging there in the air. The crowd grew silent.

He didn't know what he was supposed to do. Cray had taught him to always continue the fight until it was over, but this was his teacher. He reached down to help him up, and Cray used his sword as a hatchet to smack it across Darius's left foot, making Darius stumble and almost slip himself. He peeked down into Cray's eyes. The sparkle in them made them look as if they were enjoying a private joke. Darius decided there would be no second chances, and he kicked off Cray's hands with his boots and watched him fall through the air.

He stood breathless for a moment, watching the man tumble in silence toward a group of men ready to catch him. Time stood still as he argued within himself over and over about what he should have done.

Some of the men threw pointed dirty looks at Darius, but silence continued for a moment as the crowd waited for Cray's reaction. The old swordsman had never been thrown from the wall before, at least not that any of them had heard. They watched and Darius watched. Cray landed into the arms of a few men and then took his time standing back up on his own.

Darius's heart was beating hard, from a combination of his ordeal along with the guilt of what he had done. Cray wasn't a bad person. He was not the enemy. He was a hard trainer, but he always treated Darius fairly.

Cray looked around at the crowd and then up at Darius. "Behold your new team commander."

The crowd applauded and cheered.

Darius held up his hands in the air and soaked up the cheers. It sounded good. The roar of the crowd was addicting. Once he had made the decision to do his best, he had thrown all his energy into his training, and now it had paid off.

King Edward, unknowingly, but through his trainers, had now chosen him, Darius San Williams, to be the first team commander in the King's Elite Army. Darius had pushed himself, proving to everyone that no one would get the best of him. Now he would be always honored for being the first. It was what he always wanted.

He looked down into the faces of the men he had come up into the mountains with. Some he had known before; most he had not. After letting his power slip into his sword a few times in camp, there had been whispered talk and remembrances of when his sword had glowed in the castle the day they all were chosen. Some, because of his age, thought he was only there because he was the privileged son of a councilor. Some feared his abilities. But more and more soldiers were allying themselves with him out of respect for his accomplishments and drive.

His mind returned to the present and he looked down again at the still-cheering crowd. He had shown them what he could do. He had shown them who was in control. But this would be just the beginning. *Soon I will be ready to protect the Realm with an army behind me!*

Darius lowered himself slowly back down the tree ladder, slowing his descent so as not to show the soreness in his legs and arms. Cray continued speaking for a few moments. The man would never miss an opportunity to teach something.

He had probably talked to Cray more than anyone else in the time he had been in the mountains. They had had some good talks about traveling the Realm. Cray had been everywhere, but he never seemed to answer why. He walked with a slight limp that was almost unnoticeable to someone not paying attention. Darius didn't see anyone pushing him around. This was not due to his physical size, but to his sense of being. The other older trainers walked in respect around the man. Someone had heard that he had been a general at a young age in King Charles's army.

"Darius has been the first, but I hope not the last. The King has great plans for all of you. Many of you should be able to take a command position on a permanent basis before we leave from here. What you saw today was some of the finest swordsmanship I have ever witnessed. Each of you should become as good." He paused as he peered into each of their eyes. "But don't think I will fall as easily the next time. There has only been one other with as much skill. He too was a man of extraordinary talent . . ." He paused a moment, as if remembering. "Anyway . . . I expect a number of you to challenge me soon."

Darius continued down the ladder and walked over to stand next to Cray and shake his hand.

"An awards ceremony will be held three nights from now," Cray announced, and he walked away. The others came around to Darius to congratulate him. At first his shoulders tensed with the attention, but eventually he relaxed and accepted the glory and accolades.

The ceremony boosted his pride even more. He was rewarded the first junior team command of a group of twenty-five other young men. He looked down at them, sitting on the ground, from where he stood behind the fire. Darius released a little of his power outwardly. Sometimes his power needed release. It was just enough to give an additional glow around him, but not enough that they wouldn't rationalize it away as a trick of the firelight. It held their attention for a few heartbeats and solidified their acceptance of him as their commander.

Darius glanced behind the group. Cray stood against a tree, arms folded. It was hard to make out his facial expression in the dark, but Darius saw him shake his head and walk off. Darius let go of the power.

After the ceremony ended and most of the men had gone back to their duties, Darius sat next to the cooling embers of the fire, thinking by himself about what he would do next. His breath floated out with a white mist in the cool mountain air. He put a few more logs on the fire, sat back down, and let the smell of the campfire help him relax. He turned his head at a sound and noticed a mountain pine with giggles coming from behind its large trunk. Two young women were talking and looking toward him. When they got his attention, they came out from behind the tree and approached him.

"Hi, Darius," said one of the girls with a cute, flirty smile. "Congratulations."

"Thanks." Darius looked down and shifted himself on the log he sat on. He always felt shy around women. There were about ten girls in the camp to help cook and sew and clean clothing.

"My name is Leandra Roux," said the second. She stood closer to him than he was comfortable with.

Darius repeated the hello unenthusiastically, then added, "How do you know me?" *That sounded unintelligent!*

"Oh, everyone knows you," laughed the first girl. She was too full of giggles for Darius. She wasn't much older than fifteen or sixteen, and with her dull brown hair set in curls, she seemed even younger. She wore a plain apron with her hair pulled back. He guessed she worked in the kitchen.

"Everyone in camp talks about you," continued Leandra as she sat down next to him on the same log, her leg touching his. Turning back to the other girl, she motioned for her to leave. "You need to get back and finish your chores, Cynthia."

"Yes, Leandra." Cynthia's smile turned down into a pout.

Leandra glared at her and Cynthia scuttled away.

The fire popped and crackled, sending a few sparks into the air. The evening was starless, with a blanket of clouds and mist settling over the mountains. Leandra shivered in the cool air. Darius shifted with discomfort, but he offered her his new officer's jacket. She draped it over her shoulders, her short brown hair laying slightly over the collar, her neck looking smooth and soft. She looked right at him, into his eyes.

Her large, almost-round eyes were brown, soft, and inviting. They were the highlight of her fair face. He turned away, then slowly looked back. She was still staring right at him, and now she added a devious smile to her lips. He noticed the dimples for the first time.

"You are an incredibly handsome man, Darius." She moved even closer to him. Her body was warm and radiated a slight hint of lilac. "I have been watching you since you arrived."

Darius was sweating with nervousness, but also shaking with excitement. Her eyes penetrated into him, while her perfumed scent swept the night air around him. She dressed in a bright-colored bodice that was indicative of the city of Mar. It fit over a long silk blouse. A skirt of geometric patterns accented her obvious femininity, riding a little higher in length than was proper in the capital city.

"You . . . don't really know me," said Darius, trying to regain his composure. He was not used to being handled quite this way. He hoped none of the other men had observed how he was acting. Not very commander-like or manly. *Why me? Why do I get so nervous?* Kelln had always been more comfortable around girls.

"I saw the way you knocked old Cray down a few days ago. I watch the way others walk around you. You are a noble and brave man; a warrior."

Darius laughed a little, as if trying to thin the emotion. "I am not even twenty yet, Leandra. Hardly a warrior. And Cray is an old man."

"Age does not matter in bravery or command. All it takes is a certain type of man. I can tell that the King picked the right man in you." She smiled at him and he once again became all flustered. "You will be the first commander. You will always be the first, no matter when others gain a command. You will run the King's Elite Army, Darius. You will go down in history for this. A new breed of warrior."

Darius thought for a moment about what she was saying. He surmised that she was trying to flatter him for her own reasons. Yet she was right. He had gained the first command. Anger built for a moment as he tried to figure out if he was indeed in charge, or if the political machine of the Realm had manipulated him again. He felt his power well up inside him. It always happened in response to his anger. He thought about how much he still disliked the King and his father for sending him here without any notice or choice in the matter.

Darius laughed.

"What is so amusing, Darius?"

"Oh, nothing," he smiled. He thought about how he would eventually confront the King as full commander of his Elite Army and with his magical powers developed. Then there would be a reckoning.

"Darius," smiled Leandra, "you must find something humorous."

Darius stood up. "You are right, Leandra. I will be commander of the greatest army the King will ever have. If he only understood what that meant, he may regret bringing me here."

Leandra gave him a strange look. He didn't care. She didn't understand all of this. She was a pretty girl who was lonely. She stood up next to him and reached for his hands. She was taller than he had first thought. He felt a tingling sensation inside of him that he hadn't experienced since Christine . . .

Christine! He had missed her so much in the beginning. Training, however, had been grueling and exhausting, and soon he had found himself thinking about her less and less. Not that he didn't want to think about her, but the pain was still too much. He had boxed up his feelings for her and hidden them away deep in his heart and soul. Now, once again, he felt an ache grow in his heart. He pushed it back down, deep down, and sealed it with his power.

He didn't know when he would be back to Anikari, or how things would turn out when he did. With the power getting stronger in him, he may have to go somewhere else to learn to control it better. She would be better off without him, he justified. It hurt him to think it. He still cared for her, and even loved her, but being around someone with his growing abilities might be too dangerous for her.

Darius turned and glanced at Leandra again. She leaned into him, stood up on her tip toes, and offered him a soft kiss. Darius hung there for a moment, suspended in time. Thoughts of Christine tried to break through the power he had sealed them under. He cleared his mind once again and with an abrupt move pulled away. It was hard. She smelled like lilac and her kiss made him tingle.

A few cabins away a voice called for Leandra. She gave him another small kiss, said good-bye, and ran off toward an older woman's voice calling her in. Darius stood for a moment, watching her exquisite silhouette grow smaller in the facing light of day until she faded into the misty darkness. He felt confused. He didn't even know this girl. She surely didn't know him, except for who he was here. Darius knew there was more to him than what she saw. Or was that who he was now? Just a commander in the King's army? Is this what life had in store for him now? It had been what he had wanted growing up, but was it enough?

Darius turned and walked back toward his cabin, noticing but ignoring Cray standing behind the corner of the firewood pile with a disapproving look on his face.

The next day Cray lectured him on fooling around with the girls. He reminded Darius there was no time for extra activities.

"King Edward will be wanting this group ready soon, Darius, and you still have much to learn. You may be good at the sword and the bow, but now you must learn how to use your mind to survive."

"What do you mean?"

"This army is expected to be small and nimble. To go places where other larger armies cannot. Later in the winter you will be sent into the mountains alone, without weapons or food. You will be allowed to carry one small knife and enough water for one day. You will be dropped off days away from here and required to find your way back . . . alive."

Darius didn't like the way he emphasized the last word. It made him shiver in the morning air.

Cray moved to take Darius's sword, but a strong hand stopped him.

"What are you doing?" Darius's mouth tightened.

"Set your sword down. We have other things to learn today."

Darius put his hand on the pommel of the sword. "It's fine where it is."

Cray turned his head to one side and shrugged his shoulders. "Seems hard for you to put that thing down."

"It's comforting to me," Darius said with a smile.

Cray laughed out loud. "Better a sword than a girl, I guess."

Darius joined in the laughter, and soon Cray proceeded to teach him about various plants that might help him survive. Many of the things that Cray taught Darius he had already learned in school, yet Cray seemed determined to teach him again. He was nothing if not thorough. With patience, each day Cray personally led him around the mountainside asking questions and awaiting answers.

One day after a small argument on the edibility of a particular thorny plant, Darius strutted off with a pout. After a dozen feet, Darius turned around. Cray followed him with his eyes.

"Cray, it looks like you've seen a ghost."

"Something from a long time ago. The way you turn and move looks so familiar, like someone I once knew. He was a little older than you when I last saw him."

"A friend?"

"Yes, one of my closest friends."

"What happened?" Darius moved closer. It was rare to get Cray to open up about his past.

"We used to practice sword fighting together." Cray rubbed his stubbled chin and looked thoughtful. "He also possessed other special gifts that were just beginning to develop."

Cray had not answered his question about what had happened and Darius wondered what the man meant. "What special gifts?"

Cray lifted his greying eyebrows over his dark eyes and gave him a look that made Darius look down. *How could Cray know about my powers?*

When Darius looked up again he steeled his face. "Let's get back to the plants, Cray."

Before Darius knew what was happening, Cray picked up a fist-sized rock and threw it in a straight line at Darius. With instinct taking over, Darius threw up his hands and let his power deflect the rock away. Sending out a thrust of air he pushed the rock back to the ground between the two of them.

Cray laughed out loud.

"You're crazy, you know that? Crazy! You could have killed me." Darius breathed heavily.

"Like I said, *special gifts*." Cray's voice grew soft and quiet.

"But how did you know?"

Cray walked over and picked up the rock. "As I told you, I knew someone once with the same abilities."

"What happened to him?" Darius asked for the second time. Maybe there was hope for him. Maybe he could be accepted in Anikari with magic.

"His father told me personally he died at sea in a battle."

Darius remained silent.

"At least that was what we were told." Cray said in a soft whisper so quiet that Darius strained to hear him.

"Just so you know, I didn't use it to beat you on the bridge," Darius said defensively.

Cray raised his eyebrows, "Oh, I know. I know. You beat me fair and square that day. Though I don't know how much longer you can maintain the difference, Darius. You have to let it become you, a part of you. You can't pretend it isn't there most of the time. It will tear you apart."

"You don't understand how it is," Darius snapped back. He broke a branch off a leafless birch tree and threw it end over end through the woods. "I'm a freak. I'm not always aware when it will flare up, though I am getting better at controlling it. The worst part is, I don't know what it can do. Like that rock you threw at me. I didn't know how to stop it until I had to."

"What choice do you have?"

"Why do you act as if it is fine? Most of the Realm fears magic, and for good reason. The wizards almost destroyed the Realm."

Cray walked up closer to Darius. "It was not always that way. I remember my grandfather telling me about stories from his grandfather. Magic used to be a part of life in the Realm, Darius. Just like it is in other kingdoms around us. Someday it will be that way again."

"That could be dangerous talk, Cray. I have heard my father's aversion to magic, and his thoughts follow the King's."

"And I take it you follow all the same ideas as your father?" Cray's eyes twinkled in amusement.

"You know I don't, Cray. This is crazy. I don't even know who I am anymore."

"My friend wondered the same thing."

"And look where it got him," Darius retorted back.

A look of pain slid across Cray's face.

"Sorry," Darius apologized. He felt bad for causing his trainer pain. Cray wasn't a bad person.

Cray grew more serious. "It's in you. It's a part of your reflexes, Darius. I would guess there is no limit to what you might be able to do, and that is a danger for all of us. You are a dangerous person, Darius. A very dangerous person indeed. But maybe one the Realm needs at this time and place."

Chapter Sixteen

"**D**ad!" Kelln yelled. "Get away from him."

His father didn't answer. Kelln went closer. His dad fought with a man half his age. *What kind of madness is this?* His dad was a master at making swords, but not at using them. The soldier lifted his sword to strike his father, who had fallen to the ground. Out of instinct, Kelln drew his bow and arrow and shot. He watched the soldier fall to the ground – almost as if in slow motion. His father rolled away, got up, and continued fighting another Realm soldier without even looking at Kelln.

Kelln stood dazed. The raging battle faded from his view. He had never killed another person before. The bile rose in his throat and he tried to breathe in deeply to keep from vomiting. He leaned over, hands on his knees, trying to stay conscious. He was numb and dizzy.

He had killed a Realm soldier! One from his own city of Anikari, most likely. He wondered if he knew the soldier's family. He stepped backwards a few steps, watching the continuing fight, but not really seeing what was going on around him. The screams faded away as his heart pounded louder. *What am I doing here?*

It had been four long months since arriving in Belor. Over the last month Kelln had seen the Preacher showing off his powers more often. First it was moving something heavy, and then catching a thief. Now he was rumored to be on the front lines with air and fire coming from his fingertips against the soldiers.

Kelln thought of his family, his father, and Alessandra as he began to move away from the fighting. He felt numb and couldn't think well. He wondered where Alessandra was. She looked different now from when he had first met her. Her eyes were still riveting and her smile astonishing. However, after they had arrived in Belor, he had noticed her blind following of the Preacher. The things she said in defense of him didn't make sense. It made her less attractive, but more than ever he wanted to convince her of the cruel man the Preacher really was.

Back in his present mind, he deliberated with himself again about what he was doing in Belor. Fighting swirled all around him and he began to walk back toward the city gates. He needed to leave the madness and get help. Darius would help him. He had tried to send notes, but he never received a response back. They hadn't let him leave in person, but he would have to find a way to sneak out. He couldn't handle it any more. He and Darius could talk to Darius's father and explain what was going on.

"Kill him!" A command came from a Belorian commander to jar Kelln from his scattered thoughts. He stopped and turned around. He watched as a young Realm soldier ran through the line of Belorian men and continued on toward where Kelln stood. Kelln heard the others yelling for him to kill him and not let him through.

"Please," the soldier begged. "Help me."

Time seemed to blur. Kelln tried to force his mind to concentrate. Somehow, he could not kill another man. Especially not even knowing for sure, or believing, what he was fighting for. He tried to step aside as the man pushed him down while running for the city. Kelln just watched as others ran past him to chase the young soldier. He would never get away, he thought.

Someone came up to Kelln and grabbed him. "Why didn't you kill him? He may reach the city now."

Kelln just stood speechless.

"Oh, you are the sword maker's son from Anikari. Maybe you are with them," the man continued as others gathered around.

Soon the skirmish ended, with the Realm soldiers moving back down the road. They hadn't overtaken the city, but they didn't leave either. Kelln surmised they were waiting for reinforcements to come.

His father walked up to him. "What happened, son?"

"I killed a soldier to save you." Kelln's voice felt numb.

"Yes, that was good work ," his father praised. "But why not the other one?"

Kelln didn't answer and some of the others started calling him a traitor. His father waited for an answer.

"I don't know," Kelln said, looking up at the crowd. "I don't know about any of this. I don't know who is right."

Men grabbed him and took him off to the Preacher. His father looked like he might step in to stop them, but then he turned and walked away. Kelln was still confused over the entire matter. His father had been so sure of himself an hour before, when they had received the message to go and bring swords to the front line. His father had pulled him along, trying to explain to him the importance of what they were doing. Kelln still didn't see the purpose. It just didn't look like a religious issue, or that the Belorians were being treated badly. This felt political, and full of power plays. The kind of activities that Darius used to talk about that his father would be involved in.

They dragged him to the Preacher. With hands tied behind his back like a common criminal, Kelln faced the large man. He had never met anyone in his entire life who scared him as much as this man. He had watched and observed the Preacher over the last few months and found no redeeming qualities. He had even tried to get letters to Anikari, but no help came, so he was sure they were intercepted and never delivered.

"You are the sword maker's son, correct?"

"Yes," was all Kelln could say. He knew that the Preacher knew who he was.

"From Anikari?"

"Yes."

"Are you a spy?" The Preacher leaned down to look Kelln straight in the eyes.

Kelln felt some kind of hypnotic power forcing him to answer. Luckily, there was nothing to hide from the man. "No. I am not a spy."

"We have been looking for a spy among us who seems to want to tell those in Anikari our plans. It would be a most unpleasant thing to find one of my loyal subjects not so loyal. War is dangerous, and someone could get hurt very easily."

Kelln felt blood drain from his face and wondered if today was going to be his last.

The Preacher took a few steps away from Kelln and turned his back. Others in the room looked on at the proceedings with a mix of wonder and fear in their eyes. Kelln wondered how many of them really believed in this dangerous usurper of power, and how many were kept back by fear.

Suddenly the Preacher turned around, and with a loud voice bellowed, "Why did you not kill that soldier when you were commanded?" The Preacher seemed to grow taller. His face reddened and the effects of power seemed to ripple around his body. "Answer carefully, because your answer could determine your earthly fate."

Kelln wondered what he could say that would save him at this point. The power of the Preacher bore into him, forcing the words from his throat. He could not lie. "I don't want to kill anyone. I don't believe in your cause. I never have."

The admission left gasps around the palace room. They couldn't believe that someone would admit as much to their leader.

Kelln glanced around at the others, a sorry lot of followers, he thought. If you couldn't think for yourself, what good were you? The crowd seemed to move back to the edges of the room, the smooth, plastered walls hitting their backs. Gold lamps and crystal vases sat above them on shelves. Kelln shifted his feet on the large, ornate rug in the middle of the room.

The Preacher sat down on his throne. Power sizzled in the air. He pointed a long finger at Kelln and flicked his wrist to the side.

Kelln began to feel lightheaded. His heart beat faster. He was hardly able to hold his head up, it was so heavy. He fought it, but to no success. He couldn't think clearly. He remembered the Preacher telling him something else, but he didn't know how he had answered. Everything seemed to be closing in around him. His vision went dark and he fainted.

The next thing Kelln remembered was looking up from the cold, stone ground in a strange room. The light from the one small window shone through the bars and gave Kelln enough light to distinguish he was lying on the floor of the dungeon. He sat on the ground a few moments longer, letting his head clear. He heard footsteps coming down a hall, and Alessandra appeared with a few pieces of roast beef and bread.

"I'm sure glad you're here," smiled Kelln with as much excitement as he could muster up. "What happened?"

"Here's some food. You've been out quite a few hours."

"Where am I?" Kelln tried to rise to his feet, but he sat back down when the ache returned to his head. He remembered feeling strange when the Preacher had flicked his hands toward him. He had done something to Kelln. He had used the power on him. It made Kelln's skin crawl.

"You are in prison for being a traitor." Alessandra's eyes flashed in anger.

"But I . . ."

"Until you have a trial, you will stay here," she interrupted.

Alessandra turned to walk away and stopped. Kelln looked up at her as if hoping for some type of compassion. "The man you let get away killed two soldiers before they stopped him. You should have stopped him when you had a chance." She turned around without waiting for Kelln's answer and walked back down the hall.

Kelln's stomach knotted up and he felt nauseous. He had let the soldier kill two others. *It was my fault. I could have stopped him.* Would it have been better to kill the man and let his own conscience suffer that he had killed someone else? The soldier had just been doing what he was told and was trying to uphold the law in defense against Belor. The questions of ethics whirled around in his foggy mind. He could only control his actions, not others.

Kelln scooted on his hands and knees to a far corner of the cold, damp cell, sat up wrapping his arms around his legs, curling himself into a small ball. The room seemed larger than he had first thought. He was scared and alone in a strange city. He thought of his friend Darius, and how he would react in a situation like this. Kelln tried to find hope in his thoughts but for once he couldn't.

Kelln tried to remember the confident self he had once been, but he wasn't able to find the carefree, laughter-filled young man anymore. Belor had taken his life away from him. The city had sucked him dry of all sense of adventure and rational thinking.

Am I going to die? Why didn't my father help me?

He had definitely not found God in Belor.

Chapter Seventeen

Darius continued training with Cray over the next few weeks, but no other mention of his power entered into their conversations. However, Darius took time each day on his own to try and do new things and control the power within himself. More often than not he was frustrated with the results.

After a particularly grueling and frustrating day Darius was walking through the camp to go to his cabin. A few snowflakes lay on the ground, but the skies were clearing to a clear, cold blue.

Without him noticing, Leandra snuck up next to him.

"Have you been hiding from me?" she asked.

"I have been . . . busy." Darius looked down at the ground. He couldn't figure out how he was so tough and in charge around the other men and held so much power within himself, but when Leandra came along he seemed to lose all intelligent thought. She seemed to enjoy making him squirm and get embarrassed. So had Christine.

"Let's take a walk." Leandra grabbed his hand and they walked toward the lake. She wore a warm, multicolored cloak wrapped around herself. There were thicker patches of snow in the shadier parts, but the ground was frozen and hard, allowing them to easily walk around.

Darius glanced around for Cray, whom he thought would be watching him from behind a cabin or tree. He didn't see anyone, so he consented to the walk.

They walked in silence for a few minutes, with only the breeze rustling the pine needles, interrupted only by the calls of a few nearby birds out scavenging in the winter air.

"Why are you so quiet around me? Do I scare you?" asked Leandra in a straightforward manner.

"No . . . I don't know. Maybe I'm a little nervous."

"But why?"

Darius turned and looked back at her. "Girls in Anikari are not so direct."

Leandra stifled a giggle. "Well, girls from Mar are."

Darius had heard rumors of that. He blushed despite the cold.

They approached the small lake and stood together at its uneven edge, with only the sounds of the rippling water and an occasional rustle of wind to break the silence.

It doesn't compare to our lake next to the field. The thought came unbidden to Darius's mind. He pushed it down. Thoughts of Christine were still painful, and he knew that he may never get back to her, so he continued to deny thoughts about her.

Leandra pointed to something in the water, motioning for Darius to have a closer look. As he squatted down to gaze more closely, a handful of cold mountain water splashed him in the face. He yelled and fell backwards, breaking the fall with his hands. Leandra stood laughing. He pushed the now-wet brown hair from his eyes.

"Why did you do that?" Anger flared in him as he wiped the water with his shirt.

"You're too serious. You need to have more fun," played Leandra. "Don't you ever have fun?"

Before Leandra finished the sentence, a handful of water splattered across her face. Darius stepped back a few steps and enjoyed a good laugh. She came after him playfully and tried to push him down, but Darius squeezed away.

"Come back here," she yelled after him.

"Sorry, I don't need to go swimming today. It's a little too cold," Darius laughed. He felt like a young kid again. It was good to let go, if only for a few minutes. The laughter washed away the stress. He finally let Leandra catch up to him, once the water had drained out of her hands. She was breathing hard, the flush on her face highlighting her high cheekbones. Her short, dark hair held a few drops of water. The look was alluring.

"That was . . . fun. I knew . . . that . . . I could get . . . you to smile," she said between breaths. "Better not let your men see you smile. They all think you're just a mean and hard commander."

"Well, maybe I am," mocked Darius, putting his hands on his hips.

Leandra reached over to push a lock of wet hair off of Darius's forehead and took a step forward. She stood dreadfully close to him. Her warm breath fleeted across his face, heating up the air around him.

"Darius . . ."

"Shh." Darius quieted her as he turned around in silent movements. Leandra tried to speak again, but Darius put his finger to his mouth in an urgent request to keep quiet. He had heard someone or something behind them in the nearby shrubs. He walked closer, with Leandra a few steps behind, holding onto the back of his shirt. The birds and the water seemed to grow still, waiting to see what would happen.

"Are you playing games?" Leandra whispered.

"No, I heard something."

As he neared the shrubs, out ran a wild rabbit almost running into Darius and Leandra. Darius breathed a sigh of relief, and felt a little foolish. Leandra let out a small laugh, and they turned to walk away.

Without any additional warning he heard Leandra scream. Two arms tried to pull her into the bush where the rabbit had run from. Instinct settled in. He jumped to intercept the arms that he now saw were connected to a large, muscular body with strange painting all over the face. Darius had never seen anything like it. The colorful designs confused his senses. He froze for a moment physically, yet his mind was already steps ahead in what he must do.

He dove under the bush, reaching for the attacker's legs. He grabbed onto the man's shin and pulled the attacker down into the bushes. He heard a yelp and, from the corner of his eyes, saw Leandra fall and scramble away.

"Run, Leandra!" Darius commanded. A second body jumped onto him from behind before he could get up and pull out his sword. He bucked his legs to throw this second assailant over him and into the bush. He didn't quite make it, but was successful enough to get up off of the ground, only to see the first man starting to run after Leandra. She started to run toward the lake and would soon be trapped between the water and the painted man. He wondered if she knew how to swim. Maybe the stranger did also. Of course, even a few minutes in the near-freezing water could cause problems.

Darius sprinted toward her as he searched the ground for something to throw. He spotted a thick stick and scooped it up without breaking his stride. The second man was gaining on him from behind, but Darius didn't dare break his concentration.

Darius realized he wouldn't be able to reach Leandra in time, so he skidded to a sudden stop and drew upon his growing powers. The back of the man's head seemed to grow in his vision, as his bow targets always had. He threw the stick with ferocious speed, end over end toward the attacker. As soon as he did so, he dropped to the ground just in time for the second man, who thought he had Darius, to fall over him. When the man stood up Darius pushed his right hand toward the second attacker, knocking him back with a hard push of air. Darius reached over to grab the wild-looking man, but the man's head had hit a rock and he wasn't moving.

Leandra yelled, a high-pitched scream splitting the air.

Darius turned his attention back to her. His earlier stick-throw had hit the mark and knocked the first man down, but he was starting to get up again. Darius covered the distance with inhuman speed. Pulling out his sword, he brought it above his head and was about to slice the man when he heard a voice emerging from the trees.

"Darius, stop!" A deep, gruff voice echoed through the valley.

Barely controlling his sword arm from running through the man, he turned just in time to only scrape the man's shoulder. It was still painful, and the man howled out in anguish. Ready for another fight, Darius turned toward the voice.

Cray stood beside a tree, arms folded. Anger and pleasure crossed over his face at almost the same time. Leandra came and grabbed hold of Darius's arm, almost sobbing with fright. She was shaking, and he felt the need to comfort the poor girl. Marks of tears spread down her unblemished face.

"You did well, Darius," said Cray as he started to approach. "Better than I would have expected given the distraction." Cray glared at Leandra. "Much better."

Darius breathing hard and feeling bewildered, asked, "What are you talking about? They tried to attack us."

"I sent them, Darius. They are part of your test."

"What!" yelled Darius becoming furious, "Who do you think you are? Don't I have any privacy?"

"You must learn to defend yourself in any type of situation. You actually did do quite well," he said to Darius as he motioned for the other two men to join him.

The first man, whom Darius had knocked down with the flying stick, had been trying to help the other man up. The second man had a large gash on his head and shoulder and barely stood without fainting. They did not look well.

"I am sure my two friends here wished you weren't so good." Cray motioned to the two attackers.

Darius started to bring his hand up toward Cray in anger. The power began boiling in him. It needed a release. He did not like getting tricked. The power made him want to lash out.

"Darius." Cray's jaw tightened and his eyes narrowed. "Make sure you know who your friends and enemies are. You do not want to make enemies out of friends."

"And who are you, Cray . . . friend or enemy?"

"It depends on whose side you're on, doesn't it?" Cray mocked with a crooked half-smile.

"My friends don't attack me!" Darius shook with rage. *Who are my friends? Do I have anyone I can trust anymore?*

Darius wanted to be alone, but he felt the need to make sure Leandra was all right. This was not her doing. He grabbed her hand and with large steps walked back toward the camp.

"Sometimes friends must attack to make you stronger," yelled Cray after the young commander. "Far worse are enemies who hide and deceive until it is too late. Sometimes the enemy is even within."

Darius turned back around so quickly Leandra lost her footing and would have fallen if Darius hadn't caught her with his arm.

Cray turned and helped his two men back to the camp. They would both need medical attention.

Leandra walked beside Darius, shaking and afraid. Darius wondered how much she had seen and what she was thinking.

"Thank you for protecting me, Darius. You're very brave." She snuggled up closer to him.

Darius stopped and wondered if he should try to explain anything. His physical body was exhausted and drained. All he wanted was sleep. Leandra must be tired too, and he was not in the mood for any explanations or for any romance.

"I'll walk you to your cabin. You need to rest," said Darius with exhaustion apparent in his voice. "I'll talk to you later."

Standing at the large cabin that housed all the female staff, Leandra rose up slightly on her toes and kissed Darius again on his cheek. It was soft and warm and lingered as if wanting more. He wished it was Christine. He could use her support right now. She would understand him. He sighed deeply remembering that he had never had the chance to tell her about his powers. *Maybe she wouldn't even like me now.*

Darius wanted to say something more, but his mind was too tired. Instead he gave a short nod. "My lady, I hope you were not hurt. I'm sorry that you didn't get the walk that you wanted."

Leandra smiled back and reluctantly removed her hand from his and walked into her cabin. "You are definitely exciting to be around, Commander. I look forward to our next walk, hopefully in less strenuous circumstances."

Darius just nodded. He wouldn't mind another walk. It had been nice at first. He smiled slightly, remembering the water she had thrown in his face.

Within five minutes, Darius found himself back in his own cabin. Everyone else was out training still. Every time his power surged and was used he felt tired. He lay back on his bed and thought about what had happened. Before long, he fell asleep.

Chapter Eighteen

Mezar sat in the ante-chamber of the lavish palace, high on the hill overlooking Gildan, the capital and royal city of the Gildanian Empire. The young man had been made an officer in Emperor Alrishitar's army just six months earlier. His father, the general, currently met on the other side of the door with the Emperor himself. They were deciding on Mezar's first mission.

The young man stood and smoothed down his red uniform, shifting his silver sword to lay in a more comfortable manner on his hip. An arched window stood opposite him, and he made his way over to the opening. He opened the glass casement and let a slight breeze blow across his brown skin and ruffle his shoulder-length dark black hair. With a young-looking face, and only of average build, he looked older with his hair down, although it was not in keeping with the current fashions of tying it back.

The sun spread its morning rays through the late autumn air, sending sparkling reflections onto the domed white rooftops. Mezar had lived in Gildan his entire life. He knew the city well and loved his homeland. Gildan was clean, secure, and beautiful, unlike some of the other cities in neighboring kingdoms. His dark eyebrows furrowed over his slightly tilted eyes at the thought that at least that was what he had been told in class. He was somewhat sheltered in his young life, and as yet had not been allowed to travel outside the empire, and hardly into the other provinces of his own kingdom. He knew it was for his protection due to his family line, but he still wished to see more for himself.

A serving girl walked through the room, with a tray of breads and meats from the kitchen being taken to some noble somewhere in the palatial complex. Mezar smiled at the girl and she began to curtsy. As she did so, the tray slipped from her hands. Mezar, with a graceful, unmatched speed, caught the tray within inches from leaving her hands, steadied the silver platter, and gave it back to her with another smile. The girl, all flustered now, turned red and headed out of the open chamber.

Mezar tried to remember her name, but there were too many to remember. He felt bad, but most of his time of late had been spent outside the palace at the training camp south of the city. He put his hand on the hilt of his sword and smiled. He thought about the time away. He had enjoyed it and had learned a lot. Many young men his age, if they did not have another trade to apprentice to, went into the army for a few years. With his father, the general, he didn't have much choice in the matter, but it really was what he wanted to do anyway.

Even though the empire hadn't fought a major war in a very long time, he did get a sense that tensions were beginning to run high with some of its closest neighbors. The King of the Realm didn't have an heir, the Kingdom of Arc had started military drills on their borders, and the smaller United

Territories to the south had shown more bickering among themselves than usual. For these reasons the Emperor had taken steps to strengthen his army in recent months.

Mezar, still standing and reminiscing when the door to the throne room opened, jumped out of his thoughts. His father marched out, lips held tight and his face red, his anger barely held in check. "Mezar, the mighty Emperor will see you now."

Mezar's brown eyes opened wide at the comment. The sarcastic reference to the Emperor by his father, the general, showed more than anything the obvious outcome of their meeting.

Mezar decided to say nothing, walking past the general into the larger room. Gold and silver adorned the throne room. Ancient vases, sculptures, and weapons hung around the gold-trimmed, red-painted walls with an obvious show of the empire's wealth. He remembered coming into this room as a small child, yet even at twenty-one years old, he still felt dwarfed by its overbearing opulence.

Emperor Alrishitar, dressed in his royal red robes, sat on his golden throne, flanked by leopards made from silver. He looked almost as frustrated as his father had upon leaving the room. Mezar wasn't sure if he wanted to meet with the Emperor or not in this current mood. He decided that protocol necessitated his greeting.

Upon approaching the throne by way of the red carpet leading to it, he stopped mid-way and bowed himself low. Keeping his waist bent and head down, he recited a royal greeting that should suffice in the present situation.

"Emperor of the Sun, brighter than the stars, your wisdom guides us in the light. May thy humbled servant enter thy presence?" The words were spoken in ancient Gildan as ceremony dictated. More modern Gildan was simpler, and though different from the languages of the Realm and the Kingdom of Arc, some newer, common words were used throughout the three western kingdoms.

Mezar heard a deep sigh emanate from the Emperor, then, "Mezar, my young boy, no need for such formality between us. Rise and come forward."

Mezar rose, but still proceeded with caution. This was the supreme leader of all of the Gildanian Empire. His moods could be fickle, and even though peace had reigned for most of his time, his moments of rage were also legendary. Mezar cringed at the thought of seeing that rage firsthand, when as a young boy he had snuck to the back of the throne room and hidden behind the curtains. He moved his hand over his backside, still feeling the sting of the memory in his mind. He had behaved after that and won the heart of Emperor Alrishitar.

The Emperor smiled. "You no doubt saw the general's face as he left my chambers?"

Mezar only nodded.

"Do not be alarmed. Haven't I always told you, you were my favorite?" The Emperor chuckled to himself.

Mezar was surprised at the admission in the throne room. "Your Highness, you should not say that here."

"And why is that, young Mezar? Are you afraid of your brother's ghost coming to haunt you?"

"No. No." Mezar stumbled a moment. His older brother had died of a fevered sickness the prior year. The wizards had done all they could for him, but they had suspected some kind of poison that had been beyond their powers to heal. His brother and the emperor had not seen eye to eye on things. His brother had been a lot like his father.

The Emperor stood. "Come, let's take some refreshments in my study, where prying eyes will not overhear our conversation."

Mezar looked around the room, wondering whom the Emperor referred to. He stepped up to the elderly monarch and held out his arm for the older man to use as support. The emperor's mind was still bright and fresh, but his aged years had begun to catch up to him physically.

They entered the private study, and with a flash of his hand, the Emperor lit the lamps in the room. Mezar smiled at the use of the power.

The emperors of Gildan were in a long line of those who, besides accepting the monarchy, were also wizards. Emperor Alrishitar, while not one of the most powerful in recent times, was known to have a fine finesse of the powers that he did hold. Out of the powers of the heart, mind, and earth this emperor was strongest in the powers of the mind.

Mezar poured some fresh pomegranate juice for the two of them and sat down opposite his leader. The Emperor took an apple and cut it with a long knife, then sat back, and after eating a few pieces looked with intent at his young friend.

"Mezar, your father and I disagree on the course of action to take at this time. I am always wont for more caution, while your father, the general, tends to be more aggressive in his desires. I am afraid there are many who follow his lead. However, for the time being, I am still the Emperor while I am alive."

"Your Highness, you have a long time still." Mezar rushed to defend the sole ruler of Gildan.

The Emperor waved his hand at Mezar. "We never know how much time we have, though I agree with you. I am not yet ready to give up my throne. Don't worry about that for now. I can rein in your father's cronies."

Mezar didn't like the division he observed occurring between his father and the Emperor. Things could get dangerous for the empire, and for him personally if the army split from the throne. "Sire, what is it you would like for me to do?"

The Emperor smiled. "Now, I do temper things with caution, but I am not above stirring the pot a little and seeing how others react. We do need to know what is going on with our neighbors, and you have some unique capabilities that I would like to draw upon for your first assignment."

The ultimate authority in the Gildanian Empire then proceeded to tell young Mezar what the plan would be. At first Mezar sat astonished, but then he smiled at the wonderful opportunity he was being given. At last he would step foot outside of the empire. Finally he would see the world around him. Finally he would see the Realm.

Chapter Nineteen

A month after the first visit to King Edward, Christine and Martin, the older man who had accompanied her before, left the farmlands to return to the castle to receive the answer to their petition. Alvyn stayed behind because of his lack of control over his tongue in the previous meeting.

Christine wore the same dress she had previously, but this time she had a thick white cloak wrapped around her for warmth. Her fur-lined boots crunched on top of fresh snow.

The two of them walked through the merchants' quarter, with its brick houses lining the narrow streets. Upon entering the nobles' district, she saw that the houses turned to stone and the roofs became sturdier. Early-morning sweepers were clearing the snow off the widening cobblestone streets. The walk to the castle took longer, but finally they climbed the large steps and gathered in line behind other petitioners.

The line extended longer this week, and as usual, no place was afforded them to sit in the large hall. After waiting for some time, a steward brought them back into the throne room. With a sweep of her eyes around the room, Christine realized Richard wasn't here today. One of the other councilors helped King Edward with the proceedings.

Once again, she stood in awe of the room as well as the entire castle. She noticed things she hadn't spotted on her prior visit: the delicate carvings high up on the crown molding, the strange geometric designs carved in the hard floor, and the gold inlays around the opened windows. She could only dream of ever living in a place so big.

They soon found themselves at the front of the line. The King looked up from the Throne of Power and surely noticed them. She smiled at him, but he gave no outward acknowledgment he had seen her. Without any preamble, he stood up and announced to those in line that he was finished for the day.

The small crowd began to mumble at the unfairness, but the stewards began ushering them out of the room. Christine moved around two ushers to get the King's attention before he went out of a smaller side door. She assumed the door went to his private study or rooms. Outside of the stories her father had told her, she wasn't familiar with all of the rooms a house or castle might have.

"You promised an answer today, my King," she said politely but with confidence. It was a boldness that had only emerged since being bonded with her Cremelino. The power that her horse shared with Christine helped her to realize that she might be able to make a difference in things. Her voice echoed off the walls. Others stopped to watch the exchange.

King Edward stopped mid-step. "I promised you nothing," said the King. "You demanded, as I remember. You are not the only people in the kingdom who want or need my help." He turned and continued walking to the side door.

Go ahead, Christine. You can do it. You need to try! Lightning's voice was faint. Due to the cold, they had left her on the farm that day. But it still gladdened and emboldened her.

"You can't ignore the situation much longer." Her voice was amplified and echoed around the chamber.

The King whipped his head around.

"Peace is a fragile thing, King Edward. You will not be remembered for it unless you deal with these things." She knew they could detain her for such words, but she was compelled to say what the King needed to hear. Everything seemed so much clearer now. "You will give us an answer, or troubles that you cannot stop will arise."

"How dare you," Edward bellowed, and he stepped forward. His face went red and his eyes bulged.

Christine stood in front of King Edward, defiant and proud. A hush filled the room, and those leaving turned back around.

Her eyes pierced his, daring him to look away.

May the power fill you, and the dreams you desire come true for your boldness, my child, Lightning spoke to Christine's soul, and she felt more alive than ever before.

Hope and light filled Christine and her fear diminished. She smiled at the King and curtsied, never taking her green eyes from his. She had said all that needed to be said at the moment.

The next move was up to King Edward himself.

Christine took her surprised companion by his arm, turned, and walked out the large doors. Small whispers followed in her wake. The stewards kept control and continued ushering the rest of the petitioners out.

* * * *

After the two farmers left the room, King Edward turned with heavy feet toward his private chambers once again. His head hurt horribly. He put his hand there to quell the pain. The headaches had been coming more frequently lately. He motioned his councilor back and entered his private study by himself.

Without really seeing anything in the room, he dragged his feet to his large red chair. He hated red right now; it was Belor's colors and reminded him of the troubles there. Maybe one day he would change the furniture. He fell into the stuffed chair and leaned his head back. Slowly his heartrate returned to normal and he took a deep breath.

How can this girl have such an effect on me? Who is she? He would have to ask Richard to get more information. He was sure he had glimpsed an aura of light around her this time. That's what frightened him more than anything else. And the look in her eyes. It was pure, and full of boldness. She seemed so assured that what she was doing was right. He felt power, but didn't know what to do about it. The only real power he knew of that still existed in the Realm was the Throne of Power. Wizards and other magic hadn't been seen in a century. Well, there were rumors that the madman in Belor had magic.

His world felt like it was spinning out of control. Was this his punishment for not being the rightful heir to the throne?

He had always done his best, but a nagging in the back of his mind had always told him he was not meant to be the king.

"Peace." He banged his hand on his chair. "What does some young wench from the farmlands comprehend of how fragile peace is?"

Today had been a frustrating day. Earlier in the week he had sent a group of men to Belor to seal the city until things settled down. A messenger had arrived today to inform him that the situation had turned into an ugly and bloody battle. Peace had reigned through most of his kinghood, but all of a sudden things seemed to be happening on all sides. His life was unraveling.

Besides Belor, the normal bickering of the guilds was flaring up again in Mar, and now he had just learned from his spies that the Gildanians were marching toward Denir.

Edward wondered what the old emperor was up to this time. They had traded in peace since the treaty over twenty years ago. Rumors held that the man was becoming senile in his old age, and his eldest son had begun running the empire for him—a son who didn't always agree with the more peaceful ways.

The King kicked the small table over with his large, black leather boots. A book and two cups crashed to the floor. On top of all the troubles in the kingdom, he now had to deal with a pair of petty petitioning farmers from Anikari's own backyard. He admitted he had let things get out of hand with the treatment between the farmers and the city. He justified that he hadn't known the extent of the persecutions. His mind had been on other things. The fighting in Belor, the heir to the throne, his health.

He wished he had known more about the farmlands earlier. Now there was little time to remedy that problem until other important things were taken care of. His councilors should have taken care of these types of things for him. But now he knew some of his councilors were also conniving behind his back, setting themselves up for the next monarchy. *At least that is taken care of. Darius* **will** *be the next king!*

Richard walked into the room after a small knock on the door. Seeing the King's apparent distress, his face grew concerned. "Are you feeling well, Edward?"

"No!" he yelled, then he continued more softly, "I have been having these outrageous headaches. They almost put me in bed. And this winter weather does nothing to help, not to mention all of those petitioners out in the hall. And just now I thought I might be having a problem with my heart."

"Did the farmers come back?"

"Yes they did; that's what pushed me over the edge. I left without talking to them. Well, I tried to leave. That *girl.*" He held his head between his hands. "What do you know about this Christine? She cannot be altogether what she appears to be. She is not just a farmer; there is too much power there. Who is behind this? Somebody must be putting her up to this.'

Richard sat down across from the King. He reached down and picked up the table that had been knocked over. "She and my son, Darius, were good friends, even though I tried to forbid it."

"Why?"

"Why what, Edward?" His voice rose louder than he intended.

"Why did you forbid them to be together, and how close of friends were they?"

"Edward, she is an outsider. A farmer. You do remember what Darius is going to be?" Richard was nervous, looking around, making sure no one else was listening. "They were close friends, from what my wife tells me. Very close. They held strong feelings for each other."

"I have a sense about her, but I can't grasp what it is. The way she spoke today. The power she held. I felt something. Powers that haven't manifested themselves in generations are here in Anikari again."

"My King, am I not your councilor? If so, I now counsel you to get her out of your mind. She is just a poor, silly farmer. She means nothing to us."

"Richard . . ." The King paused. "You must not be so hard on them."

"But . . ."

"But nothing, my councilor and friend. Someday you will appreciate things differently. Mark my words . . ." Edward was so tired of late. It was so much to juggle. He had so much information he wanted to share with Richard, but for his sake, he had to only give him bits at a time. He didn't want to see his first councilor and friend destroyed.

"What are you talking about, Edward? You had better lie down. You aren't making much sense."

Richard helped Edward to his bedchamber, then left the King, telling him he would be in his office if he was needed.

* * * *

Out in one of the hallways of the castle, Christine and Martin stood talking.

"They will not listen to us," said the older man sadly. "But you did try. We will have to think of another way. Let's go."

"I am not going until I get some answers. I want to know if they even looked at our petition."

"Christine, he will not talk to you. He's the King. He does what he wants. You saw him. That's how the nobles are. You might have been taken and bound for what you said to him. I promised your dad I would keep you safe. Now let's go!"

"You and my dad have been friends for a long time, haven't you?" reflected Christine, walking down the long stone hall. Lamps flickered on the high wall, sending shadows onto the marble floor. Paintings and tapestries hung on the stone walls every few feet, between the lamps. The hallway seemed to narrow as she looked down its long corridor. "I can tell my father doesn't like the city, but he wants all of this settled peacefully."

"We need to get out of here, Christine." Martin looked around for guards. He was the opposite of her father physically. Thin and serious, with graying hair. The only hint of his former hair color was the touch of black right above his temples.

He grabbed her arm and pulled her along. Christine stopped and pulled her arm away from him. "What is this secret that no one is telling me about? I want to know about my father."

"He's the only one that can say. I cannot. Now let's go back."

"I am staying until King Edward or his councilor sees me."

"You will need an appointment, and they will never give you one. Now be reasonable. We tried, and I hoped with all my heart they would listen. But they didn't. They don't care. It is only a matter of time before we start fighting," he said in a fatherly, lecturing way.

"If that's what it has come to, then all the more reason for me to try even harder to keep the fighting from happening. Now you go back to my father and tell him I am fine. I am going to find the King. Nothing will happen to me in the castle."

Martin sighed, realizing that Christine wasn't going to budge. He told her to be careful and left to go back to the farmlands.

Is this a good idea?

Christine felt Lightning's question probing her. *I'm not sure, but I have to do something.*

Christine sat down on a lone chair in the spacious hall to try to think of what she was going to do. It seemed strange to her. For some reason, the hall was empty except for her. In the shuffle of getting everyone out, she and Martin had become separated from everyone else.

She looked up at the massive stones that fashioned the ceiling, and down at the marble floor that was pieced together in large rectangles. She felt alone and afraid, but was determined to talk to the King. She looked at the gilded mirrors and large paintings and began to get angry. They lived in such opulence while many struggled just to barely live out in the farmlands.

She would see this thing through right now.

Be careful!

She abruptly rose off the chair and started to walk down the hall, leading deeper into the castle complex. More than once she ducked behind a large pillar or corner before someone spotted her. Her heart pounded with adrenaline-filled excitement. She was not the one to opt for adventure but since the night she had gone with Anya and Stephanie to the barn, her whole life seemed to be taking a direction of its own.

Thoughts of adventure made her think of Darius's friend, Kelln, as she slid through the hallways, looking for the King's quarters. He would have found a way through this maze. The thought made her smile and relax. She let her boldness still smolder beneath; it gave purpose to her actions.

She passed a few servants who eyed her but said nothing. Acting the part of a noble and ignoring them seemed to work, though she hated herself for it. Her white cloak was nice enough to blend in, and it covered her homespun dress. No one wanted to ask questions and risk offending someone who may be a guest. Discreetly, she asked a few questions of servants to learn where the king and councilor's offices were.

With cautious movements she headed toward the east wing. The halls became narrower and there were fewer places to hide. She began to catch a glimpse of more nobles in this part of the castle. Her heart raced with nervousness. She ducked into a closet as she heard voices reach her from around a corner.

The small closet was full of clothes. A small window opposite the door let in a stream of dusty light. She noticed the clothes to be those the servants wore. "They must be extra clothes," she mumbled in a whisper. She started grabbing some off the shelves as a plan formed in her head. It was bold and dangerous, and could land her in the dungeon, but she had to try.

Chapter Twenty

Farther down the hall of the castle, Sean San Ghant entered into councilor Richard's private study. Richard wasn't necessarily fond of the young man, but he knew as long as he kept rewarding him more than another would, he would be true to his needs.

"How are you today, sir?" The young man bowed, almost in a mocking motion.

"I am fine, Sean. Now what is your report?"

"I hear that the farmers have been giving you problems."

"I didn't ask you to report on the farmers. I am familiar with their concerns." He walked up closer to Sean and glared at him. They were of similar height. "What about my son?" He was not in the mood today for Sean's arrogant manners.

"You do know he became the first junior commander over a month ago."

Richard let himself almost smile.

"He has continued to work with a fierce determination and is preparing for his final wilderness test to become the first full commander of the Elite."

"You must keep an eye on him. He must be kept safe."

"I have someone else helping me. Someone that will keep close, very close to him. But it's hard sometimes sir, he is not making a lot of friends there. They . . ."

"And who are they?" Richard raised his voice. "I assigned you this mission Sean. Don't mess it up. If anyone questions you, I will have him or her in this office within the week. Now go and make sure my son stays safe. Let me know when he is ready for full command."

Richard pushed him toward the door, but before he opened it he added, "And take this. I am sure you could use the coins, couldn't you?" He threw a velvet pouch of money toward Sean. He knew money was only extra insurance to ensure that Sean followed his commands exactly.

Sean turned back to him before opening the door. "Ah, councilor. One more thing."

"There always is with you."

"There are rumors about your son."

Richard gave his full attention. "What rumors?" People couldn't possibly guess about his son and his heritage. No one knew except for the King and himself. Where would rumors come from?

"Some think he has powers."

"Powers?" Richard relaxed. "Is that all? He has had a lot of training. You know that. The men are just jealous of him. He is good at most anything he sets his mind to."

"Maybe that's all it is." Sean shrugged. He seemed to be holding something back.

"But?" Richard prodded.

"The men talk of a glow about him sometimes, and the power in his sword. He excels at every test placed before him. He seems to push people back with little physical touch or effort, almost as if summoning the wind to do his bidding."

Richard's mind jumped back in time to the day Darius had left Anikari. While escorting him to their home he remembered his son putting his palm on Richard's chest and pushing him backwards. *Was the force more than normal strength?* His son was strong.

Sean continued. "People say he may be a wizard."

The notion was so ridiculous to Richard that he actually laughed.

"Sir?" Sean seemed flustered for the first time since Richard had met him.

"Sean. You are still young, aren't you? You must learn that whenever one rises to leadership, others try to discredit, ruin, and tear him down. It's human nature. Things like this happen all the time. Someday there might even be rumors about you."

"Me?"

Richard stroked Sean's ego. "Yes, Sean, you. There are surely those who admire you and want your position of trust. They will try to bring you down."

Sean puffed his chest out. "Yes. Yes. Of course you are right, councilor. Surely they will."

"And they will try to say lies and other ridiculous things about you. But you won't believe them, will you?" Richard asked.

"About me? Lies? No. No. Never. I am a loyal servant of the Realm. "

"I'm glad to hear that. It's the same with Darius. Others are jealous of him being the first commander and being my son. They are spreading rumors to discredit him. Now, no more childish talk of wizards. We haven't seen wizards in the Realm for generations and more. We will leave those likes to the other kingdoms to deal with."

"I understand now. Thank you for teaching me, councilor."

Richard was irked by Sean's patronizing tone. He knew that the young man wanted power and prestige; it was not a hidden fact. He didn't trust Sean, but it was all he had to work with at the moment.

Sean moved toward the door, opened it, and stepped out in a hurry. He had only taken a step when someone ran into him from the side, almost knocking him over. Money spilled from out of the pouch he was holding. Richard heard the loud noise and walked toward the door.

"I am sorry, sir," said a soft female voice. "I will help you pick it up."

Sean barely glanced at the servant. "Get out of my way. I will get it myself."

She turned to continue on her way as Richard reached the hallway.

"What's going on here?" He looked at Sean.

"Some blind and stupid servant ran into me." He pointed at her as she continued to walk away down the hall.

"Come here," Richard commanded. "Where are you going?"

The girl started to run down the hallway.

"Get her, Sean!" yelled Richard, as Sean took off running toward her.

She had started to turn the corner when Sean caught up with her.

Sean took her face between his fingers, and with a slight force of his hand turned her toward him. "What is your name, girl?"

Richard couldn't see the girl's face through Sean's body. She said nothing.

"How did you?" Sean stumbled on his words. "Aren't you a farmer? I recognize you . . ."

She recognized him also and shuddered, but kept silent.

"I think the senior councilor would like to speak to you." She squirmed again but his tight squeeze on her arm made it impossible to get away. He dragged her to Richard's doorway and they all went inside.

Richard was astonished and immediately recognized who it was. "How did you get in here? You cannot be here Christine." Richard remembered what he and Sean had been talking about. "What were you doing outside of my door? Were you listening to us? You could be imprisoned for this, you realize."

Christine stood shaking at the obvious failure in whatever plans she had conceived.

Richard watched the young woman smooth her dress and close her eyes for a moment. She breathed deeply as if to calm herself. Then her features sharpened and her eyes popped open.

Richard almost stepped back at the look in her eyes, but he held his ground. The King was right; there was power there. "I heard that the King dismissed you. I ask again, what are you doing here?"

Christine held herself up tall and straight. Her eyes blazed deep into the councilor's own. "I needed to talk to the King or to one of his councilors." She nodded her head toward him. "King Edward was supposed to answer us today. He didn't have enough time earlier."

"The King has other things to think about besides you," Richard interrupted. "Are you sure you didn't overhear anything outside of the door?"

She smiled at him with force. "Would you believe me anyway?"

Richard's head snapped back as if being pushed. He fought to keep control.

"How can you trust her? She's an outsider," Sean said with disgust. "What do you want me to do with her?"

Richard was happy for the distraction. "Nothing, Sean. This isn't your business. Just go and take care of what we talked about. I will take care of her. "

Sean turned and gave Christine a leering look of utter disgust. "Sounds fun."

Richard saw a look of anger come over the girl. She stopped, almost as if listening to someone. Then she calmed herself down and relaxed. "You're not worth it anyway." She directed her comments toward Sean as he turned to go.

"What?" Sean spun around.

"Oh, nothing." Christine gave him a sweet smile. "Just trying to convince myself not to hate you too much."

Sean grunted and left, leaving only Christine and Richard standing face to face. Christine stood in defiance, not moving a muscle as Richard closed the door. He smiled inside at how she treated Sean. Maybe he had misjudged his son's choices. She was definitely more than she seemed.

He closed his door and motioned for her toward some chairs. They sat down and he watched her look around his study and take in the surroundings. Dark cherry wood, with maps of neighboring lands, covered most of the walls. A semi-circle of chairs, a couch, and a small table took up about a third of the room. This is where he led her.

"What do you know of my son?" he asked with a softer tone after they sat.

"I know that he went away," was all she said.

"You are trying my patience, young lady. You're not allowed in this part of the castle. There are men who, if they behaved like you have done, would be sitting in a dark room awaiting punishment. Maybe even death."

"You sent him somewhere to train," she said, keeping her composure.

He could tell his words had affected her like he had wanted. "You have not heard from him since?"

"I didn't even see him the day he went away. I had gone to Forest View with my father. From what I do know, he was only given a short time to prepare." The last statement, Richard realized, was an individual attack on him. But he kept his mouth closed.

"I did not like the influence you had on him when he was here, and you could be punished, but for the sake of my son, though he will not believe this, I will let you go. Besides, the King is intrigued by you." He wondered why he had offered that to her. Why was her presence comforting?

Christine smiled. "How so? I am just a poor farmer girl." Sarcasm was becoming more natural to her in the councilor's presence.

"That is what I told him. But now . . . ?"

"Now what, councilor? Do you actually see a person rather than just an 'outsider'?" She used his terminology boldly.

Richard had to admire the girl. She was better at trading barbs than many nobles he had met in a long time. "The King thinks there is something more; however, I think it is just your level head and sweet disposition that has made an impact on his thinking."

Christine just smiled. "Now who is being sarcastic, councilor?"

"There isn't anything else, is there?" Richard raised his brows.

The girl froze for an instant. Only for a blink of an eye, once again as if listening to something. But before he could question it, it was gone.

"Now what else would there be, councilor? I'm not an evil wizard or sorceress sent to put a spell on King Edward," Christine laughed.

For the third time that day, Richard was involved with someone mentioning the old magic. He hoped it was only a coincidence, but something tickled the back of his mind. The King had mentioned a power before. Was this young lady bewitching them all?

"I think I should leave now," Christine interrupted Richard's thoughts. "But the reason I came here was the petition."

Richard didn't believe the daring of this young lady. "As I told you before, we will get to your petition when we have time."

Christine stood up and her eyes flashed brightly. "Councilor, time is running out," she began. "I am only one of a few that want to settle these matters of inequality and unfairness with peaceful means, though that idea is quickly becoming unfruitful. I am probably the simplest, easiest one you have to deal with."

Richard laughed. "Nothing about you is simple or easy, my dear." He stood and motioned her to the door.

"Others are planning to take you to battle. I think it's ridiculous. But others don't. We will be heard one way or another."

"To battle?" Richard said with laughing hostility. "Do you not recognize that our army is the mightiest in all the lands? You would bring us into battle? We would squash you like gnats on a horse. Now get out before I change my mind." Richard's voice boomed as he opened the door. "And tell your friends if they try to fight us, there won't be any of you left to write a petition."

The councilor called for a steward standing at the end of the hall to escort the young lady out of the castle. He stood watching them until the two turned a corner, then headed back into his office. He had a feeling that it was not the last time he would see Christine.

Chapter Twenty One

"Good luck," smiled Leandra as she leaned into Darius. With a quick rise onto her toes she gave him a kiss. He tried to move backward but hit the back of his head against a tree. He was about to leave for his last field test to become the first full commander of the Elite Army. It had been four months since arriving in camp and almost three since becoming a team leader. Others had become team leaders since then, but no one else was being invited to take the final field test yet.

"What did you do that for?" Darius asked, rubbing the back of his head. Ever since he had saved her from the men that Cray sent to test him she had clung to him whenever she could.

They had enjoyed additional walks together since then, which were in fact relaxing and far less exciting than the first one. Darius admitted that he had begun to like having Leandra around. She praised him and smiled at him, and was quite alluring with the looks she offered him. Above all, it seemed to make the other men envious of him.

"Why do you think?" giggled Leandra, her soft brown eyes sparkled with her usual mischievousness. "Why do you think people kiss, Darius?"

"I uh . . ." Darius watched some of the other young men from afar. Some were jealous of him, with all that he had accomplished at the camp in the few short months, but having Leandra on his arm really seemed to irk them. What would they say if they knew how nervous he actually was around her? Some of the men looked over toward the pair to see what was happening.

With an unexpected move, Darius grabbed Leandra around the waist and pulled her back toward him with force. Letting her feel a trickle of his power, he returned her kiss, letting his lips linger just a brief moment longer than hers had.

Leandra's face turned multiple shades of pink as Darius turned and walked toward Cray, who waited with men and horses to begin their ascent into the Superstition Mountains.

The other men behind him snickered and whooped and hollered. Maybe kissing her had shown them he was more like them than they thought.

"Don't say anything," he said to Cray as he jumped on his horse.

"Who, me?" laughed Cray. "What would I say to a young man who just about made a girl melt to her knees?"

"I did not." Darius looked a little embarrassed.

"Look back there." Cray pointed toward Leandra, who still stood in the same place Darius had left her. She had a dreamy look on her face and smiled at Darius as if nothing else in the world mattered.

"Girls . . ." was all Darius said as he kicked his horse and headed up the mountain and out of the camp. Cray and two others followed shortly behind.

As Cray had promised, they stayed on the horses for two days as they climbed higher into the mountains. The ground and branches were covered in snow, but the days were clear. As they climbed to a higher altitude, the temperature dropped and Darius wrapped a red cloak around his leather vest and pants. He could see his warm breath in the frigid air. Towards the end of the second day they stopped.

Cray took out a thick piece of wool fabric and moved closer to Darius. "You will now go blindfolded the rest of the way."

"What?" Darius was surprised at the direction. "What will that accomplish?"

"It will make it more of a chore to get back to camp." Cray smiled.

Darius looked around for the other men that accompanied him. They were off to the side, feeding the other horses. "You do know that I have other abilities that will help me get back?"

Cray smirked at him and hopped off his horse. "Don't let everything hinge on that, Darius. You are here at the training camp for a purpose. To be trained in the King's Elite Army, and then to follow the King's direction in where he wants to send you and what he wants you to do. This final test of getting back to camp on your own, in the mountains in the middle of winter, will convince me and the other leaders you are really ready to have a full command of men under you."

"I don't need a lecture, Cray." Darius furrowed his eyes at his trainer and tried to relax his clenched fists as he dropped to the ground. His legs still felt like he was riding the horse.

Cray walked closer to him. "I don't pretend to understand what goes on in your mind." He put a friendly hand on Darius's shoulder. "I know this was not your choice to be here, but you have done well and I am proud of you."

Darius took a deep breath and let it go, wisps of warm fog escaping into the cold air. "I am not mad at you. I just want to control my own life without others pulling the strings."

The other men came over toward Cray. "Sir," one of them said. "We need to keep moving before it gets dark."

Darius reached over and took the blindfold from his trainer then tied it over his eyes. With a smirk he said, "Lead me on, men. Let's hope you don't dump me off a cliff somewhere."

A few hours later they stopped, removed the blindfold, and gave Darius a small knife and a day's worth of water.

"You are on your own now, son." Cray shook his hand. "Make a camp here for the night and then return to us at the base camp as soon as you can."

Looking around himself, Darius saw he was next to a small creek with a large rock face behind it. Large pines surrounded a small meadow of snow. "Looks inviting."

Cray smiled. "Use the knowledge of your training. There is plenty of food and shelter here; just be smart about it."

The men took his horse and left Darius to head down the mountain, trying to get a head start to camp before darkness forced them to settle in for the night.

"And no cheating!" Cray yelled from around a corner.

Darius looked toward him with surprise, but he couldn't see the men anymore. He could now instinctively bring up the power within himself. *It isn't cheating to use something that belongs to me.* The power flared again. He pushed it back inside. He knew what Cray meant. He had been trained and had passed all the tests up until now; he could do it without using his power. It wouldn't be hard, except for the fact that it was now a part of him, and he hardly had to think to draw on it in a time of need.

Darius looked in more detail at his surroundings. He could tell he was much higher than the base camp. The trees were not as dense. At this height and time of year, all but the evergreens had lost their leaves. He walked around with some difficulty in the snow and found himself on a large plateau, looking east. As far as he could see, the jagged mountains filled his vision, growing smaller and smaller in the distance, eventually disappearing into the fading purplish mists. He knew Anikari was in that direction. Thoughts of home invaded his thoughts, but before they got too painful he shoved them back down inside of him.

Down by the stream a dozen yards away was an overhang of rock. With a few branches from the pine trees, he was able to make a small shelter for the night. Soon, with his flint and steel, he built a small fire and felt more comfortable. He didn't worry about getting back too soon. He could survive out in the mountains. This was what he had trained for.

Darius had, in fact, already decided to stay out a little longer than would be expected. It would make Cray and the others worry for him a little longer. That would make them appreciate him more when he did arrive back in the camp. The men would admire him and he would now be their leader—the youngest of them all. He would be ready to march!

He thought of Kelln. This was the kind of adventure they had dreamed of as young children, and into their teen years. Maybe he would find a lost cabin or hidden cave. He felt better than he had in months. He wondered where Kelln was. The last he had heard of his friend was before he'd left to Belor to find out about his family and the troubles there. Darius smiled at the thought of the trouble Kelln could always find, no matter where he went.

He breathed in the cold air, relaxing, and his power pulsed. It gave him clarity of thought. The pine needles seemed clearer, his memory sharper, and the possibilities of what he could do started to open up to him. *I really am going to become a leader in the king's army!*

This was the first time that he had felt free since leaving his home. He grabbed a dead branch and started to whittle as he pondered what to do to find some food.

He was finally in control.

Chapter Twenty Two

Christine, sitting atop her large Cremelino, raced through the trees. She weaved her head back and forth, trying to keep pine needles from slapping her face. She was glad it was winter, or the oaks, maples, and smaller brush would have made her ride more dangerous. Lightning kicked up dirt from the soft ground, spraying mud around about her and dirtying her white coat.

Taking advantage of a warmer than usual winter day, she had ridden Lightning out to the Field of Diamonds earlier that morning. Being there always brought solace to her soul.

The field reminded her of Darius. She missed him horribly and wondered when she would see him again. The year was coming to an end and it had been five months since he had left.

The petition had earned nothing from King Edward and trouble grew daily between the farmers of Anikari and those inside the city. Taunting and beatings had become more dangerous and frequent. The talk of retaliation on the part of the farmers continued to grow. Christine grew more and more unsure of a peaceful solution.

Sitting at the edge of the Lake of Reflection she had seen what she'd first thought were clouds. But on second glance she had recognized them as smoke. Dark, thick clouds of it coming from the direction of the farmlands.

With a silent thought to her horse to ride quickly, she jumped up onto Lightning, and now they rode quickly through the forest between the lake and the farmlands.

Emerging out onto the road once again she sucked in a deep breath and clutched her chest with one hand. The smoke was thicker and billowing over the thinning trees and closest fields. It was in the direction of her family's farm.

Lightning rode faster than what Christine had thought possible. Green and brown blurred around her as she streaked frantically down the road. Before turning around a bend she heard the voices of others and the loud crackle of the fire. The air seemed to warm and thicken.

The sight sickened her and she almost fell from her horse.

"Stop," Christine voiced to Lightning.

In front of her blazed a fire, spreading across fields where spring vegetables would have been planted in a few months. Other farmers were running around, trying to keep animals safe. What grabbed her attention, however, was the bright inferno at the back of their own property, which used to be their family barn. The orange and yellow flames licked high into the sky with billowing smoke pouring from it, burning wood, hay, and food.

Their own house, at the far end of the property, looked safe for the time being. The wind seemed to be carrying the fire away from any homes at the moment.

Christine didn't know what to do. Her eyes were burning from the smoky air and she wiped the tears from them with the sleeve of her coat.

A loud yell turned her attention to the side of the barn. It was a horrific scream that tore her soul. Squinting through the smoke, she saw her father running from the burning barn. A horrid sob escaped her as she urged Lightning forward and over a fence.

Keeping the edge of the spreading flames to her left, she spurred her Cremelino faster. Her father had fallen to the ground and the flames were quickly turning toward him. The back of his clothes looked singed and dirty.

The dry winter grass was instant fuel for the raging fire. A loud cracking sound followed by a crash alerted Christine to the fact that the barn was about to topple over. Nearing her father, she called his name.

He rose up on his elbows and looked at her. His face was streaked with soot and tears, with a large gash on the side of his head. "Go back," his weakened voice yelled toward her.

"No, Daddy. Get up. Get up."

Christine jumped from her Cremelino before she had even stopped. She fell down and reached an arm over her father's body. "We will take you back to the house, but I don't think I can lift you up."

The barn creaked louder and the wall furthest from them fell with a loud crash to the ground. Only about thirty yards separated them from the building, and the heat was becoming unbearable. The grass nearest them was starting to smolder and the fire moved toward them at a quicker pace.

Stefen got on his hands and knees and tried to stand. "I can't do it, Christine. Leave me and save yourself. You need to get away." He coughed and almost choked as he tried to get a clean breath but couldn't.

Christine bent down to him and Lightning moved over next to Stefen. The Cremelino then lay down on her stomach.

Roll him over on top of me.

Christine felt infused with hope as she helped her father back up on his knees. As she pushed him over, he fell across the back of the horse. A loud groan escaped his lips. Portions of his clothes were burned away, revealing multiple burns along his back and legs.

Lightning stood up, with Christine's father draped across her neck. Christine jumped onto the horse, sitting behind her father.

The rest of the barn rumbled and fell, collapsing to the ground, sending sparks of burning wood out into the air. Christine batted them away, with a few sparks burning quick holes through her coat. Turning around, they raced back across the field, away from the fire and toward their home. Her father hung lifeless in front of her. She held one hand to steady his body.

Turning back around as they rode, tears filled Christine's eyes. Their entire farm was burnt. The fire now raced across their neighbor's farm and would continue, she presumed, until it reached the river a few farms away. She could see others running around, trying to save what they could. She wondered how it could have started.

As they stopped suddenly at their back door, her mother and Emily came running outside. Upon seeing her husband's condition she covered her mouth and silent tears ran down her face.

"I will ride to get a doctor," Christine told her mom.

"The city people won't help." The voice of her younger brother, Jain, came around the corner of the house. "They are the ones who set the fire in the first place."

"What?" Christine couldn't believe it. "You don't know that."

"Yes I do. I saw two of them running across our back fence just before the fire broke out." Jain raised his voice. "I tried to chase them, but they were too fast."

"It could be anyone!" Christine retorted.

"Enough arguing." Their mother stepped between them. "This solves nothing. If Jain said it was men from the city, then I believe him. Why would he make it up?"

Christine was about to argue when a groan from their father interrupted them. Christine turned around. "I will get you to a doctor shortly. Lightning is fast."

"No." Her father groaned. "No. It is time I speak to you of things. Jain, help me down."

"What things?" Christine jumped down and moved to his side.

Stefen lifted his face and coughed again. "I will be leaving you soon. My wounds are too great. You must know the truth before I go."

Jain moved to his side, next to Christine, and helped his father sit up. "What truth?"

"Get me into the house. Are we safe here?"

Christine looked back toward the fire. A slight breeze seemed to be blowing the smoke and flames away from their home. "For the time being."

They helped their father into the house, laying him down on an old cloth couch. He winced as his back hit the cushions.

"I love you, Dad," Jain knelt down next to his dad. "I'm sorry for how I have been."

"I know you do, son . . . I know . . ." He trailed off in a weak whisper. "You are just trying to protect us."

Caroline brought water down to his lips in an old ceramic mug. He sipped a few swallows, then laid his head back down. Emily leaned down to him also and just held his hand. She was the youngest, and most of her work and chores were done in the home. Since their dad had been indoors for the past months, in weaker health, they had developed a closer relationship.

"It is time," whispered Stefen. "My children, it's time that you know."

"Know what?" asked Jain.

"Of my boyhood and my family."

An excitement grew inside of Christine to finally hear her father's secrets, but she could hardly stand to see him in this condition. He had never spoken much of his growing-up years.

"I have not always lived in the farmlands," he began as surprised looks popped up on the children's faces. "My mother was a farmer, and my father came from . . . the . . . city. He was a teacher."

Jain looked at Christine with surprise. She didn't know what to think.

"We lived in Anikari in a large house when I was young. My father, although not a noble, was treated well, as he taught the children of nobles. He was a nice man, and generous from what I can remember, and very intelligent. He died when I was only a young boy. About eight years old." He stopped, his breaths slow and labored.

Stefen closed his eyes and winced again. Emily came in with a cool cloth and put it on his forehead. He smiled weakly at her, his blue eyes dull and pained.

"My father's sister moved in with us to help my mother with the children. I had a younger brother and sister. My aunt did not like my mother, since she came from the farmlands, and somehow they kicked her back out to the farms, and my aunt and uncle kept the three children with them. My mother did it because she thought we would be better off that way . . ."

He paused again and asked for a drink.

"Let us get a doctor for you," Christine pleaded. She couldn't stand to see her father like this. "You need to get the smoke out of your lungs, and you need something for your burns."

Her father weakly moved his arm and dropped it down onto her hand. He rubbed his fingers across her smooth skin. "I am sorry, Christine. I have been weak already, and now this. A doctor won't help me. I . . ." A deep, hacking cough brought pain to his face.

"Daddy," voiced Emily, trying to hold back the sobs.

After a moment of silence their father continued, his voice softer. They all leaned in to hear better. Christine's mother stood behind them.

"With my mother gone, my aunt and uncle started to treat us badly. They made us do all of the work around the house and stables. They sent us to school, but always insisted we would never be able to learn as much as the other kids would. We were treated differently because we didn't have a mother and father around, and because our mother was from the farmlands. I, being the oldest, had to somehow try to console my younger brother and sister." Tears came to the big man's eyes.

Stefen began to cry at the memory. "It was so humiliating. We ran away a few times, but they always caught us, brought us back, and beat us. We saw my mother at times and she would always assure us that she would bring us to her someday, after we were done learning in the schools. My brother ran off, never to be seen again, and a year later my sister died from a childhood disease."

"One day the house caught fire and some men pulled me out. I was sixteen by this time. My aunt and uncle died in the house while sleeping. To this day I don't know how the fire started, but I think it was from one of my mother's friends. They killed my aunt and uncle to bring me back to the farmlands." He began to grow paler. He paused for a few minutes.

"I blamed myself for their deaths, though I was glad it happened."

Emily leaned in and wiped the tears from her father's eyes with the cool cloth. Jain stood still, not moving. Christine felt her chest tighten, and anger began to rise as she thought about the years of useless violence that had destroyed so much.

"Then why didn't you want to fight?" Christine whispered. "You were always the leader of peace. That is what you taught me. But now another fire and more violence. When does it end?"

"There has to be a peaceful solution. Somewhere. Somehow. Life can't continue like this. If we go killing city people, we are killing a part of me and a part of you. Even though I don't like to admit it, I am part of the city of Anikari. I went to school there, I learned a lot, and some of those people living in the city are my relatives . . . and yours."

He stopped talking, and everyone sat in silence for a few minutes, just soaking in what Stefen had revealed to them. Christine guessed that their mother already knew, but for the rest of them it was a new concept that they may have relatives in the city.

Stefen started coughing hard again. Jain lifted him up slightly, but still their father had trouble reaching for a full breath of air. Caroline tried to give him more water but he just pushed the cup away. He became more pale and weak. His lungs wheezed as he struggled for each breath.

"Dad, don't die. Please," pleaded Jain.

"I love you." Emily grabbed his hand.

Christine stood next to her mother, both with tears streaming down their pale faces. They both knew the time had come. Stefen's life was fading out, and there wasn't anything else that they could do about it.

"I'll take you to the doctor on Lightning. There is still time," offered Christine as she began to run out of the house. She had only gotten a few steps into the next room when her mother softly called her back.

When she came back in, silence enveloped the room. Time stood still. She looked at everyone's faces. Emily covered her eyes. Jain stared with a look of horror. Her mother, Caroline, was leaning over Stefen, stroking his graying hair with one hand and holding his hand with the other. His eyes were closed and his chest still.

"They killed him." Christine wailed uncontrollably.

"It was his time," whispered her mother.

She is right, Christine. We all have our time. Now it is your time to take up the cause.

Christine shut the Cremelino out with such force that she heard the horse neigh loudly and stumbled outside. Christine didn't want to be consoled. Not now.

"It's not fair. They took his life from him once and now they took it away from him permanently." Tears streamed down her face.

"It's all right, Christine. Things will be better." Jain put his arm around his sister. She had barely noticed how quiet he had become during the words of her father. "He is better now in the hands of God. He will watch over us."

"They never listened and they never will," she shouted uncharacteristically. Tears slid down her face. "His aunt and uncle, the boys that beat us up, the King that does nothing, and the cowards that burned our farm today. They all deserve to burn. I am not part of the city. I am a farmer, and I am happy to be an outsider, if that is what they want to call us. They will pay for what they have done to my father."

Christine pushed Jain's arm away, making him stumble backwards. Anger boiled up inside her. All the feelings and frustrations of dealing with the King and Richard, of the persecutions, of Darius leaving her, of her father dying, all built up to a point that could not be contained any longer. It was too much for her. She had finally hit her breaking point.

"Christine. Please sit down," said her mother.

"I hate them. The King, his condescending councilor, the stewards, the noble Sans, all of them. They don't want peace and they don't want us." She ran toward the front door, with Jain chasing after her.

"Christine." Jain embraced his sister. She fought him at first, then stopped and cried against his shoulder.

"I hate them. I want to kill them," she kept saying. "They don't deserve what they have."

"We will find a way for peace," said Jain, knowing that his words sounded hollow against his recent feelings of wanting to fight.

Christine barely registered his change of behavior since their father had died. "There will be no peace for us." Christine pushed away. "There will never be peace!"

"You are just upset now."

"Yes, I'm upset. Our petition failed, I have been threatened by the councilor, and now my father is dead. What is happening to my life? What am I supposed to do?"

"Don't push us all away, Christine. We are all in this together."

She looked at him through teary eyes. "You are a good brother, Jain, but I don't know what I will do now."

"Now your family needs you. Now your neighbors need you, Christine. Look around you."

Smoke still stood in the air, and the fire was farther away. Their barn stood burning and smoldering. She knew the fire had hurt other farms too, but she couldn't help them. Not right now. Not today.

"I can't, Jain. I can't help anymore. I have nothing left to give." With that she turned and dragged her feet slowly in the opposite direction of the fire. She couldn't believe how her life had crumbled in the last five months. She felt hollow and hurt.

A while later she found herself, for the second time that day, in the Field of Diamonds. The grass, brown during the winter, supported patches of snow in the more shadowed corners. The large oak stood like a skeleton in the now-grey sky.

Anger grew, boiled, and steamed inside of her. She breathed out and watched a rush of fog escape her lips. She walked aimlessly around the lonely field. Her tears stopped. There was nothing left. She ended up next to the pond, standing in the mud. She picked up a large rock and hefted it through the air as far as she was able. "They will pay. They will pay!" was all the sound that escaped her trembling lips.

The soft sound of someone walking on the stiff brown grass made her turn around. Her Cremelino was walking down across the bare meadow. Compared to the anger Christine felt inside, the beauty of her white horse lifted her spirits. She seemed to give off a soft glow that trailed behind her as she walked with cautious steps toward Christine.

Christine reached out her hand and ran it in loving patterns across the top of Lightning's nose, moving down her beautiful, soft, snow-white mane. Bright light erupted in her mind. She closed her eyes and once again felt a reassuring, calming presence.

You pushed me out, Lightning said softly.

I'm sorry. I'm so sorry. Tears rolled again down Christine's face.

I miss him too.

Miss who? asked Christine.

A light laughter ran through her mind. *Darius.*

How did you know?

Oh, I know. He is very special. More than you know.

You talked to him, didn't you?

Yes, I did. It surprised me. That hasn't happened in a long, long time.

What does it mean? Christine asked her Cremelino.

Get on, let's ride, was Lightning's only answer. *We have some work to do to get ready.*

"Ready for what?" Christine voiced out loud. She jumped onto her Cremelino and began to ride.

But Lightning didn't come forth with any further answers.

Chapter Twenty Three

Darius batted away the large birds that swept into him as if to consume him alive. They were so close he could make out the individual thick black feathers of each bird. The giant vultures came swooping out of the large trees as if they had been hiding for days, waiting for something to eat. Darius stumbled as he tried to run. His hand scraped against a large ice-covered boulder. A large crooked branch on the ground became his only protection from being pecked, and even that was working less and less.

One sleeve of his tunic hung off his arm. The screeching birds tore away at the thick fabric. Small scratches dripped blood down Darius's tired arm, attracting the birds even more. He swung his stick in wild circular motions while he searched for cover, but none could be found. Large trees and small bushes wouldn't stop the ravaging birds.

The exhaustion of fighting the birds overcame his senses. The power began to respond to his needs and build up inside him. He pushed the urge back down. He told himself he wanted to do this on his own.

All of a sudden an arrow flew through the cold afternoon's winter air, piercing one of the birds in its breast. Large black feathers drifted away in the mountain breeze, landing as a stark difference on the white snow. The other vultures hesitated a moment, as if deciding whether to turn away or continue attacking. Darius stood still, breathing hard, not yet knowing what was happening. Another arrow splitting one of the other large birds seemed to make the decision for the rest of them, and with a noise of protest they flew off over the tall pines.

Darius began to let the power die down.

He looked around with wonder to find out who had shot the life-saving arrows with such skill. To his surprise, out walked Sean from behind a large tree. Darius's mouth, dry from the fight, just hung open in apparent surprise. Sean's lips curved into his cocky smile as he sauntered toward Darius.

"You're lucky I came when I did."

"Where did you come from?" Just seeing Sean made the power come alive again inside him. Sean represented everything he hated about the attitude of the nobles. He had taunted Darius since he was a young man.

"I came to help you and find out what you were doing up here for so long. I've been following you for a few hours. Wasn't hard. It was obvious you weren't trying to hide your tracks."

"A few hours?" Darius finally got hold of his senses. "Why did you wait until now to help?"

"I'm not supposed to be here, you know. But you looked so desperate with all of those vultures bothering you."

The adrenaline from the recent fight with the birds still raced through Darius's veins. Sean drew out the anger in him as usual. "If you're not supposed to be here, why are you?" *Don't lose control. He's not worth it.*

"Let's get your wounds cleaned and the blood wiped up, then we can talk. Any smell of blood might bring worse things than those birds after us."

Darius knew Sean was right, so he found a nearby stream, which, although it had ice around the edges, still flowed freely in the middle. Cleansing himself with the cold mountain water, the water felt like ice to his warm skin. One of these days, Sean was going to push him too far. He glanced over at him through the corner of his eyes. Sean set up a small fishing pole and tried to catch something from the stream. He smiled with thoughts of just pushing him into the stream.

He took another step toward Sean and let out a deeply held breath. He felt the power recede, but it was always present now. A prickle at the back of his mind. He knew now he could summon it with a moment's notice; he just wasn't always sure how to direct it or what its limits were.

"I bet Cray and the others are quite worried by now," said Sean.

"You mean they didn't send you?"

"No. If they knew I was here they wouldn't like it very much. It's against the rules."

"Then who sent you, Sean?"

"Settle down, Darius."

Darius walked away from the water's edge, rethinking again whether Sean deserved another reprieve.

"Not much appreciation for saving your life," Sean mocked.

"I would have survived without you, I'm sure. I always have." Darius turned around in a blur.

"Now, Darius, let's not get hostile. I came here to help you. We don't have to be best friends, but I may be able to help you."

"Who sent you, then, if it wasn't Cray?" asked Darius one more time, trying to regain a hold upon his patience.

"Your father," Sean said. "He sent me to make sure you remained safe."

Darius smiled inside. It had been ten days since his test in the mountains began. They had expected him to return after three or four days. He wanted to show them he could do what he wanted. And he had. In fact, Darius had begun to enjoy the quiet mountain surroundings, staying below the worst of the snow. Plenty of fish filled the cold mountain streams and he was able to catch a few wild rabbits with handmade traps. He smiled with the small triumph.

"What do you find so funny, Darius?"

"Are the men in the camp worried?"

Sean raised his shoulders up and down. "I suppose that they are. I haven't been in camp for quite a few days. Like I said, they don't know I'm here." Sean lit a fire with wood he had gathered from nearby. "I know why you are still here, Darius. You and I are a lot alike, you know."

Darius raised his eyebrows, "And how is that?"

"We are both independent people, not wanting others to order us around."

"But you want to be where I am. You want politics and power."

"And you are trying to escape it," concluded Sean. "Is that what you really think you are doing? You are now more a part of this big game than you or I probably know. You are going to be the youngest commander in the King's Elite Army. How does that make you feel?"

Darius thought for a moment and then actually smiled. "It actually feels quite good."

"See, having power isn't all that bad. It's about how you use it and what you do with it." Sean paused a few moments before turning back toward the fire. "Your father cares about you far more than you think, Darius," whispered Sean. "He was truly concerned with your safety up here. Don't hate everything that you are. Many are not given the privileges you have."

Darius sat back and ate a few bites of the fish Sean had caught and cooked for them. After the battle with the large birds, the food renewed his energy. He had never seen birds so large back in Anikari. He was tired of eating fish, edible roots, and rabbits. He felt a cold storm coming in the breeze. He should begin heading back to the others. He couldn't stay in the mountains forever. Though it was a little tempting, he didn't have the provisions or fortitude for that kind of life.

Darius knew this final test was more symbolic than anything. Being on his own and fending for himself was just a way to solidify all that he had already accomplished in camp.

Darius wondered why his father had sent Sean. Darius did not trust Sean now and he never would. He thought enough of his father's senses to know that his father wouldn't trust Sean either. *Something is going on that my father is not telling me.*

They finished eating without much conversation, each deep in his own thoughts of what his part was in the whole plan of the Realm. The full moon rose from the east over the giant evergreens as darkness settled in around them. The cool wind picked up and began to blow down through the nearby canyons. Despite their differences they decided to work together, and they built a small lean-to to block out as much of the wind as possible.

Through the rest of the evening conversation became lighter. They talked of Anikari and of things happening since Darius had left. Sean mentioned the problems in Belor and in the surrounding farmlands, which made Darius think of Kelln and Christine. Sometimes he longed for those simpler days back in Anikari. He knew they were never to be that way again. His position and his powers now changed all of that.

The fire died down and the mountains became quiet as everything seemed to drift off to sleep, including Darius and Sean.

All of a sudden, something woke Darius. He found Sean already standing up, turning his head as if listening for something.

"Something woke me," whispered Sean, "but with this wind I can't tell for sure."

The full moon lit up the tree-filled mountain landscape as far as a sharp ravine on the west and a thicket of large trees on the east. After studying the area for a few more minutes, they sat down once again behind the lean-to. Since waking up so suddenly Darius's heart beat a quick rhythm. The power, always a heartbeat away, heightened his sense of awareness. Someone moved out among the trees. Or something.

"Who's there?" yelled Darius, hoping it was something that would answer back, but his voice was lost in the wind.

Silence followed. Sean motioned that he would circle one way while Darius circled the other. The moonlit forest made an eerie kind of darkness, casting uncertain and hidden shadows.

Darius crept along, being careful to step on the soft snow-covered portion of the ground, where no branches or leaves would give him away. His sight sharpened as he took in the surroundings. Despite the cold wind, sweat beaded from his taut body. With deliberate slowness he moved. A dark shape became visible to him up ahead, between two weathered trees.

Darius stood still, next to a tree, as if one with it, putting into practice all he had ever learned about tracking. The shadow moved. It appeared to be a person. A man, by the way he stalked. He came closer. Darius's muscles held tight and still. He feared that the man, whoever he was, would hear Darius's loud heartbeat. A twig snapped on the other side of the figure, and the man turned.

It must have been Sean. Darius wasted no time. He sprang from the tree, covering the distance quicker than a normal man should have, and flung himself on top of the dark figure.

The man was strong, but when Sean joined in he became no match for the two of them. They flung him to the ground.

"Stop," they heard the man say. "Stop. It's me!"

Darius recognized the voice and pulled the man's head up off the ground, pulling back his hooded wool cloak. With a stern and bewildered gaze, Cray looked up at him.

He turned to Sean in gasping breaths. "What are you doing here? I thought you went back to Anikari days ago."

Sean just smirked in apparent joy at the man's reactions.

"What are you doing here?" Darius asked Cray.

"If you will let go of me, maybe we can sit down and talk about it," mumbled Cray.

They moved back over toward the lean-to and threw more wood on the fire. It seemed the mountain had come awake with Cray's apprehending. They saw a few ground squirrels scuttle by and heard smaller birds take off in a midnight flight.

Cray looked sternly into Darius's eyes. "The camp is worried about you, Darius. You have been gone longer than expected."

"Are you worried also?" Darius challenged.

Cray shrugged, laughed and settled onto the ground more comfortably. "I am only anxious that you figure out what you really want, Darius. After a slow start, during the last few months you threw yourself into training, and I don't think anyone will challenge your right to be the first commander. But what do you want?"

"That's what I've been trying to ask him," Sean piped in.

Cray glared at the young noble. "I am more worried about why you are here, Sean, than why Darius didn't come back yet."

The fierceness of Cray's face made even Sean straighten and take notice. "I don't report to you."

Even with Sean's never-ending arrogance, Darius was surprised at how he stood up to Cray. Not many men could.

"We will discuss that later." Cray continued to stare forcibly into Sean's eyes until finally turning back to Darius to continue talking.

Darius learned that the camp indeed was worried about him. Rumors had him escaping or being eaten by wild animals. Cray had been sent to find him and bring him back.

"King Edward has sent notice that he wants a group of the Elite soldiers in Denir as soon as possible," said Cray after they had discussed all of the reasons why everyone was there. "You are the only one to lead them at this time. After watching the Gildanians building up a small army on their side of the border, our spies have said they have finally crossed over into our lands."

"Don't we need more training?" asked Darius.

"Apparently not," said Cray through tight lips. "But everyone is more than capable. The King doesn't want a war; he wants to settle this as quietly as possible."

Darius sat back, lost in thought about his new command opportunity. He had stayed in the mountains longer to think about what he wanted. He didn't know everything, but for now, yes, he would take the command and be able to make his own decisions. He would be a leader that others would watch and look at. He'd wanted to visit Denir anyways. This would be a good way to start seeing the Realm and protecting it from outside influences before he turned his attention inward.

The three men decided to sleep for a few hours before heading back to the base camp. Cray took the time to continue to brief Darius on the tools of leadership, and how he should organize the group. The return trip was not long with Cray leading them back through the valleys of the mountains. They reached the camp in a day and a half.

When they returned, the camp was in turmoil. Some of the young men did not want to actually fight in the King's army and had left during the previous night, escaping with many of the horses.

Cray shook his head in disgust. "It's up to you, Darius. You must lead them to follow the King's commands."

Darius wondered if the King actually knew that Darius would be leading the men on their first excursion. No matter what he felt personally for the King and politics, he couldn't deny the sentiment of pride and honor that had swept through him since being asked to lead the King's Elite Army. The first commander of a new special unit of young fighters! It was what he had always wanted. He was not a general yet, but being a commander before he was twenty was a great start. He would lead a decisive victory in Denir!

After Darius finished cleaning up, shaving, and changing clothes, Leandra came up to him and offered a big hug. She told him she had been worried and didn't want to see him leave again. She pleaded for him to take her with him to Denir. Darius wasn't sure of the depth of feelings he had for Leandra. She excited him in a way that at times was exhilarating, but he seemed to lose control over his thoughts when she was around. He couldn't have that happen around the other men. He was their commander now. He must be strong and not be distracted. At this point, he didn't need another distraction and so he told her no.

Darius met with Cray and a few of the other men that night in one of the large cabins. They spread maps of the area out in front of them. Darius traced his finger along the main routes to Denir. They talked and planned as the candles burned down to the ends. Darius would take all the men with him that hadn't deserted camp. In the next few days, supplies would be put together. The march would lead them east out of the Superstition Mountains and straight south down the road toward Denir. Darius would lead the army into the city and stop the Gildanian aggression.

Leandra and Darius talked once over the next two days. Darius had been walking out of his cabin when off behind a tree he noticed Sean and Leandra talking. They conversed in low whispers. Sean's hands flew out in the air around him as they appeared to be arguing.

Darius approached them. "Leandra, are you all right?"

Leandra breathed deeply and tried to compose herself. "I'm fine." She glanced quickly at Sean and then back to Darius.

"We were just talking about things going on in Anikari, Darius," Sean said, looking at Leandra for confirmation.

"Oh. Yes," Leandra agreed. "Sean was telling me about the happenings back in Anikari." She forced a laugh.

Darius glared at Sean, not trusting the truth of the exchange. Without anything better to go on he nodded his head and walked away, without saying anything more to Leandra.

The next morning the camp awoke with an excited fever. Young men covered the open meadow, practicing their swordsmanship and restringing their bows. A late-winter cold snap settled into the air. Everything was just about ready for the march to Denir. The trek would take them two weeks, depending on the weather. With the temperature dropping, they hoped to get out before additional snow dropped to their level.

Darius climbed up onto a high ridge overlooking the camp. Men were running everywhere, churning the ground into a mix of sludge and mud. Snow still hung on the branches of the tall trees and the smell of campfires being doused filled the air.

He turned and looked south toward Denir. The morning sun cast long shadows across the dark mountains, turning them into mounds of fading grays and purples. Darius looked past the tall snowy pines and the purple mountains standing in majestic forms around him. He looked past the rising mists clinging to the distant snowy peaks. Darius envisioned himself peering into the city of Denir itself. He imagined his army marching into one of the oldest cities in the Realm. He would now get to travel and find out what was out in the Realm for him. Anticipating the honor he would receive from the people as he rode at the head of this elite, trained army made him smile to himself.

He breathed in and let his power flood into him. A slight shift of focus came. Everything around him became more clear. A cold wind blew at Darius's back, making the tall pines sway as if to silent chords of music. The chill clung to him and dug into his breast. He wrapped his cloak around him more tightly, trying to shut the cold out, but it penetrated deeper.

Darius closed his eyes and took power from the cold. He thought of the mighty wind, the drenching rain, and the numbing snow that winter brought. He thought of the icy lakes that kept fishermen away. He thought about the dark, foreboding clouds that took over the mountains. And he drew strength from them. *Yes, there is strength and power in all of them.*

Opening his eyes he thought about the King and his father and how they continued to try and use him. There was power in anger and darkness. He finally recognized that. He would lead and fight and win and show them who was in control.

Darius found himself holding his sword, flames dancing down the blade. He felt the power raging once again and pushed it back out of him with all his might. Lightning darted down behind him from the sky and struck a tree up against the mountains. He was in control of so much power he could hardly contain the force. A sharp crack of thunder rocked the ground after the lightning.

The men would think it was the storm, but Darius knew better. His power could do anything and he let it fill him to the breaking point. He let the anger take control. It gave him strength.

Now he was hardened. Now he was ready for battle.

The sound of a loud, shrill whistle tore Darius from his heady thoughts—the signal that it was time to depart. He stood for a moment, trying to remember what had been going through his mind a few seconds before. He shook his head to clear his thoughts and glanced back down toward the breaking camp.

Cray, standing alone in the middle of the camp, stood still in his black jacket and looked past Darius. Darius twisted his neck slightly and watched the needles of the large tree behind him quickly burn off the tree. When he turned back around, Cray's eyes had widened somewhat and he gave Darius a questioning look.

Darius offered a grim smile and Cray beckoned him back to the camp. Darius walked down off the ridge, rejuvenated and alive now. The power brought clarity to his mind and increased awareness to his senses. He understood now what he would do. Darius turned toward the camp and into the cold wind. He didn't sense the cold anymore however. He only felt the raw power burning inside him. All other feelings were insignificant compared to that.

Chapter Twenty Four

Kelln groaned and rolled over. The thin blanket did nothing to ease the pain of his tortured body on the hard, rocky floor of the dungeon. The odor of stale food and urine whiffed at his nostrils. He couldn't keep track of how many weeks he had been in the cell, though he surmised it was much longer than he thought, maybe even months. Everything had become a blur of time. There were many moments he wished he were dead. It would be easier that way.

The cell door creaked and Kelln held his eyes closed. He couldn't do this again. Maybe if he kept his eyes closed they would leave him alone. Some part of his mind screamed with the absurdity of the thought. They didn't care if he was asleep or awake.

Two large hands hauled him up from the ground. "Open your eyes, traitor."

Kelln slowly opened his eyes, the right one still swollen from last week's beatings. He groaned out loud. One man held him on his feet, arms behind his back. The other staring back at him gave him a wicked grin, showing he only had half his teeth. But Kelln didn't care about the man's teeth; it was the large muscles and whip he held that would inflict the damage.

"Ready to admit you were wrong and swear to the Preacher, traitor?" the man asked.

Kelln knew he couldn't hold out much longer. He yearned to say yes and accept his fate as a follower of the Preacher, but some kind of stubbornness stayed buried deep inside his injured soul. Enough that he wouldn't fold. At least not yet.

"Never," Kelln said through gritted teeth.

The lash cracked across his legs and he cried out in pain. He found no shame in showing how much it hurt. The man holding him turned him around, with his back facing the torturer. Another lash across his back, another across his shoulders. Pain seared through his body and tears flowed freely from his eyes. If this day was like others, they would whip him until barely conscious, then put salve on his wounds and allow it to barely heal over the next few days. Then it would start all over again.

They were careful in their beatings, spreading the pain around to different parts of the body each time. His mind receded as deep as it could. Through the fog of delirium he noticed that the beatings had stopped and that someone had asked him a question.

"Who were you sending messages to in Anikari?" came a softer, yet deeper voice.

Deep in his mind he recognized the voice, and fear spread throughout his body and mind. The Preacher. He hadn't seen Belor's proclaimed leader for a while.

The Preacher stepped up and touched his hands to Kelln's head. Evil tendrils seemed to scour though his skull. Kelln shrieked at the invasion. The Preacher was searching for something. Kelln tried to think of other things, tried to stay firm, but it was becoming too hard. Finally, with a push, the pain became too much and his head flopped forward, unconscious.

In his unconscious state he heard voices in his mind. Images flashed through. Memories. They seemed to go backwards in time. First standing paralyzed in front of the Realm soldier he had been told to shoot, then seeing the Preacher speak to the growing crowds. He watched in his mind as he and Alessandra escaped Anikari and came to Belor. Seeing her face again, even only in his mind, made him feel longing and pain at the same time. He couldn't understand her. How could she do the bidding of this evil influence?

Suddenly his mind moved more rapidly back to Anikari and to Darius. Visiting White Island and seeing the Cremelinos seemed to bring more intense pain, and loud voices just outside his conscious reach. Someone became angry at his memory.

The next few minutes saw him with Darius holding the sword, and power crackling down the side of it. That brought a feeling of surprise to whomever was forcing the memories. After going back a few more years, his mind finally collapsed and all was dark once again.

A boot kicked him in the side and he winced. It held nothing compared to the whippings. A cool salve and bandages had already been applied. He tried to curl up and go back to sleep but a voice commanded otherwise.

"Who is Darius?" boomed the Preacher's voice, "and how does he have such power?"

Kelln opened his eyes and looked up. The Preacher brought his hand forward and helped Kelln sit up. "Bring the boy some water," he commanded one of his men.

A cup of cool water met Kelln's lips, and he drank greedily. He didn't want to look at the Preacher, but he couldn't help it. "What did you do?" he croaked.

"I sifted through your memories. It's easier to do when you are unconscious, and if you have been trained properly by the Eastern Lords, as have I."

Kelln tried to snarl and spit out venomous words at the Preacher, but he just couldn't do it anymore.

"Who is Darius, where did he get his power from, and where is he now?" the Preacher asked again.

Kelln couldn't hold back much longer. "He is my friend. Last I knew he was still in Anikari."

"Does he know he's a wizard?" The Preacher loomed in closer to Kelln, his large face intimidating him.

Somewhere inside, a lost laugh emerged from Kelln. It hurt his stomach, but he found it amusing that the Preacher was asking if Darius was a wizard.

"You find something entertaining?" The Preacher raised his voice.

"You asked if Darius knew he was a wizard. I kept asking him the same thing, but all he did was fervently deny it over and over again. My friend has been very stubborn in accepting his power."

"How can he deny such things?" asked the Preacher.

Kelln only shrugged.

"Maybe he could join me and we could rule the entire Realm together with power and might." The Preacher's eyes widened with an excited fervor.

Kelln knew his best friend would never agree to that. The Preacher was evil. Darius would see at once upon meeting this man that their powers were not the same.

"I will have to find your friend. Seems like we have much to talk about." The Preacher rose from the ground and motioned to the guards to come with him. Outside the cell door he turned back to Kelln one more time. "Thank you for the information. Your trial will take place in one month."

Kelln opened his mouth to ask a question, but the Preacher beat him to it.

"I want you strong again, so that the people can watch me tear you apart." The Preacher's eyes bore holes into Kelln's soul. "Rest up."

As soon as the Preacher was gone, Kelln collapsed back onto the ground once again. He had one more month to live. One more month to try and figure out how to get away. He dug backward in his mind, going deep inside his own memories. They were all he had now to keep him from going totally insane.

Chapter Twenty Five

Some rode horses, others walked, and a few took the supply wagons as they headed down out of the mountains, trying to beat the coming storm. Down the rugged trail, they marched at a pace full of excitement. This was what they had been trained for. To serve the King. They were all lost in their own worlds while silently walking over the rough, muddy road. A few squirrels and a stray rabbit or two scurried out of their way. The march would take a few weeks to get down the mountain and all the way south to Denir.

Darius glanced back at the lower, billowing clouds and realized they would not make it through the night without sleet and new snow. Winter weather had begun late in the season, but now it seemed to be in full force. Darius smiled. The cold would make the men strong. They had been trained as elite soldiers for battles just like this.

Sometime in the middle of the darkened night, he heard rain begin to descend outside of his command tent. For a while it seemed the howling wind would rip his tent apart and send him sliding down the mountain. However, the tent held up and the monotonous, steady sound lulled him back into his dreams.

During the night the temperature dropped and the next day the camp woke to a brilliant covering of white, being held in contrast to the darkened mist still hovering over them. Darius ordered the camp to eat quickly so they could depart. A few of the men mumbled that he was not being fair with them in regard to the weather.

In answer to one of these remarks, Darius pushed through the men to find the complaining soldier. "What don't you think is fair, soldier?"

"The storm is still upon us. We should be making preparations to stay safe," whispered the young man as Darius stood above him.

"Maybe you think it's fair that the people of Denir have an army at their backdoor. Maybe we should just wait here until winter is over. Then instead of saving them we can bury their bones."

The young man cowered back, seeing the anger stream from Darius. "I'm sorry, sir. I wasn't thinking."

"I like someone who can admit when he is wrong," Darius continued, lowering his voice. "But if this happens again I will let you stay here for as long as you want, by yourself in the freezing snow with a dishonorable discharge. You were chosen as an elite soldier. If you can't face a little snow then maybe you will have to go be a grunt in the larger army."

He knew he was being unreasonable, but the foul weather made him cranky also – and it fueled his anger, which in turn increased his powers. Powers that he was finally beginning to understand.

The group packed and started on again. The going was slow. Their feet dragged in the previous night's snow. It would take them a week to descend the mountain passes before reaching the main road to Denir. As they moved on down the mountain, the snow turned into slush, and then mud that covered half the way up their knee-high boots. When night came again they found themselves a few miles farther but still a ways from the foothills.

A brilliant light woke Darius the next morning. He squinted in the clear sunlight. The sky, a clear blue, looked as if an artist had painted its far reaches during the night. Much of the water had soaked into the ground during the night, and even though it was still cool, the day found the young army full of enthusiasm.

After a quick breakfast of biscuits and fried meat, the group started out again. The supply wagons would catch up to them at midday. A group had already started out before dawn to set up for dinner later that evening. After six days of slugging through the mud and combatting a few rainstorms they eventually descended the foothills and camped at the base of the Superstition Mountains for the night. Darius could see the road leading to Anikari from the camp, and he wondered what his father would think of him now.

After setting up camp, Darius sent two men ahead to search for any advance scouts from the Gildanian army and to determine their plans.

Before beginning the march south the next day, Darius rode back to the far wagons to see how they were doing. Without strong wagons, an army would starve and not be useful to anyone. A small figure marched next to one of the wagons. Darius thought the person looked too small for his army, but maybe they were one of the cook's helpers. He almost turned away, not wanting to bother with it, when the sunlight caught something on the figure's wrist. Curious, Darius approached him. As he did, the figure bent its head closer to the ground.

"Soldier! Stop!" Darius commanded, but the soldier continued walking even faster. "I said stop!" he repeated as he jumped down off his horse. He walked over and turned the soldier around.

Darius stared in astonishment. "What . . . How did you?" he stuttered in surprise. He couldn't tear himself away from the eyes for a moment. "Leandra!" he finally exclaimed.

"I needed to come with you, Darius. I couldn't stay in the mountains without you. I was so afraid when you left before," she rambled on.

Anger flooded into Darius's eyes for a moment, but he couldn't seem to find the words to match it. She gave him a hug, which caused others to glance over and see what was going on. Darius became embarrassed and confused. "I'll talk to you later," Darius said briskly as he jumped back on his horse, turned quickly, and rode back to the front of the line to contemplate what to do. He was angry she was here because he didn't need her distractions right now. At the same time, the one hug from her and the smell of her sweet lilac scent brought back feelings he wasn't sure how to deal with. Darius wanted Leandra with him. He wanted her touch and her kiss to comfort him. *Why now?* he thought. *I have an army to lead.*

She came to him later in the day and Darius told her she could stay, but she had to take care of herself. She asked if she could set up her tent next to his and he consented, knowing it might be a mistake, but not wanting a distracting argument. A few of the men made whistles and catcalls behind his back, but he ignored them. They were most likely just jealous anyways.

They made slow progress down the road. Later that week the advance scouts returned. They had been to Denir and seen the Gildanian army. It actually turned out to only be a small battalion of about five hundred men. The foreigners had taken land in the southern end of the city, just over the border, and looked to be preparing to go further. They had not fought anyone yet. Darius couldn't figure out why they would only bring such a small battalion into the Realm. They would know that the Realm army would mount their own attack with many more soldiers.

The Realm army, however, would take more time to assemble and march to Denir. The reason for the Elite Army was for things just like this. Darius dismissed the scouts and sat out on a log by himself to think. It was warmer here, being out of the mountains. Personally he was hoping for an early spring.

After a few minutes of silence someone touched him from behind. He turned, and Leandra stood above him. She looked beautiful, silhouetted in the firelight, with her breath making small wisps of fog that circled her face then disappeared into the cold night. She wore a long, dark-blue wool cloak around her slim body. She pushed the hood back off her face, smiled, and bent down to him. *I have to think of my army. I have to decide how to beat the Gildanians. I can't have this now.*

She leaned down and kissed him. It had been a long time since she had kissed him like that; it had been before his trek into the mountains. It felt warm and exciting. Her scent lingered around him. *I can't. I can't be distracted like this.*

She rubbed her soft hands on his sore neck. She seemed to take the tension away. *No! No!*

"No, Leandra!" He tore her hands off his neck and stood up. "I can't. I have to think."

"I can help," she offered. Her sweet voice whispered through the night air.

"No. You distract me." He walked further away from her. "Leave me alone. I don't know why I let you stay. Maybe I should send you back. I don't want you here."

Darius's back was to Leandra. That was the only way he could talk to her. He had to be strong or else she clouded his thinking. He heard her begin to cry, turn, and then leave. He wondered why he had let her stay. He wondered why he had let her kiss him.

Darius walked further away from the camp, disappearing into the dark, misty night. The night posed no problem for his eyesight. He seemed surprised by how the natural flow of power reacted to his needs now.

The Gildanians outnumbered him by more than double. He knew his soldiers were probably better trained, but this was their first battle and he couldn't be too careful. He climbed up on a large rock and stared out into the endless darkness, wrapping his cloak around him to keep out the cold. The trees seemed to take on shapes of their own, looking like monsters guarding the ominous mountains. Shadows looked real, and what looked real might only be shadows; however, he could see better in the dark than he used to be able to. The camp began to quiet down as thoughts and plans came in quick succession to his power-enhanced mind.

Darius watched as a small sliver of moon highlighted the large pine trees against the nearby mountains. The fires around the camp all died down and only an occasional sound made him look around. He looked up at the glowing stars and exhaled, watching his breath frost up the air in front of him. *We will win!* he assured himself. *I didn't go through the training to lose everything now.*

He strolled back toward his tent, pausing for a moment in front of Leandra's tent. He stood gazing at the enclosure a moment, not knowing what to think then turned and moved into his own tent by himself.

The next morning Darius gathered everyone together. He unveiled part of his plan. The rest would have to wait until he actually saw the enemy camp. A small part of his army would branch off and go into the foothills of the Superstition Mountains, coming around on the far side of Denir. The rest would continue to march as if going straight to Denir as planned, making sure that the Gildanians knew they were coming.

Darius announced that he would lead the smaller party of twenty-five men; men that were the best at combat training and following orders. They would travel two days and most of a third day over a rough terrain, with little rest, to get to Denir before the main army did. Many of the soldiers wanted to know what he was going to do with only twenty-five men, but Darius said they didn't need to know yet. Some of the men became angry at the sudden change of plans, but in the end, as things were forever throughout the Realm, soldiers followed their leaders into battle, and the men quieted down. With it being their first battle, they had to trust their new commander.

Darius was aware of the quiet, whispered complaints under their breath. He placed two other men he trusted in charge of the main army, handpicked his twenty-five men, and left, leaving Leandra with the main army. He thought about leaving without telling her, but she still seemed to be brooding over the previous evening's encounter, so he talked to her for a few minutes and gave her a small farewell kiss. Her scent lingered in his mind as he left the main camp. He wondered how she managed to have perfume with her in an army camp.

Quickly and quietly, the small group spent the three days crossing the muddy foothills, bringing them to the west side of Denir late the third day. Their feet were soaked and the men were cold to their bones, but excitement filled the air.

Darius sent two men out of his group to scout out the perimeters of the Gildanian camp. He found out that it appeared that the Gildanians had indeed been fooled and were anticipating the main army marching in from the main road, with anticipation of having more time until the fighting would begin.

Chapter Twenty Six

There seemed to be a pre-celebration of victory already among the men in the Gildanian camp. Darius could smell the wine mixing with the roasting of meat over their open fires. They looked to be planning on going north out of Denir in the morning and meeting Darius's main army before they entered the city.

"We must act tonight," said Darius to his small group, as he laid out the plans for them to follow. They sat a few small hills away from the Gildanian army. He was full of confidence and smiled as he ordered his men in their respective roles. One part of the plan he kept to himself. He had to work his magic covertly for the time being. He was beginning to realize now it was part of him, but not a part he wished to expose too much or too soon.

That evening, as dark settled like a heavy blanket over Denir, twenty-six men dug ditches to the west of the Gildanian's camp. The air was cool, but the previous storm had gone north of Denir, leaving the ground wet, but not muddy. A small grassy knoll separated them from the camp. Their sentries stood on the north and east side, not expecting trouble behind their backs.

Darius experimented with his power by reaching out with his mind toward the edge of the enemy camp. He pulled some of the water out of the ground in the form of a light mist. His men would think it was natural. He was excited with what he could do and looked forward to seeing the look on the Gildanian commander's faces. The mist helped to hide their activities. They spent the next few hours digging multiple ditches with tools and shovels they had borrowed from the city. As each ditch was finished, the men headed off toward their next assignment.

Darius sat crouched behind a tent at the corner of the enemy camp. The Gildanians had stayed up late, drinking and talking, but now with a minimal amount of guards they slept with overconfidence. Darius still couldn't figure out why the small battalion had come across the border in the first place. It seemed like a trap, but he couldn't figure out what it would be a trap for. He would send a few of his men south in the morning to make sure another larger army wasn't coming from Gildan.

The others should be in place by now. It was time to see if his plan would work. Rather than outright killing, his plan required stealth. He didn't have the stomach to kill unnecessarily.

Even though the evening was cool, his head beaded with sweat and his arms ached from the digging. He wiped the sweat off with the dirty arm of his long wool shirt, leaving streaks of mud across his face. He let the night settle around him and he closed his eyes. Without any hesitation, he brought the power up inside himself. He wrapped himself in a cloak of silence and crept into the camp. The power receded a few times but he brought it back up. His control was still very new.

He held his sword tight in his right hand. It glowed faintly. He began cutting the strings that held the tents to the ground. He also entered as many tents as he could and took their bows and swords. This he did in silence, swathed in his power. Once his hold on the magic slipped and he made a noise. A bleary-eyed soldier stood up, but Darius knocked him on the head with his sword and the man fell back to slumber. When he gathered as many weapons as he could carry, he headed back outside of the camp.

Two more times he crept in using his power to silence all his sounds. He stumbled once in exhaustion, but caught himself without making much noise.

One by one, each of his men untied the ropes holding the Gildanian horses. At dawn they gathered together again and took the weapons that Darius had taken. The men were smart enough to not question his accomplishment. Darius smiled at how easy this was turning out to be.

Time for phase two of his plan. Half of the men went around to the north of the camp, into the outskirts of the city, and half of them to the south of the camp. At the appropriate time, the men up north made enough noise to begin waking the Gildanian soldiers from their drunken sleep.

Darius put on a stolen uniform that he had taken during the night over his own clothes. The Gildanian army was much better dressed than his group was. He would have to talk to the King about that.

In the early morning hours, just before the sky would lighten with the early dawn, Darius snuck into camp and, with the stolen uniform on, lifted his sword high in the air and yelled.

"Ambush! We are being attacked!" Darius hoped he remembered his Gildanian language well enough. He had studied languages in school at the academy. Gildanian was not a lot different from the language of the Realm or the Kingdom of Arc, more like a different dialect.

Men stood, bewildered, rubbing sleep from their eyes, tripping over one another, and trying to get out of their tents. With the strings cut, they weren't as taut, and they collapsed inward, making it difficult to find the door. They held their aching heads, trying to regain consciousness after the late night drinking.

"It's a trap," Darius continued telling the enemy soldiers. "They are on the south side of the camp." At that time of the morning, the men didn't think to question who was calling the orders. All they saw was a man in uniform with a bright sword held above his head. They had no reason to question.

The Gildanians scrambled for their swords and bows, not finding their weapons where they remembered placing them before going to sleep. Darius and his men had let those camped on the edge of the camp keep their swords, so as not to arouse total suspicion. Confusion and mud filled the air. Men began running south out of the camp into the misting winter morning, unwittingly relaying Darius's false orders to each other. Some of Darius's men let themselves be seen through the thin fog. This spurred the men on with hollering and yelling.

As the enemy soldiers left the confines of their camp, those in the back began seeing the men in front of them fall and disappear. The dark ground over the small rise seemed to swallow them up and they were gone. As men neared where others in front of them fell, they too tumbled into the ditches the elite army had dug during the night. No matter which way they went they tripped and fell into freshly dug ditches, only to find themselves looking up into the eyes of one of the elite soldiers and his sword.

During the chaos, Darius continued shouting commands as he searched for whoever was in charge. He threw the flaps of each tent back, ripping them with his sword until he found the right tent. He was certain it belonged to the Gildanian commander. A colorful flag hung from the point of the tent. Darius hid outside of it until someone came crashing out.

"What's going on?" the man began to yell in Gildanian, only to be shoved back inside the tent by Darius.

"Who are you?" the captured commander asked in astonishment. "You are not one of my men."

"That's right. But you are one of mine now. My prisoner, that is." He turned the man around and poked his golden sword into the back of the commander, pushing against the skin enough to hurt but not enough to draw blood. "I want you to get out there and tell your men to surrender."

"Surrender? To whom? Where did you come from?" The young commander voiced his concerns.

"That doesn't matter right now," Darius informed the commander. "Call your men down or we will kill them all, starting with you." Darius pushed the sword harder, feeling the skin break as the commander stiffened. Darius's head rushed with the excitement of battle. He stared at the back of his prisoner. A simple gold band held black hair back from his brown-skinned face.

"But we saw your army on the road. You don't have enough . . ." The Gildanian commander switched to the language of the Realm.

"Don't always believe what you see, Commander. Remember there is a sword in your back. A few minutes ago you did not think that was possible, did you?"

"You can't threaten me . . ."

Darius spun the man around, so hard he almost tripped. The man's dark, tilted brown eyes widened, but to his credit, he held steady and seemed to show more anger than fear. He stood eye to eye with Darius, though obviously a few years older. Darius gripped the sword with two hands and let the power flow into the ancient weapon. The glow started at his hands and moved to the tip, engulfing the entire sword. "I am a peaceful man, Gildanian, but have been accused of losing my temper recently. I have no desire to kill anyone and would like to settle things peacefully."

The commander stared at the sword that Darius held in front of him, his eyes going wide once more. He took a deep breath, brought his hand back slowly and removed the band out of his black hair and shook his head, letting his hair fall back down to his shoulders, then proceeded to walk out of his tent.

"Fall back," he yelled out to his men. "Drop your weapons and surrender."

Those who didn't already have their swords and bows taken away put them down on the ground. A few tried to fight back, but with additional words from their commander, they fully surrendered. When the commander found out there were only twenty-five other men in Darius's group he was furious and embarrassed.

"The older men thought not to listen to me last night. They stayed up too late drinking to victory before we even fought." The young Gildanian seemed to be trying to justify his loss. "Many thought I was too young to be in command."

Darius just grunted. He understood what the Gildanian commander meant. He still struggled with some of his older soldiers taking him seriously.

"This should have never happened," the Gildanian commander yelled to his guards and soldiers.

"You will be my prisoner until we meet King Edward Montere, King of the Realm, in Anikari. We will see what he has to say about this incursion," said Darius

"You deceived me, threatened me, and used the power of a wizard in front of me. Who are you?" The young commander said in low, whispered Gildanian, obviously noticing that Darius understood his language.

Darius ignored the man's remark, although he saw questioning looks on his men's faces. Some of them understood Gildanian and overheard the comments. He spoke to the captured army. "You deceived yourself with all of your celebrating and drinking last night. You should never celebrate victory before the battle. I am sure your generals would be disappointed in you."

The young Gildanian showed some sense of embarrassment at that last statement, but composed himself. "Where is the rest of your army? We had reports of you coming down the main road."

"They will be here in short order to make sure your army is held prisoner until we sort this out. So, Commander, what is your name?"

"Mezar. Commander of the Gildanian twenty-first battalion." This he spoke in the tongue of the Realm.

"Just Mezar? No other titles?"

"Commander Mezar will do for now," the man noted in defiance, not willing to give any more information. He looked around at his men, silencing them with his look.

"Well, Commander Mezar, now you are prisoner of Darius, first commander of the King's Elite Army."

The rest of the solders began to be herded into organized areas to await the remainder of the army. Darius watched his prisoner and studied him for a moment, still wondering about the purpose of this incursion. He found himself alone with the young man and tied his hands behind him.

In a perfect Realm accent he asked Darius, "Where have you been hiding? We hadn't heard the Realm had a wizard again."

The question surprised Darius and he looked around nervously. "Will you stop referring to me as a wizard?"

"Ahh. I understand." Mezar looked around with a tiny smile on his thin face. "Your men do not know, do they?"

"I am not a wizard. And no, they don't." Darius was getting confused by this enemy commander.

"Which is it, Commander Darius? Do they not know you are a wizard or are you not one?" Mezar smiled, bright teeth in contrast to his golden brown skin.

Darius pushed Mezar to one of his soldiers to watch, and headed off through town. He was not in the mood to spar with his Gildanian counterpart. He didn't yet know what he was and was uncomfortable with that line of questioning. But he did know he had just won his first battle, without the loss of one life on either side. He felt great!

After removing the Gildanian uniform, Darius jumped on one of the Gildanian's horses and rode through Denir, yelling victory and waking up everyone in the early dawn hours. They jumped out of their homes thinking another fight was upon them to find Darius, a lone man galloping up and down the street with his golden sword raised high. He seemed to fly above his horse with the overpowering sensation of power that came with victory.

Early the next day the rest of Darius's army arrived to find, surprisingly, the battle already ended. Many of the men were disappointed, some because they couldn't fight, others because Darius's plan had indeed worked. Darius met with Denirian leaders to receive praises and banquets in his honor. He had captured, with only a small group of men, an entire battalion of the famous Gildanian army. He gloried in the praise. His plan had worked.

Stories began to spread of what had happened that morning, growing more spectacular with every telling. Riders rode from town to town with rumors of the man with the glowing sword. The commander of the King's Elite Army.

Darius sat at an evening banquet held in his honor. He had finally accomplished something in life. Something on his own. He had won his first battle as a leader in the army. He had secured peace for the Realm. The townspeople were invited to pay tribute to the army that saved them. Music was playing and many were dancing. He sat at the head table and looked out over his men, enjoying the evening because of him. Darius relished the power and the glory.

Heady thoughts swirled his mind. *This is what I have been looking for. The power is mine now. I won this battle. My father and the King sent me away from my friends with no warning. They have kept me from Christine, and they sit instead with their nobles and make decisions, not understanding our people. Now I have risen above all the other recruits. Now I will choose my own path!*

Leandra walked toward him. He stood and took her willingly into his arms this time, pushing thoughts of Christine far away. She was not here now, and he might never see her again. It pained him to think so, but it was true. Leandra had been nice to him and had complimented him, and he needed someone who would stand by him among his men. She cleaned up at the governor's private home and now stood in a resplendent long silk gown of pale blue. Dark hair in curls cascaded across her bare shoulders. It seemed to be part of the expected prize for being victorious. His power made it seem natural to have such a beautiful woman in his arms. Darius held Leandra close and kissed her with power and passion.

"Oh, Darius!" Leandra giggled and sighed under his attention.

The next day a stand was erected in the town square and local dignitaries praised Darius and the King's army. Darius spoke briefly at the end.

"My men, you have won a great battle against the famed Gildanian army. You have trained for this these past months and now you can see the fruits of this training." He left out any mention of the King. To add to the already growing legend, he raised his sword high in the air, and let it glow with a bright light. "Hail the glory of the Realm. May peace prevail in its borders and understanding reign from within. "

The crowd yelled and clapped in a deafening roar, echoing back, "Hail Darius, Commander of the Realm."

Standing in the back of the crowd, held by two of Darius's men, stood Mezar, the captured Gildanian commander. Darius looked directly at him and let his power continue to build. His grey eyes grew brighter and a hazy glow intensified around him. What was power good for if he couldn't intimidate and glory in its sensation? Mezar's eyes held surprise and awe, and in deference to the power he gave a short bow of his head to his captor.

Darius returned the acknowledgement with a short nod of his own head. Mezar didn't seem like such a bad fellow. He just happened to be on the wrong side of the battle. Anyone opposite Darius would be on the wrong side. That included

Mezar, and depending on their actions, maybe his father or the King.

Darius would now be his own man and make his own decisions. He had finally seen that it was anger and purpose that gave him the power to do what he wanted to do and be what he wanted to be. He would restore the glory of the Realm and choose the path of his own destiny!

Epilogue

King Edward DarSan Montere paced around his private study. His head hurt. It seemed to always hurt these days. His kingdom seemed to be falling apart around him. The farmers and their petty petition, the lunatic preacher in Belor, and the conniving Gildanians in the south. There were even rumors that a prince of the Kingdom of Arc was having practice maneuvers near the border.

"My Lord, it's freezing in here," Richard said as if stating the obvious.

The curtains and casements were opened wide. The fresh, cool air of late winter helped the King to think. "Richard, what is happening to the Realm? We had peace for so long, and now events seem to be collapsing the Realm from all sides."

"We have become too complacent, I fear. The children are soft and don't take their studies seriously, the nobles only care for their coin, and the army has poor recruits," Richard answered.

"Except for my Elite Army," the King said, turning around and facing his senior councilor. "They were handpicked to be different. To be the best."

"Yes, it seems that way. Though based on the information and rumors we have received over the last two weeks about the battle in Denir, there was not much fighting to test their prowess and combat skills."

"Still a decisive victory led by your son, Darius." The King fell down hard into his overstuffed red-velvet chair. He let out a long breath of air to calm himself.

"Yes, my son," Richard echoed. "What do we do with him now? You heard the rumors as I have. A glowing sword, strength more than many men. And arrogance."

"Rumors are all they are, Richard. Others are just jealous of his position."

"Edward." Richard slipped back to a less formal name with his old friend. "I am still not comfortable with his future. He hasn't been trained for this. You should take another wife, a young woman who can quickly give you children—an heir to the throne."

"We have already been through this. I should never have sat on the throne. I need to restore the throne to the proper line. It is the right thing to do."

"But the right thing to do is not always the best thing to do," Richard reminded the King.

Edward poured himself some wine and sat back, swirling it around in his mouth a few times before swallowing. "Ahh, my friend, that is one of the oldest arguments alive for a king to consider. Right versus best. I must admit we have chosen the best over right sometimes for the good of the kingdom, but not with this. This was an injustice that needs to be righted. For the good of the Realm. For the strength of our kingdom."

"So back to the question at hand. What do we do with my son and his army?"

The King sat up straight. "It is not his army, Richard, it is mine! And he will need to remember that he follows my orders in all things."

"The rumors say otherwise. They are calling him the Commander of the Realm, and referring to *his* Elite Army."

"It's a dangerous balancing act we play at, Richard. He is just living in the glory of his first victory. Let him have a moment."

Richard growled low. "You do not know my son. He cares nothing for politics, but he is smart. He has naïve ideals at how things should work in the world and in the Realm. He will use this to get something that he wants. Probably to get in the good graces of that outsider girl."

"Richard! You are as bad as all the merchants and other nobles. Have some respect for these hard working people. They provide us a great service in growing our food and handling our cattle."

"But they are still outsiders, disorganized and weak. They rebelled against the throne once." Spittle came from the force of Richard's words. "I will not have my son stirring up trouble and encouraging them in a new rebellion."

King Edward stood again and walked to the window in the direction of the farmlands. Through the low-lying clouds he could see the outline of the leafless trees and a few brown fields. "They are only outsiders because we allowed it. They are getting organized. Have you so soon forgotten their petition?"

"Forget these farmers for now, my King. They can be dealt with later."

"Maybe you are right." The King sat down again and thought for a few moments. "Let's bring your son back here to Anikari, with his prisoners in tow. We will parade his victory around the city, build up his reputation, then send him down to Belor to quickly and decisively take care of that problem. We will allow him to gain popularity with the people, but under our terms and direction. He must be ready when the time comes, Richard, but not be in a position to take power any sooner than that."

"We should hold the council and let all weigh in on these matters. I know we can't say anything about Darius, but which wars we fight, the petition of the outsiders, this Preacher; they should be consulted in these matters, my Lord. We need the other councilor's thoughts to make sure we take the right course. Why don't you convene a full council to deal with these problems? You can't handle everything yourself. That is probably what is giving you these headaches."

Edward drank more wine. "Richard, I don't trust the council."

"What? You appointed them. Who don't you trust?"

"I'm not sure, but until I do, I cannot hold a council and share information. I worry some are sympathizers with the preacher from Belor, and others may be dealing with the Gildanians or Arcs. But most of all I fear the ones that are undermining my position as king and are trying to set themselves up as the next ruler when I die."

"Then what can we do?" Richard said in exasperation. "Do you have a plan?"

"Yes. We trust in your son. He must learn to be a leader on his own and to gain the respect of the men."

"My son?" Richard bellowed. "That is your plan?"

King Edward DarSan Montere, rested his head back on his high, stuffed chair and whispered so softly that the councilor had to lean in to hear. "That is my plan Richard. We must continue to prepare him to be the next king of the Realm."

To continue the adventures of Darius, Christine, Kelln, Mezar, and their friends,
*Read **The Path Of Decisions,***
Book II of the Cremelino Prophecy.

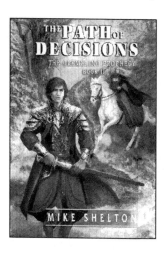

**Cutting betrayal. Increasing powers.
Complicated decisions.**

A wizard walks the land once again, but he struggles with how to use his power.

Darius San Williams, now the first commander of the King's Elite Army struggles with his emerging powers. After winning his first battle against external foes, he must decide now to follow the King or to take matters in his own hands.

Back in Anikari, Christine wrestles with how to confront oppression against her people, while in Belor, Kelln must escape the clutches of an evil wizard and warn Darius.

Mezar, the captured Gildanian quietly watches everything closely and harbors a secret of his own.

Each of their decisions will determine the fate and destiny of their friendship and their kingdom.

Other Series By Mike Shelton
The Alaris Chronicles

15 years later and a few kingdoms to the south...
Three young wizards. A magical barrier. Civil war.

The fate of a kingdom rests on the shoulders of three young wizards who couldn't be more different.

Bakari is a brilliant scholar wizard who's more at home in a library than a battlefield.
Alli is a beautiful young battle wizard whose grace in battle is both enchanting and deadly.
Roland is a counselor wizard with a seemingly limitless depth of untapped power -- and the ego to match it.

As the magical barrier protecting the kingdom of Alaris from dangerous outsiders begins to fail, and a fomenting rebellion threatens to divide the country in a civil war, the three wizards are thrust into the middle of a power struggle.

When the barrier comes down, the truth comes out. Was everything they were taught about their kingdom based on a lie?

Will they all choose to fight on the same side, or end up enemies in the battle over who should rule Alaris?

Sign up on Mike's website at www.MichaelSheltonBooks.com and get a copy of the prequel novella e-book to The Alaris Chronicles, Prophecy of the Dragon.

Protect the youngest heir of the Dragon King. That is the mission given to Imari in this prequel novella to The Alaris Chronicles.

The TruthSeer Archives

On an island far out in the Eastern Sea join a new adventure of magic through the stones of power.

The lies could kill her, but the truth could destroy a kingdom.

Given a rare TruthStone, Shaeleen suffers immense agony with every lie she hears or tells. While struggling to control her new power and curb the pain she learns a powerful truth that could thrust an entire continent into civil war.

The stones of power protect the five kingdoms of Wayland - and have done so for two hundred years. Now those stones are failing and a dark power threatens to take control. With the help of her brother, and a young thief, Shaeleen sets out on a dangerous journey to gather and restore the power of all the stones.

Shaeleen can either reveal the truths she finds and stop the physical torment or hold on to the lies and sacrifice her own well-being for the sake of the kingdom.

Will she succeed before the endless lies destroy her?

Readers of YA fantasy, unique magic, mighty wizards, reluctant heroes, and magnificent kingdoms will enjoy the TruthSeer Archives!

About the Author

Mike was born in California and has lived in multiple states from the west coast to the east coast. He cannot remember a time when he wasn't reading a book. At school, home, on vacation, at work at lunch time, and yes even a few pages in the car (at times when he just couldn't put that great book down). Though he has read all sorts of genres he has always been drawn to fantasy. It is his way of escaping to a simpler time filled with magic, wonders and heroics of young men and women.

Other than reading, Mike has always enjoyed the outdoors. From the beaches in Southern California to the warm waters of North Carolina. From the waterfalls in the Northwest to the Rocky Mountains in Utah. Mike has appreciated the beauty that God provides for us. He also enjoys hiking, discovering nature, playing a little basketball or volleyball, and most recently disc golf. He has a lovely wife who has always supported him, and three beautiful children who have been the center of his life.

Mike began writing stories in elementary school and moved on to larger novels in his early adult years. He has worked in corporate finance for most of his career. That, along with spending time with his wonderful family and obligations at church has made it difficult to find the time to truly dedicate to writing. In the last few years as his children have become older he has returned to doing what he truly enjoys – writing!

mikesheltonbooks@gmail.com
www.MichaelSheltonBooks.com
https://www.facebook.com/groups/MikeSheltonAuthor/
https://www.facebook.com/mikesheltonbooks/
http://www.Twitter.com/msheltonbooks
http://www.Instagram.com/mikesheltonbooks
https://www.pinterest.com/mikesheltonbooks/

Made in the USA
San Bernardino, CA
09 December 2019

61100076R00190